OPEN WOUND

DEAD ENDS
BOOK 2

BECK LEWIS

1

"Fire!"

I generally pride myself on my ability to control what comes out of my mouth, but this exclamation comes from some deep, primitive part of my brain that knows death when it stares it in the face.

"Fire? Where? What's on fire?"

Tyrese Jali's on the phone – Tyrese Jali, centre back for Leicester City – *that* Tyrese Jali. I think he's still drunk from his idiotic exploits this evening. Or rather yesterday, now. He's the reason I'm out at this hour, driving into the city.

"You're fine, Tyrese," I say. "The fire's at my end." I stop the car as I placate him over the hands-free.

"When will you get here? I need your help. They won't even let me have a private room."

"You really are fine, Tyrese. The hospital will look after you. I'm on my way."

Three o'clock on a Monday morning and the Narborough Road into Leicester is quieter than I've ever seen it. Any other time, it's a logjam of chaos. The main road from the motorway into the city centre would be a dual carriageway in any other city, but here it's a riot of tiny shops and takeaways. Food from every continent is here.

I end the call to Tyrese and lower the window.

There's a loud roaring sound.

The fire's across the road, in the row of houses that extends down one of the side streets. It's one of those in-between buildings. A series of extensions off a Victorian house. There's blanked-off windows and roller shutters that make me think it's commercial, but I can't be sure. Right now, it's burning like a candle. I can feel it, too. There's heat on my face, which is insane given that it's a good distance away.

I reach for my phone to call it in. My hand lands on two phones. One of those is for Tyrese. I need to take his regular phone away from him. He's not going to like that.

I call 999 on Tyrese's phone and use mine to record video as I step out of the Jag to take a better look.

"Emergency service operator. Which service?"

"Fire," I reply as I cross the road.

"Connecting you now."

I can really feel the heat now. The height of the flames makes my stomach flip.

I'm connected to the fire service. *"What's the full address of the fire, please?"*

I'm not certain what the side road is, and I can't see a sign from here.

"Just off the Narborough Road. Not far from the KFC."

It's the best I can do for now.

"Is it a house, flat or a commercial building?"

"I'm not certain."

"Possible mixed-use, then. Is anyone inside the building?"

"I don't know."

The question fills me with sudden horror as I look up at the place. It's completely engulfed by flames. Even in the time I've been on the phone, they've grown huge, roaring above the roof space by a good fifteen feet. Taller than trees.

The sound of it is immense. It stokes some primitive fear in me, as if my hindbrain knows how deadly it is.

I can see windows, up above. There's a sticker on one of them. It looks like a unicorn, but it's charred now, and peeling away.

And the smell... It's a dense, cloying version of a bonfire smell, but this smells dark and terrifying, thick smoke billowing across the skyline now.

I try to approach, but the heat's intense.

I yell. "Hey! Hey, is anyone in there?" I'd bang on that shutter, but it must be red hot. It's padlocked from outside.

"Can you see flames or just smoke?" says the operator.

"Flames. Massive ones. There was a bang a few minutes ago, too."

"How close are you to the fire?"

"I'm on the street outside."

"We're sending fire engines now. Stay well clear."

But how can I stay clear, knowing that there might be people in there?

I end the call, standing in the street, wondering what I can do. I make more noise, shouting up at the bedroom windows, although the fire is so loud surely it's woken everyone?

I can see lights coming on in some of the other nearby houses.

Then I see something that seems frankly impossible.

The door opens and someone emerges from the property. Fire frames her in the doorway.

It's a woman.

2

A woman has just stumbled out of the burning building and I have no idea how she's not on fire.

"Fucking hell," I whisper.

As she stumbles out, there's a blast of heated air from the doorway.

I rush over to help her. She's walking, but her face is streaked with black marks. She's got a limp canvas duffel bag and I realise she had it over her head and shoulders as a shield as she came running out.

I touch her and she almost instantly collapses against me.

She carries the smell of the fire so powerfully that I instinctively recoil. Is it burnt hair that I can smell? It's horrendous.

"Come. Come on, away from the fire."

I need to get her to safety. She looks stunned. My face is cooking. I can feel it prickling.

I guide her away. Away, away, to the roadside and my car.

"Is anyone else inside?" I say.

She turns to me, her face a blank. Her hair falls in curls around her round face and large eyes.

"Anyone else?" I ask.

"No." Her voice is very croaky.

She's wearing jeans and some sort of blouse, but it's melted away in places. Completely gone.

How on earth did she walk out of that fire? It was like watching someone walk out of an oven.

"Are you burned? Are you hurt?"

"No," she says and coughs. "Have you got some water?"

"Yes!"

I'm glad that there's something I can actually help with. I pull open my passenger door, get her to sit down and hand her my Stanley cup, filled with filtered water. She takes a long drink and sits back in the seat. As she does so, I can hear a tiny crackling noise from her hair. Can it still be smouldering?

There are freckles across her face under the streaks of dirt.

"Are you sure you're not hurt?"

She takes a long moment to answer. "Don't think so."

"Still, though." My mind casts around. "Shock. Smoke inhalation. God knows. I'm going to call for the paramedics. They should check you over."

She straightens as though waking. "I must be lucky." She looks over at the burning house. "Jesus."

I see tears pricking her eyes.

I grip her hands. Such bravery to come walking out of that blaze and not be a bawling wreck.

"I'm Hannah," I say.

She nods. "Natasha."

"Right, Natasha. Let me find you a top to wear, at least."

She looks down at her ruined blouse. As she raises her head, she looks confused, as though it's not normal to be carrying spare clothes. She has no idea of the things that my clients get up to.

I pop the Jaguar's huge boot and have a quick riffle through the wardrobe emergencies bag.

"Here." I hand her a folded garment. "Should fit."

It's a white Sunspel t-shirt. They're not cheap, but some of my clients – precious darlings – won't tolerate tacky brands. Normally I'd recover it on expenses, but this lady needs some dignity, so I'll take the hit.

She sits in the passenger seat and pulls it on over her blouse. Small fragments of crispy blouse fragments drift to the floor as she does so.

"Thank you. You're a life saver."

She makes a noise that's somewhere between a sigh and a wheeze.

I try not to stare, but I'm worried about her breathing. She inhaled that super-hot air. I don't know what that does to a person's insides, but it can't be good.

She does it again and I think it's just a sigh. The small exhalation of disbelief that a person makes when they realise they're not dead.

I'm still staring.

She brushes her hands over the leather interior of the Jaguar X351.

"Nice car," she says.

I nod. "Yeah. What can I say? I work in PR. Image is everything."

She nods.

I feel oddly shallow. I talk about image all day, every day, but talking about image to someone who's just walked out of a fire feels all kinds of wrong.

"Have you got somewhere to go?" I ask her.

She makes a small, throwaway gesture, like she's not just walked out of a burning house. One tear track is the only evidence of the upset she must have gone through. "I'll be fine." She pauses and a look passes over her, like she won't be fine. She's hugging the canvas bag close. "I just grabbed it. It's my dirty bloody laundry."

Her eyes go to the building. There's a crowd building up on the pavement. There's shouting, a sense of urgency, but also a sense of excitement like it really is Bonfire Night.

"I've got nothing," she says. "My phone, my cards..." Still sitting in the front of my car, she puts her hand in her jeans pocket. This Natasha moves delicately. She might say she isn't hurt but she's moving like she's got all-over sunburn.

I can see her pull the tip of a fiver from her pocket and she gives a dry chuckle. "Not even enough for a King Richard breakfast."

I feel overwhelmingly beholden to this young woman. She's early twenties at most. I've yanked her away from a nightmare and now she's sitting dirty and hurt in borrowed clothes while I stand over her. I feel like she's a cat I've pulled out of the canal and now she's my responsibility.

"Hang on," I say. I dip into my purse and pull out nearly a hundred quid in tens and twenties. "Will this help?"

Natasha coughs again as she looks at it. "It really will."

Can I afford to give that money away. No.

"I really don't want to be a bother," she says.

Am I over-compensating, feeling inadequate in this situation? Oh yes.

I hear the sound of the approaching fire engines, and

relief floods through me. It's time for the professionals to make this all better.

I really need to get on my way. Tyrese needs me at the hospital.

Again, I question my priorities as I try not to stare at the woman in my passenger seat. My eyes are drawn back to the building. Surely it's now burnt to a crisp?

Two fire engines and a smaller Fire Service vehicle pull up over the road, and then a police car pulls up behind me.

The two officers are talking in the car.

I take a step towards them. I just need to hand over Natasha, let them deal with her injuries and whatever happens next, and I can get to Leicester Royal Infirmary and my needy client. My lucrative client.

One of the police officers approaches me. He holds his ID. "Was it you who called in the fire?"

"It was," I say. "I really need to get on my way now, though."

He pulls out a notebook. "Can I please get your details first?"

I check the time. "Fine. Yes. But I really need to get going. I've got a situation."

"Name?"

"Hannah Douglas-Jones."

He makes a note. "What situation?"

"A client who doesn't know it, but whose career will be going down the pan if I don't step in and wave my PR wand."

"Dave!" calls the other officer from the car. This guy, Officer Dave, saunters back to his mate.

Fire fighters are clearing a path through the growing crowd. In only seconds they've got a hose connected and are starting to tackle the blaze.

Officer Dave comes back to me.

"That's your job then, is it?" he asks. "PR? It's why you're out here in the middle of the night?" His tone is sceptical.

I nod.

"And this car?" he says.

"What about it?" I say. "Shouldn't you be focusing on the woman who came out of the building?" I shake my head, and thrust my hand towards the car. "She needs some actual help."

"What woman?" he asks.

I turn to indicate Natasha in the passenger seat, but she's not there. The door is open and all that remains are some blouse fragments and a dusting of crispy brown powder.

I can't see her anywhere.

"She was just here. Like ten seconds ago."

"Uh-huh," says Officer Dave.

"You have to believe me."

"Actually, what I'd really like to know is what you're doing driving a stolen car."

I don't have an immediate answer to that.

3

"It's my dad's car," I tell Officer Dave.

"Oh, is it?" he says, still with the heavy scepticism. "Because the owner has reported it as stolen."

I know exactly what has happened. And this is bad. "What time?" I say.

"Sorry?"

"What time was it reported stolen? This is important."

Officer Dave frowns. "What is important is that you're driving a car that's been reported sto—"

"Yes, yes! I see that's what's important to you."

I'm trying not to snap. I try a smile, although I don't feel like smiling.

Deep breath, Hannah. Dealing with people is what you're good at.

"What's important to me is what my dad's doing," I say. I keep my tone reasonable, but I underline the urgency with little finger jabs. "He has dementia. If he's up at this hour and he's looking for his car, then his welfare is at risk. Do you understand?"

"We can look into that," says the officer.

That's a nothing statement, a non-helpful statement.

He opens the driver's side door and takes the keys out of the ignition. Just like that. Confiscates them like I'm a naughty little girl.

I get out my phone to call the house phone at home.

"Hey! No phone calls!" says Officer Dave.

"I'm trying to get hold of my dad!" I snap back at him.

He dithers and then gives me a curt nod before he walks back to his car and talks to someone on his radio. I can't hear anything over the noise from the fire and the shouts of the firemen.

Dad doesn't pick up the phone. It rings out.

"Shit."

He's fine if he stays in bed, but he could be up to anything if he's gone wandering off. I pull up the number for Marissa, the carer.

At least she answers, I tell her the bind I'm in. "I'm stuck somewhere and I think that Dad's got out of bed. I'm worried about him. Any chance you could pop over and see that he's all right?"

She is silent for a beat too long. I am really pushing my luck.

"I will go." It's a very terse reply by Marissa's standards. She's not best pleased.

"Thank you." I hang up. There will be fallout, but that's a problem for later.

I call Tyrese again.

"How's it going Tyrese?"

"I asked for morphine and they gave me paracetamol. You need to get here and sort them out."

"On my way."

"How long? You were going to be here by half past."

He's sobered up enough to check times. I sigh. "I've been held up, Tyrese. You are my number one priority and I'll be there very soon."

"When though? Do I need to call the Bourne Agency?"

"Whoa, whoa. No. You don't. Hold tight and let the hospital staff treat you."

I end the call.

I spend a moment imposing serenity upon my face. It's an important life skill, and has served me well. People shouldn't be able to see my agitation, they simply see a calm, controlled, well-groomed professional woman.

Thirty minutes they keep me waiting there, doing nothing.

The firemen have started to subdue the fire. I'm very late now.

"Any chance I might have a word?"

I didn't see this person walk over. He must have parked in a side road and walked up. Things are quite congested on the main road now.

"Hello?"

He holds up a police ID badge. *Detective Sergeant Rob Joseph*. A detective? At this hour?

Detectives investigate crimes. They don't turn up for house fires.

I wonder what's really happened here.

4

Detective Sergeant Rob Joseph wears a shirt and tie, which makes him instantly look like an old soul, even though he's no more than thirty-five.

I'm not certain whether his haircut is edgy or just bad. He has a fringe that sits high on his forehead, as if he's trying out for the role of 'ironic monk'.

"I need my car keys. I need to get along to Leicester Royal Infirmary." I name the hospital to try and drive home the severity of the situation. "Let's hurry this up."

"Yeah? Someone's in trouble are they?"

"A client, yes."

"Uh right." He has his notebook out. "Who's that then?"

"What does that have to do with anything?"

He inclines his head and looks at me gently. "I'm trying to understand what situation we have here. Help me understand, will you?"

There's a sincerity in his face that clashes with the neck tattoos that slide into view as he moves. The shirt and tie is a disguise, then.

"Fine." I huff mildly. I don't like sharing stuff like this. "The client is Tyrese Jali."

"The footballer?" he asks.

"Yes."

"Centre back for Leicester City."

"Yes."

"Cool," he says.

I fix him with a stare. "Do I need to hit you with a non-disclosure agreement?"

He holds up his hands. "Christ, no. I'm a fan, that's all."

That's all I need, but I bite down on any retort.

"And the car? What's the story there?" he asks.

"Urgh." I roll my eyes in frustration and try to give him the shortest possible version. "At a guess, he's seen his car wasn't there and he's got in a tizzy. I'm really worried about him."

"We're doing a safe and well check," he says.

"Oh?" I'm impressed that the other officer has followed up on this. It will be another annoyance for Marissa, but that can't be helped.

Of course, by safe and well check, they also mean that they are checking on the story that I told them. I don't care about that. Another pair of eyes on Dad is the important thing.

"Right. Tell me about the fire," he says, flipping over a page in his notepad. "You in this area a lot?"

I shake my head. "I was driving up here, I heard a massive bang. The fire – well you can see the fire. It was much bigger then."

"And this was at what time?"

"Something like three o'clock."

He's writing it all down. I want to ask about the fire, and if anyone was hurt, but it seems gauche. "I opened the window and I could hear the fire. I could really feel the heat on my face. I got out to go and look. I called 999."

He flips back a page or two. I guess he has the time of my call written there.

"Then I recorded some video."

"You have footage of the fire?" His eyebrows creep up towards that too-short fringe. He looks like a little boy when he does that and I try not to smile.

I find the video and show it to DS Rob Joseph. I forward it to him, when he asks.

He seems pleased.

"I stopped the video when I started hammering on doors, because my hands were full."

"Gotcha."

"That's when the woman came out of the burning building."

His eyes flash to me. "Wait, someone came out of there?"

I nod. "Yeah. I couldn't believe it. Still can't. She was lucky to be in one piece. Her hair was actually smouldering. Her blouse was all melted."

"Definitely a woman?" he says like it's important.

"She was a woman," I say. What else could I say?

He frowns and glances around. "Did she go in an ambulance? I've not heard any report of a survivor. I mean anyone coming out."

"No, she sat in my car, then she disappeared."

He looks surprised. "Can you describe her for me please?"

"Sure. She was white, about five foot six. Brown hair. Wearing jeans and a white t-shirt."

"You just said she had a melted blouse."

"I gave her the t-shirt. She said her name was Natasha."

"What kind of build was she?" He mimes a thin person, a hefty person.

I look at him. "Is this where I'm supposed to know how many kilos a person weighs?"

He gives a small laugh. "Do it how you want."

"She'd be a size twelve, I think."

He looks at me and unless the smoke has gone to my head he's comparing that with me and my size. Right now, in flat shoes, I'm looking at him eye to eye. In heels, I'd be looking down at him.

"And did the two of you speak at all?" he says.

"We did. Nothing of consequence. I gave her some water, suggested she should see the paramedics."

"She didn't want to?"

"No."

"She say why?"

"She just said that she was fine." I shake my head. "No way could anyone be fine after that. No way."

I don't mention that I gave her money. I feel slightly embarrassed, as if I can't quite remember why I did it. It felt right in the moment.

He recaps some specifics, jotting them all down, and then he gets a call which he takes with almost no comment at his end.

He looks at me when he ends the call. "Everything checks out with your dad. There's a carer with him now."

"Marissa. I gave her a call."

"Yeah. I reckon you're free to go now."

"Oh, really?" I say curtly. "Maybe you can get my bloody car keys then?"

"Sure," he says and smiles. He goes to the uniformed

Officer Dave and comes back with the car keys. I all but snatch them from him.

He passes me a card. "Any extra detail comes to you? Give us a call, yeah?"

I'm tempted to not take it but I do.

I pause for a second as I turn to my car.

"You asked me if it was definitely a woman," I say. "Like you were expecting maybe a man to have come out of there."

"Just asking questions," says DS Joseph.

I point at the extinguished fire, the ruin of the house, with gaping black holes for windows, like empty eye sockets.

"Was there someone else in there?" I ask. "Someone you knew was in there."

DS Joseph pulls a tight smile. "Like I say, any extra details, you let me know."

That's a 'yes' if ever I heard one. Bloody hell. There was someone else in there.

5

Even though I'm incredibly late arriving at the hospital, I still need to wait around. Tyrese has not yet been released.

He's pacing a cubicle. "This place is a shithole. Let's just go."

"You do know there's worse things? People in the world are worse off than you?"

He pulls a face.

"I'm serious. I got held up by a massive fire. A woman walked out of it. She was on fire. Actually on fire."

"Cool."

I look at him. Cool? What kind of a response is that? I just told him a woman was on fire. He's picturing it as a special effect. Tyrese is not the first client I've had that I suspect of being a sociopath. I need to squash that thought down and get on with the job.

"So can we go now?" he asks again.

"No. We do this by the book and then we'll get you somewhere off-grid for a few days," I tell him.

He got into a brawl with someone who wasn't invited to the party last night. The other person is in a bad way, and this could go very badly for Tyrese. Once I get him out of here, I need to spell that out for him. I don't think he gets it.

I need Tyrese to keep his head down while I get some decent intel on the other person.

Tyrese slumps into a chair with a pout. I peer at the dressing on his head, wondering if a baseball cap will cover it.

Like all top tier footballers, he's young, fit and handsome. He ought to be a dream client for someone like me, but Tyrese has fallen foul of using his fists in the past. It's not a good look for a wholesome young footballer, which is the image he should be presenting to the world.

I run through my mental checklist, both for his benefit, but also to double check in my own mind.

"I'm booking you into a retreat for a few days. Luxury spa. Keep you out of the public eye."

"I can go home and do that."

"This place has wall to wall facilities. You'll love it. Just a few days. Your socials are locked down. I've drafted a humble statement that we can whack out, if any details leak, and then you've got a whole heap of follow-up activities."

"Oh yeah? What like?"

"A little bit of charity work. Some youth coaching."

"Coaching's fine. What charity?"

I look at him hard. "We can flex on that. What's your favourite charity?"

"Cats. I like cats."

"Fair enough." I scribble a note while I try to re-frame Tyrese as a cat person in my mind. "Cats it is."

6

It's eight a.m. before I get home. It's late June and the sun is bright as I drive out of the city along the Hinckley Road. A battery warning light flickers on the car dashboard for a second as I drive. No idea why. I'm not going to spend money on getting the garage to look at a temperamental warning light.

I pull into the driveway of the large farmhouse that has been home to the Douglas-Jones family (who are certainly not farmers) for half a century. I half expect to find a police car parked out front. Instead, Marissa's car is pulled up in front of one of the two outhouses that are now garages. The police came for their safe and well check and Marissa, the carer, was called out. Fine.

I go in through the chunky black-painted door.

Crossing the threshold makes me want to go to bed straightaway, but such things are not possible. I messaged Karolina from the hospital, then phoned and asked her to meet me at mine for eight thirty. That's thirty minutes to get showered and changed out of clothes that reek of burning building. I need to pour enough caffeine down my neck to get prepared for a full and busy day.

I dress in sloppy gym gear. Karolina is one of the few people in my professional life who I permit to see me at anything other than my very best.

I open Dad's bedroom door and he's asleep in his pyjamas, the quilt tangled round him, his mouth open to the ceiling as he snores.

The first-floor spare room door is closed. Marissa will be in there, close to Dad. I don't disturb her.

I'm making coffee when Karolina comes in.

"Well, you look like shit," she says.

This is one of several standard greetings I get from her. She's my employee – my detective/fixer/general busybody – and she frequently talks to me like she's a disapproving aunt. I could blame it on the fact that she's a few years older than me. I could blame it on the rather direct nature that comes from her Latvian background. I don't think it's any of those things. Karolina Ozols talks to me like that because she can and I happily let her.

She has a face that's thin, a little sharp. As a matter of course, she dresses in the most wonderfully non-descript manner, like a mum halfway between the supermarket and the school run. When she needs to, she can dress for any situation.

"Coffee?" I say.

"Sure," she says, like I'm doing her a favour.

We sit in the bigger living room. I like to think it's full of personality, but really it's a bit cluttered in here. It's Dad's house, and naturally contains all of his things, but my collection of books is starting to dominate. Novels by Lisa Jewell and quirky non-fiction like those English place name references are edging out his old law books. There are pictures of me through the ages. As a ballet dancer on stage when I was small right through to my days as a holiday rep on the Greek island of Zakynthos. I'd sooner take some of them down, but Dad loves them.

"You smell smoke?" Karolina says.

"Really?" I sniff myself. "Still?"

I've told her the basics about the fire. It's an episode that's going to stick with me for a very long time. The sheer impact, the sensations, the randomness of it. But we've got work to do.

"Tyrese Jali," I say.

"A naughty boy."

"Six of one, half a dozen of the other," I say. "A fight at a house party thrown by a Leicester striker, Callen Rudge. You know him?"

Karolina wrinkles her nose. "I follow basketball."

"Tyrese got into a tussle with this guy, Oliver Chambers. Blows on both sides. According to Tyrese, this Oliver character was drunk as hell. We need to get on top of this story."

Karolina is making notes in what looks like a child's notepad. She has her methods and I've trusted her well for the last three years.

"I'm going to speak to the club media liaison," I tell her. "Get them to hold fire, maybe work on a joint statement. If one is needed."

"You want me to investigate this Oliver Chambers?" says Karolina. "And maybe find who else was at the party?"

I nod. "I've been watching socials and I've not seen anything yet, but there's no way someone didn't take photos or video."

Karolina agrees. "I can do all of that. If there's footage, you want me to buy it?"

I bite my bottom lip in a show of indecision. The correct answer is 'yes'. The only problem is the lack of money to do it. "Yes," I say with grim acceptance.

"Timescale?"

I flick to my calendar for the day. Shit. I've got Harvey Kenelm coming over at nine. That's now! I'd mentally skipped over that, my subconscious focussed on a much more important appointment later.

"I've got lunch with Todd Streetly at noon," I say.

Karolina cocks an eyebrow at me.

"What?"

"He's nice," she says. "You like him."

"I like his Safe As Houses campaign and his genuine desire to make something of this city," I say, perhaps a little too quickly. "Him personally I have no interest in."

"You need more friends," she says. "All work and no fun will turn Hannah into an old woman."

"Yeah."

"All dried up and wrinkled."

"Thanks. I don't need friends."

"At least you have me," says Karolina.

"We're colleagues."

"Trusted colleagues who care very much for each other," says Karolina. Her expression says the exact opposite, but that's her manner. "But you need more in your life than this."

I hear movement from the distant kitchen. Cupboard doors and rattling crockery. Dad.

"I've got to go," I say. "Drink your coffee. You all right with what we're doing?"

"Crystal clear," she says.

I go to the kitchen. Dad is in his jimjams and dressing gown and pottering about, making cereal. Bran flakes, raspberries sprinkled on top, a good splash of full fat milk. There's a notable tremor in his hands, but otherwise he's doing a good impression of being the master of his own household. Dementia isn't a single state. It's a rollercoaster. He tends to be at his best in the mornings.

"Morning, Dad."

"Ah, you up, sweetpea?"

I go over, grip his shoulders and put a kiss on his silver head. He used to be a giant of a man but he stoops a lot now.

He looks at my attire. "You not got work today?"

"I'm just getting going. You had a bit of an adventure last night."

"Did you?"

"You did. Making phone calls to the police in the middle of the night."

He gives me a frank stare of puzzlement. "Slept like a baby."

I keep the sigh on the inside. "Glad to hear it."

Marissa comes bustling into the kitchen in plastic slippers. She's originally from the Philippines. She is a very short woman. I'm nearly six foot and I loom over her. But she's strong enough to lift a full grown man when the situation demands. She's not wearing her normal carer's tabard. Understandable given she was called out in the middle of the night. Her unbrushed hair is pulled back in a ponytail.

"Good morning, Hannah." She sounds as tired as I feel.

She goes over and starts to help Dad with a task he was getting on perfectly well with by himself.

"Thanks for coming over," I say.

She grunts in response.

"Do you know how Dad managed to get hold of a phone in the night?" I ask.

"What do I need a phone for?" says Dad.

The doorbell rings.

"Postman?" says Dad.

I go to the front door. Karolina passes me her coffee cup as she opens the door.

"Hello," she says to Harvey Kenelm as she squeezes past to leave.

Harvey, Dad's old business partner and even older friend, turns to watch her as she leaves before looking back to me.

"Busy morning?" he says.

"Like you wouldn't believe," I tell him.

7

Detective Sergeant Rob Joseph thinks that there's something perfectly horrible about watching the sun come up while you're on the job.

The fact that you've missed the whole night is a smack in the face. A point of no return has been passed. It means the rest of the new day threatens to be a write off.

There are four police officers at the house fire now. Two of the constables are managing the cordon and the flow of traffic.

Rob has spoken to the Fire Incident Commander. The fire was brought under control a couple of hours ago, but the fire teams are taking it slow when it comes to actually getting inside. Problems with structural integrity. The Fire Incident Commander mentioned something about the floor in the kitchen being unstable.

The slowness of things is infuriating to Rob's tired brain.

A car pulls up along the road. Rob recognises it. It's Detective Inspector Scabbard.

"Bugger."

Knowing who the property had belonged to, Rob had radioed in for DI support an hour ago. Any DI could have turned up. It depended who was on duty.

He'd have preferred anyone other than Scabbard.

Greg Scabbard is a tall figure with dark hair that's receding, but it's at that point where it makes him look distinguished and wise, rather than just bald. He's got a look on his face that says he doesn't appreciate being called out during morning rush hour to one of the busiest roads in the city.

DI Scabbard doesn't like Rob. This isn't merely Rob's opinion. It's common knowledge. Scabbard is not sparing when it comes to letting detectives know he doesn't like them. He literally arranges them in the main office at Mansfield House like kids in a classroom. Teacher's pets nearest the DI, the naughty kids relegated to the corner.

"Sergeant," he nods to the uniformed officer nearby and then looks at Rob. "What are you doing here?"

"Morning, sir," says Rob. "Property got flagged when the call was made. It's part of Operation Chainlink."

"This?" says Scabbard, pointing at the smouldering building.

Operation Chainlink is the ongoing initiative to tackle rural crime around Leicestershire. It is a punishment, being assigned to Rob's team of three detectives because nobody else wants to do it.

"The property is owned by Paul Mulholland," says Rob. "A front man for the Degutis gang. Suspected of shipping stolen goods to Lithuania."

Scabbard doesn't seem quite able to believe him. "You're here because of some stolen tractors?"

"It's not just tractors, sir."

Scabbard snorts in disbelieving amusement. "Right. Anything to report?"

"The fire crews have not been able to go inside yet. Building's unsafe. I spoke to a witness when I arrived just after three. She was videoing the incident."

"Typical."

"She said a woman managed to escape the fire. The witness spoke to the woman, who gave her the name Natasha. She'd gone off by the time our first units arrived."

"Any clue on who this Natasha is?"

"I spoke to the owner of the corner shop just there," says Rob, pointing. "The landlord, possibly Paul Mullholland, rented rooms on the top two floors to uni students. It's out of term time so the rooms are mostly empty. I think we're going to struggle to find official records of who was renting what."

Scabbard nods. "Anywhere to get coffee round here?"

"Corner shop has one of them Costa machines."

"Okay. I'm going to get a drink. You can piss off."

"Sir?"

Scabbard gives him a steely look. "You've had your fun, Joseph. Played at being a big boy detective. If this is a suspicious fire, if this is linked to organised crime, then I will deal with it and pass it on to Organised Crime as necessary. You – you can piss off back to the nick and carry on looking for stolen tractors."

There's no point arguing. Rob nods a farewell to the uniformed sergeant and heads towards his own car.

8

Harvey Kenelm comes into our house, all red cheeks and slightly out-of-control hair. He and Dad were at Champion Fellowes solicitors together since before I was born. I don't know if it's universal but it seems that old partners don't retire but just sort of fade away. My dad was in his seventies and down to two afternoons a week at work before the dementia forced a final departure. Harvey Kenelm is not much younger and is still doing days here and there.

He wears a pinstripe suit every day as far as I can tell, although he ditched the tie years ago.

"You look like your mother more and more," he says, putting a kiss on my cheek.

He says this regularly. I can see I get a lot of my features from my mum. I got my height from my dad. My mum killed herself when I was fifteen and she was forty-five. I went off the rails a bit after that. She was married and had me by the age I am now. I think on that at times and can't imagine having children. Will I have my own demons to face when I get to forty-five?

"Come through," I say to Harvey.

"Just got some papers for you to sign and a monthly statement."

"Sure. Dad's in the kitchen."

"I don't want to disturb..."

I lead him through. Dad sits at the large farmhouse table, slurping at his cereal.

He looks up and it takes him only a second or two to click.

"Harvey. Are you—?" He looks around. "What time is it?"

"Just popping by, Donald," says Harvey. He adds extra jovial bluster whenever he sees Dad these days.

"I'm entirely unprepared," says Dad, gathering his open dressing gown around him.

"Harvey's just come for a drink and a chat," I say breezily as I go to make Harvey a coffee.

"Papers for Hannah to sign," says Harvey, patting his brown attaché case.

Harvey rocks on his heels and waits for his coffee. Dad stares at Harvey, spoon in hand.

"Harvey, why don't you tell Dad what you've been up to?"

I can see he's uneasy. As Dad's health has gradually worsened, Harvey has been more standoffish with his old friend, as though dementia is catching; as though Donald Douglas-Jones has already gone.

But with prompting, Harvey launches into a very pedestrian account of what he's been up to. His wife and two children are reduced to tiny updates. Linda is lunching with her lady friends every day. Stuart is enjoying Dubai. Alicia is still at the Foreign Office doing something complicated. Only when Harvey mentions that some new outfit has taken over the restaurant at the golf club do both men come to life. Dad is suddenly animated and, for a minute, the two of them are able to talk with ease about the shocking food and service they'd put up with for the last few years. Dad talks as though he goes to the club every day. It's been nearly a year since he last went.

As soon as the coffee machine stops spitting and gurgling, Harvey turns the conversation off and looks to me. He's done his duty. He's opened up his old friend's coffin and shown his respects. Time to move on. I want to say that we don't need to leave Dad, that he can stay and talk. But, no, Harvey has moved on, mentally and emotionally. Harvey might be a ray of sunshine in Dad's meaningless jumble of days, but Harvey doesn't want to engage. Sadness pulls inside me.

"We're just going to sort out some papers," I tell Dad and take Harvey's coffee through to the lounge.

I hear Dad slurping his cereal again before we've even got there.

I sit on the settee. Harvey sits next to me.

He breaks out the papers and the statements. If I had access to the accounts, I'd be able to look these up myself, but these are Dad's accounts and he granted Harvey Lasting Power of Attorney over his finances.

"The current account, the savings account, the long term ISAs," he says, spreading sheets on the coffee table.

It is all as expected. Dad, and therefore me with him, are caught up in a peculiar though not unique situation. Dad owns the house outright. He owns the car that I drive. He has no debts at all. In terms of property, he is a wealthy man. The house alone is worth nearly three-quarters of a million. And yet his income is modest. His private pension pays a decent amount but it was never intended to also cover the cost of a carer on call twenty-four hours a day. Or a cleaner, laundry services and a gardener. The house is huge and is expensive to heat and run. The council tax on this property is high.

In short, once everything's been paid for, there is no money for food and home maintenance. And definitely nothing for fun.

It's almost impossible to understand from the outside, but Hannah Douglas-Jones and her dad live in a six-bedroomed farmhouse with a sleek black Jaguar X351 on the drive and they are, nonetheless, somehow, poor. Clients like Tyrese Jali will provide me with the kind of income I need to contribute fully to our tiny family, but I don't have enough clients like Tyrese Jali. Not yet.

I'm working like a devil to keep Dad in the home he loves. I don't know if I'm going to succeed.

9

"These are the ISAs we've cashed in," says Harvey, sliding more paper in front of me. "That should keep you going until next year."

We could sell the house. Of course we could. But Dad's at a stage where new things are confusing and frightening. We went away for one night, to Cromer. The terror in his voice in the night was gut-wrenching. And with terror, there's sometimes violence.

I don't want to move him out. I definitely don't want him to go into care, even though I know there will come a time when he needs a level of care that Marissa and I won't be able to provide.

Harvey passes me some papers to sign.

"What about the Brascote buildings?" I say. "Any joy there?"

The Brascote buildings are some ruined barns by the side of a small lake a few miles away that Dad bought decades ago.

"Ah," says Harvey, raising a pudgy finger. "The developers

are still interested, and old Mr Chestnut is perhaps willing to sell the ransom strip to allow construction access."

"That's good."

"I expect a call from them any day now."

"I'd like to have access to that money," I say.

Harvey looks directly at me. "You? Personally? It was your father's money."

I ignore the fact that he accidentally referred to Dad in the past tense.

"There are things for it to be spent on, for his benefit," I say. "Harvey, I don't want to have to come to you, cap in hand, every time we need the plumbing fixed or a room decorating."

He chuckles in a fatherly manner. "You can call on me anytime, Hannah. You know that."

He puts his hand on my knee and squeezes. I maintain the external serenity on my face and try not to flinch.

Once Harvey has gone, I prepare quickly for lunch with Todd Streetly of the *Safe As Houses* campaign.

I shower, again, and dress. Ivory silk blouse over taupe culottes with a light blazer and tan court shoes. Accessorised with a simple gold necklace, a dark leather tote bag big enough for my laptop and notes and a spray of *Femme* – currently my favourite eau de toilette. It has more than a hint of buttery pastry about it.

I check my phone for messages. Nothing from Karolina yet. No messages from Tyrese.

I put out feelers to some friendly tabloid journalists, one of whom definitely owes me a favour. Neither have replied, but it's only eleven in the morning. This is okay. The scandal that might yet bubble up around Tyrese has not yet woken and we're in the 'holding' stage. Right now the role of Team

Tyrese is to hold, ignore, deflect and deny. Any statements going out right now will say nothing and admit nothing. Depending on how fast this thing grows, we will then move onto the dirty business of 'contextualising' – excuses, accusations, misdirection – before moving as quickly as possible onto 'rebuilding', where any necessary apologies and periods of reflection will be announced, alongside some heart-warming charitable donation.

My purse is light on cash after I gave the money to that woman, Natasha, in the night. I go to the study where I keep a small supply. The drawer is empty. I don't remember taking the last of it. But I'm tired. I'll have to withdraw some later.

I find Marissa encouraging Dad to get dressed for the day. I tell her my plans and give him a kiss before heading out.

As soon as I get in the Jag, that smoke stink hits me again. I can't believe how it seems to have impregnated everything. And the smell brings back the almost dream-like images of the night just gone. The young woman's face, dirty, filled with the rush of what she'd just experienced, is etched into my mind. Insane. I wonder where she is right now.

10

I drive into the city with the windows open and the blowers on, hoping to dispel some of the smell.

The 1573 is a pleasant lunch spot in a converted schoolhouse in the city. Todd Streetly is already there, occupying a table for two commanding a view of the rest of the bar. He stands to shake my hand.

"Sorry, I'm late."

"I'm early," he assures me. "Had a meeting about the Great Central Street apartment developments. The ones that got held up by that shooting incident at the building site earlier in the year."

"I know the ones. I knew someone involved."

"You seem to know everybody."

"I do, don't I?" I say.

We order. I go for plaice goujons, cauliflower wings and a side of chips. Todd orders a burger.

Karolina is right when she says I like Todd. I do like him. I'd say he's physically not my type, except I think that people who have a 'physical type' are unaware that people have personalities too. Todd is a big guy. He sits right on that boundary between muscle and flab. Fifteen years as a builder and even though he now wears suits and expensive shirts, he looks like a builder. Powerful hands. A neck as wide as his head. He wears his clothes well. I like him a lot.

Todd owns and runs Streetly Construction, which is one of the biggest independent property developers in the city. He did not build it from the ground up. Like most of us, he is who he is because of the leg up his parents gave him, in this case by inheriting his dad's firm, but he's made Streetly Construction his own and made something of a splash by grasping the current drive for ethical and considerate construction and accelerating it forward.

His *Safe As Houses* campaign has already made some media splashes. Famously, he zeroed in on the Oakleaf Road tragedy in Leicester last autumn, in which carbon monoxide filled a house of multiple occupancy, killing five residents and putting another in a coma that I don't think she'll ever wake from. He can speak with passion, intelligence and earthy common sense that really hits home.

It's easy to get him to talk about the campaign's goals and I want him to.

"There are so many things that still need doing," he says. "There's no universal accreditation for fire risk assessors at the construction stage. There's no legal requirement for personal evacuation plans for vulnerable residents from shared accommodation. And there's inconsistent oversight of so-called lower-risk buildings."

"There's so much I love about your campaign," I say.

"Yeah?"

"It has such clean, clear and relatable goals."

"Er, okay?"

I use my hand to chop up my points as I make them. "We all want safe homes. No one is against safe homes. The way forward is clear."

"Some people in the trade don't want more red tape."

"So it's red tape, political laziness and, let's face it, basic greed that's stopping this."

"It is. But can I be honest?"

"Please," I say.

"I get you want us to use your services, but you don't strike me as..." he makes an uncomfortable gesture "...the kind of person to get excited by construction work."

This is code. The posh bird and the builder. Is it a good fit?

"It's not about me," I say. "It's about what we all have in common. We all have homes. We want our homes to be fit for purpose. Trust me, I've got a dad in a crumbling farmhouse that's too big, too draughty and not suitable for a man in his seventies. We all care about where we live."

He pauses as the food is brought over.

"You hear about that fire off the Narborough Road last night?" he says as he picks up his cutlery.

I laugh. He gives me a funny look.

"I was there," I say. I sniff my lapel. "I think I've still got the smell of it on me."

He puts his fork down. "You're kidding me."

"I'm not. It was terrifying."

I don't have to exaggerate. Distance has given me perspective and I realise I'd never understood how powerful, how frighteningly overwhelming a house fire could be. That place was an oven. And it all comes tumbling out over our lunch. And there's a point at which it's no longer Hannah the image consultant telling it but Hannah the fragile human being. And I let her because a) I need to get it out and b) I think Todd is the kind of person who understands.

His hand comes across the table and briefly squeezes mine before retreating.

"That's shocking. And the woman you helped out?"

I laugh weakly. "I'm not sure I even helped. She came bursting through that door, using her bag as a shield and I just sat her down, gave her some water. The blouse had literally come apart on her back."

"Was there anyone else inside?"

"I don't know," I say.

"These are the kind of stories that we need to get out there. We need policymakers to understand."

I have to work to bring myself back from sounds and smells and eyeball-searing heat of the fire. "My company can help get those stories in exactly the right places. You do press releases and you look good on the TV, Todd – no, you do – but getting a story into the world in a way that makes it live beyond those few hours. That's a skillset you need." I try not to think about how much the *Safe As Houses* money will do to keep my business and my family in the black. It's hard not to think about it.

"You think we could work up something about this woman in the fire? What was her name?"

"Natasha," I say. "We didn't swap details."

"You spoke."

"To check she was all right. I gave her a T-shirt and a bottle of water. And some cash."

"You give out cash to fire victims?"

I smile. "She had nothing. A bag of laundry. What was it she said? Not enough cash for a King Richard breakfast. I don't know."

Todd grins. "Maybe a fan of the Silver Street café?"

"Huh?"

"King Richard breakfast." He marks out a huge plate with his hands.

"Is that so?" I say. "I mean if I did find her..."

"I can see that you're coming for my business, Hannah. You can smell blood in the water."

"Not the analogy I would have used," I smile back. "But I do want to be in business with you."

11

Detective Constable Josie Kaminski is making a round of drinks and she wants to make sure that everyone sees. She clatters the mugs on a tray and makes a big show of putting one on Walker's desk, one on DS Rob Joseph's desk, and then one on her own. She bashes the tray once more for luck as she puts it aside.

Walker and Rob exchange glances at her performance, but she's not doing it for them. She's really doing it to show DI Scabbard that she's a team player. He's sent her to sit with the Dead End Duncans but he has not succeeded in denting her spirit or crushing her ambition.

Yeah, like fuck.

Scabbard's not even looking. The DI has his own office space nearby: a glass partition keeping him in splendid isolation. His office door is closed, the blinds down.

Several months ago, she saw Scabbard take a fat envelope from the solicitor for the Degutis gang. It was a secretive, furtive handover, but he saw her looking and he got right up in her face – told her she'd seen nothing. That moment had stayed with her and now she was keeping her eye on him.

"Scabbard's not even in," says Rob.

Josie tuts and thumps the nearest desk.

"Steady," says Walker. He pulls a hanky from his pocket to mop up where Josie has spilled his coffee. Everyone calls him Walker even though his proper name is Patrick. DC Patrick Smith.

"A hanky," she says. "Didn't know they even still existed in the world."

He rolls his eyes. "It's because I am from the olden days, Josie."

Walker is in his fifties, surely nearing retirement age. Josie reckons that if she was Walker's age and still a DC, she'd be climbing the walls. She admires his fortitude, but has no clue how he doesn't go mad.

"But you do know they invented tissues, right?" she says. "Nobody needs to carry a pouch of their own snot round in their pocket anymore."

Rob is about to take a bite of his breakfast sandwich. He sighs and puts it down again. "Is there any chance you could not talk about bogies for a few minutes? I've already been up six hours."

Josie's about to point out the difference between snot and bogeys, but she thinks better of it and flops in her chair instead.

CID occupies a large open plan office at Mansfield House police station. Josie, Walker and Rob are relegated to the corner most distant from Scabbard's office. Occupants of that particular corner are called the Dead End Duncans, or just Duncans. The nickname predates Josie being consigned to the team. She doesn't know the origins of the name, just like she doesn't know why everyone calls Walker 'Walker'. The Duncans have a row of cupboards between them and the other CID teams to mark their territory; their own little island cluster of desks.

It's a social exclusion, being a Duncan.

"Up six hours?" says Josie to Rob.

"Mmm," he says around a bite of sandwich. "I'll tell you in a minute."

She glances at Walker. He's scrolling through his emails, rather than waiting on tenterhooks for whatever the DS is about to share.

"Right." The DS wipes his fingers on the paper bag that his sandwich came in. "Josie, remember you did some work tracing some of the stolen trailers?"

"Yeah. My intense Facebook Marketplace sleuthing turned up that fake website selling Ifor Williams trailers."

"That possibly fake website," says Rob.

"That *totally* fake website," Josie corrects him. "Looked so wholesome. Good old Charlie Bates."

The website was full of videos of this character 'Charlie Bates' showing prospective customers his wares. Josie casts her mind back, trying to remember some of Charlie's favourite phrases. "Sound as a pound, this one!" She mimics a fake geezer voice.

"And obviously there is no real Charlie Bates," says Rob. "But we did draw a line between the website, the Degutis gang and one of their associates, Paul Mulholland."

"Yes." Josie remembers it mostly as frustration. Whenever the Duncans get a sniff of anything juicy, they have to hand it over to the organised crime team.

"Well, a house belonging to Mulholland on the

Narborough Road went up in flames in the small hours of the morning."

"Bloody hell," says Walker.

"Arson?" says Josie.

Rob shrugs. He answers his phone which has begun to ring. "We'll be down there immediately, sir," he says.

Walker and Josie look at him as he ends the call.

"Scabbard wants us back at the scene of the fire. They've found a body."

12

In twenty-twelve, the body of King Richard III was found beneath a car park in Leicester. The location, how he came to be there and how he came to be found have been recounted in books and movies since then and the people of Leicester took their dead Plantagenet king to their hearts. Overnight, half of everything got renamed the King Richard. Roads, pubs and, apparently, breakfasts.

I don't give Todd any hint that I'm rushing. I enjoy his company and make sure that my offer to him and his campaign leaves a solid impression. But as soon as we're done, I go straight to Silver Street. Through Highcross, down the High Street and to the Silver Street café. I don't know it personally. I tend not to do greasy spoon cafés. But I'm thinking I can go ask at the counter about a young woman, maybe in a white Sunspel T-shirt.

What I don't expect to see is that very same young woman in a white Sunspel T-shirt sitting at a table by the wall, stirring a big cup of coffee and staring blankly at it.

I go in and stand next to Natasha's table.

She looks up and stares. She blinks.

"What the hell?" she whispers.

"Can I join you?"

She looks around wildly as though in horror that she might be seen in here with me. But no one is paying attention.

"What the hell?" she repeats.

"I hoped to find you here. Another coffee?"

She stares for the longest time. "Mocha," she says eventually.

I go to the counter and order a mocha for her and a cup of tea for myself.

"You want your money back, right?" she says.

I shake my head. "I simply wanted to talk to you."

"What for?"

"We really didn't get to talk last night." I realise those events are only twelve hours ago. The fire. The heat in the darkness. The sheer physicality of the flames ripping through that building. It feels like an age ago already.

"Was there something you forgot to say?" she asks.

There are pink marks on her neck and the back of her hands. It looks like sunburn. It isn't.

"You've not been to the hospital."

"I don't need to go to the hospital."

"They'll at least put some cream on that, or something."

"I'll be all right." She scrunches up her face and blinks hard. "Got a bloody headache, like hangover style."

"Who knows what you breathed in."

"You trying to make me feel better?" she asks sourly.

She's got fight and spirit. This young woman with attitude who walked out of a fire. She's like some sort of unkillable creature out of myth. I'm starting to like her a lot.

"Tell me about yourself," I say.

"What's there to say?"

"You're called Natasha. I don't know anything else."

She huffs and empties a sugar sachet into her mocha. "I'm a student."

"Uni?"

"Leicester Uni. That place was where I was living during term time."

"But it's summer break right now, isn't it?"

"Yeah. I haven't exactly got a home to go back to. Long story."

"Who else lived there?"

She shakes her head. "There was a business on the ground floor. Some women lived downstairs. I didn't know them." She twitches uncomfortably. "I'm not sure I want to talk about this. I've got a headache. I need to get some sleep at some point." She meets my eyes with a penetrating gaze. "Listen. Thank you for what you did..."

"Hannah."

"Right. Hannah. You're one of the good people. But, yeah, that's it."

A thought pops into my head. No, that's a lie. It's been lurking under the surface for a while and now it's finally risen to the front of my mind. This girl is charismatic. She's been through hell. She's got grit. I bet the situation with her building and landlord will turn out to be exactly the kind of thing Todd's *Safe As Houses* campaign wants to target. Todd is only one handshake away from signing up with me. The company could do with his money. I *need* the money.

"Listen," I say. "You need somewhere to stay. Somewhere to rest and recover. I'd really like to hear more from you about the story of last night."

"I'm not interested in telling anyone my story," she says. "I'm not that kind of person."

"We could do it in whatever way you like."

"I don't want to be on TV news or anything. Who'd want that?"

"Nothing like that, I assure you," I say. "Nothing you don't want to do."

My phone buzzes. I look at it. It's a video call from Karolina. She often video calls.

I stand. "Do not go anywhere," I tell Natasha. "Let me just take this."

I step outside the café where smokers sit at silvered tables and watch the world go by.

"Hey," I say, answering.

"Hello," says Karolina. I can see on the call that she's outside somewhere. She's chewing something, maybe a donut. *"You want the bad news or the less bad news?"* she says.

"It's traditionally good news and bad news."

"Well, I don't have that." She swallows what she's chewing. *"The less bad news is that I've tracked down a lot of people at the footballer's party. I found a chatty lady who was very helpful. I have reached out to most of them and made a standard offer for any pictures or video. One woman, Lilja someone, a model apparently, is being awkward. She mentioned selling what she had to the tabloids."*

"Shit."

"Yes."

"Lilja who?"

There is a judder as she juggles phone and notepad. *"Lilja Eiríksdóttir. Icelandic."*

"You're gonna have to spell that," I say but there's already a buzz on the phone. Karolina has messaged it through.

I immediately do a search.

"Model, huh?"

"Wants to be a model. Clearly thinks her path to success is hanging around at footballers' parties."

I'm not a bitch but I can see from her Instagram feed that those modelling dreams aren't likely to come true. She's got youth and a narrow frame on her side, but that's not enough.

"She needs a better portfolio, I reckon," says Karolina.

We're on the same wavelength. "Get in touch with one of our photographers. Set something up. A photoshoot in exchange for whatever she's got on her phone. I'll add it to Tyrese's bill."

"Will do."

"That was the bad news, right?" I say.

Karolina laughs. *"Oh no. This one. There is no good way to say it. The man Tyrese punched."*

"Oliver Chambers."

"Tyrese said he was drunk."

"Yeah."

"The man has cerebral palsy, Hannah."

13

This hits me hard like the punchline to a sick joke.

"What?"

"He has cerebral palsy," says Karolina. *"You know the thing with—"*

"I know what cerebral palsy is."

"By what Lilja tells me, the injuries to Tyrese's face, the guy did them with his walking stick. His crutches."

This is beyond awful. Premier League footballer hospitalises a man with cerebral palsy in party fistfight. I can't think of a worse headline.

"You can be drunk *and* have cerebral palsy," I hear myself say.

"You think that fucking matters, Hannah?"

"No, of course it doesn't," I say. "Shit."

"It is shit, like you say."

Right now I want to drive round to the De Morgan hotel spa retreat where I've relocated Tyrese and bellow at him for an hour straight.

Of course, it wouldn't do any good. I'm starting to think

that any man who can punch a person with a disability and not happen to mention that key fact to his own PR woman is the kind of person who has already morally justified the act to himself.

And yelling is not going to make the problem go away. I need to swallow down my contempt for Tyrese and work out what to do. And then add some zeroes to his fee.

"Excuse me."

The fire victim, Natasha, is on the pavement beside me. She's got her pathetic canvas bag in what I see is her less-injured hand. She stands like someone heading somewhere.

"Let me think on that," I say to Karolina. "Gotta go."

She nods.

I hang up. Natasha speaks before I can.

"This place you have? This is a place I can stay?"

"Yes?"

"What's it like?"

"Er. It's a big old farmhouse. Five miles out of the city. Just me and my dad there. If you think you might—"

"Okay. Let's do it," she says.

I stare. "Great."

"Somewhere to stay. Somewhere to rest. I really don't feel well. And maybe we'll talk – but no press, okay? I'm not doing that."

"No," I say, thrilled. "Not a problem. Let's do it."

I drive Natasha home.

Her mouth hangs open when she sees the farmhouse. "This is your place?"

"It's my dad's house. Family home. We'd sell if we could but he's not well and... It's definitely got room for one more person."

I lead her inside. I'd offer to carry her bags but she's barely got anything.

Marissa is in the hallway.

"We've got a house guest," I tell her. "This is Natasha. I'm putting her in the top floor guest room."

"Hi," says Natasha politely.

I get Natasha up to the second floor.

"You've got fucking servants?" she whispers.

"My dad's carer."

The guest room really needs airing, but the bed is made and will do for now.

"There's a bathroom just along the corridor," I explain. "You have to wait a while for the hot water to come through but it's there."

"I'm going to sleep now," says Natasha. Her voice is almost a monotone. She's seen the bed and her brain is already dragging her into sleep.

As I close the door, she lies on the bed, fully clothed.

I go downstairs and look in the first aid drawer for anything we could use on her burns. We've got a tube of Savlon and some E45 cream.

Dad is in the smaller cosier lounge at the back of the house. He's starting to doze. Afternoons can be difficult for Dad. The confusion comes on in waves and there's no point taxing him when he's not at his best.

I'd normally be working in my office during the day but this has been no ordinary day. I sit with Dad while he snoozes and work out what the hell to do next with Tyrese.

Punching a man with cerebral palsy. Jesus!

That's a difficult story to polish. Contextualising a story like that and reframing so that Tyrese isn't the biggest arsehole in the narrative is going to require superpowers.

The football club's own media team have been back in touch. I put together a suggestion for a joint press release and provide them with talking points that they can use – which is basically none. I'm starting to think that I need to deploy an even bigger scandal story so that when this stuff hits the tabloids – which it is still very likely to do – then we can deflect with something bigger and even more shocking.

What's even more shocking than a premier league footballer punching a member of the disabled community? I'm going to have to work hard on this.

I message Tyrese on the phone I gave him and put the facts to him. I don't phone him because, frankly, I don't want to hear his voice right now. He replies cagily. He uses the phrase, *I knew there was something wrong with that guy.*

Fuck. I won't be using that as a quote.

I think about my houseguest.

I send some more e-mails. I thank Todd Streetly for meeting me for lunch. The afternoon sun comes through the windows and makes the air warm.

I close my eyes, just for a second.

I wake abruptly to the sound of laughter from elsewhere in the house.

The sun is low, the light an orange glow now.

Dad's no longer in his seat.

14

I stand up groggily and look at my phone.

I've slept for three hours.

I curse myself for just drifting off like that. Sure, I've had no sleep in the last twenty-four hours, but I thought I was stronger than that. Daytime dozing while there's work to be done. It makes me feel weak and vulnerable.

I hear the laughter again. It's Dad.

Shaking myself, I move through the house. I try to force myself to feel awake, feel normal.

I step into the larger living room and find Dad there.

He's in his favourite armchair. Natasha sits in front of him on a leather footstool with one of the little nested tables between them. On another low table next to her is an open laptop that I don't recognise. It's scuffed around the edges.

Natasha puts down a playing card on the table and Dad follows.

I watch them at play. Dad is intent on the game. Natasha looks up at me. She smiles. She's got a beautiful smile.

"Hey, what you doing?" I say.

"Beggar-my-neighbour," says Dad without looking up.

"I think we used to call it Ratscrew," says Natasha. "Your dad is beating me."

He's just laid a king. "Come on. Pay up."

"I think I fell asleep for a bit," I say.

"You looked peaceful," says Natasha.

"And how are you?"

She turns over an ace. "Now you pay me, Donald," she says. She stretches out her arms and looks at me. "I hurt. Delayed reaction. I need a shower."

"I can sort you out with some clothes," I say, having no idea what we might have that would fit her. "Is that your laptop?"

Natasha nods. "Old college one. Was in the bag I grabbed to shield myself. Thought I'd see if it was still working. I'll need a charger for it, though."

Marissa comes in with a tray of fruit slices for Dad. He can use a knife and fork perfectly well, but he seems to have developed a fondness for finger food. He snatches apple slices and orange segments from the plate.

He turns over a jack. "Ha! Pay up."

Natasha turns over a card in payment and he gathers the pile of cards victoriously.

"You're lucky," she says.

"Skill," he replies.

"Used to help out at a kid's holiday club," she says to me. "Card games are an essential skill."

"Anything to keep them occupied, right?" I say, with a smile. I remember my days as a holiday rep in Greece. You soon learn every trick, diversion and game in that kind of environment.

Beggar-my-neighbour is one of those games that's almost

impossible to finish and I want to rescue Natasha from it. But, at the same time, both she and Dad seem to be having such a nice time.

I'm about to ask if she's working at the moment, then I remember she said she was at the uni.

"What are you studying?" I say.

"It's a public services degree."

"What's that?"

"Hospitality. Tourism."

"You want to work in a customer-facing role?" I ask.

She shrugs as she taps at a queen she's just laid. "I'm good with people."

"Should have a word with Ann Martin, see if they need anyone in the admin office," says Dad.

Ann Martin hasn't worked at Champion Fellowes solicitors in five years.

"I'll show you my workplace tomorrow," I say.

She shrugs again like she doesn't care one way or the other.

After the almost interminable game is brought to a close, I tell Natasha I'll find her some fresh clothes while she gets a shower. I find some drawstring leggings, a pair of shorts that can work as pyjamas or underwear, and some more T-shirts. As I bring them up to the second floor, I can hear her gasping and wincing in the bathroom.

"You okay?"

"I'm..." she pauses and hisses. "I'm peeling. I look awful."

I get her the Savlon and the E45. She comes out with a towel fully wrapped round her. Her forearms are pink and shiny. It looks alarming.

"You need this stuff. All over."

She takes them. "Thanks, Hannah."

She says it like she really means it. This young woman has the kind of face that draws the eye, that people want to pay attention to. Inferno survivor poster girl for Todd's *Safe As Houses* campaign?

That's my goal.

15

It's been a long day at the scene of the house fire.

By the time evening comes, Walker thinks that DS Rob Joseph looks so tired he could just walk onto the set of a zombie movie, no makeup required.

Walker has messaged his family to say he's going to be late home for dinner. It's mildly depressing that no one seems bothered by this fact. Helen replies to tell him that it's her book group night so she won't be in anyway. Amber, home from uni, replies that she's off out with friends to some 'fried chicken place'. Walker's son, Oscar, doesn't reply at all but that's pretty standard.

DC Josie Kaminski spends a lot of time huffing and pacing and asking no one at all why the fire people are taking so long to let them inside. Walker likes Josie, but she's got too much fire, too much energy. Her sin is that she is a loud and ambitious woman and the world still isn't ready for those.

DI Scabbard (who, if rumours are to believed, had a drunken fumble with Josie that permanently soured his professional opinion of her) has told her to shut up and stand still more than once. She's gone to stand with the waiting crime scene investigators and is now chatting with Crime Scene Manager Sanjee Baksh who seems happy to talk.

Eventually, the Fire Incident Commander, a craggy man with a cage-fighter's build, invites them all forward.

"Right," he says. "You need to see this. I'm going to show you what we've found, but you stand where I tell you and when I say 'no further' I mean it. Crime Scenes," he says to Sanjee, "you'll need to work out how to work through this."

"What have you got?" says Scabbard.

"The fire was particularly intense in the ground floor kitchen. Looks like a commercial kitchen. Ceiling collapsed from above, a lot of waterlogging. As you know, we found a severely burned body in the kitchen. It will not be identifiable by sight. Trust me. DNA or dental records will be needed."

"Paul Mulholland," suggests Josie.

No one offers an opinion.

"Survey concluded that there was a cellar space beneath the property," says the Fire Incident Commander. He's walking them in now. The place smells of woodsmoke and chemical dust. To Walker's mind, it smells unsalvageable. It smells of devastation.

"Through here," says the commander. "Only stand in the hallway."

He leads them through. The blackened walls and ceiling feel like they're closing in above them. Temporary lighting rigs have been set up to provide some illumination. A pump judders nearby, trying to empty out some of the standing water.

"Kitchen that way," says the commander. "Cellar door here."

He gestures to a door – once white, now blackened and smashed in. Walker can just about see past Scabbard and down the stairs. Brickwork and darkness below. Further temporary lights have been set up down there.

"We're not going down there now," says the commander. "Another hour to make it safe. But we have found at least four bodies down there."

"What?" says Josie.

"Looks like it was being used as sleeping or living quarters," says the commander.

Scabbard's hand touches the outside of the door frame and the remnants of a latch.

"This door. It was locked from the outside?"

"It was," says the commander with a finality that indicates this was what he really wanted to show them. "Padlocked."

"The people down there were locked in," says Rob.

They can't see into the cellar, can't see the four people dead below them, but Walker's brain conjures up an instant image of them. Four people dying in a burning, airless building.

Scabbard turns to Rob. "This person of interest you were watching, Paul Mulholland... What the hell was going on here?"

16

There's a police briefing for the house fire case, bright and early on Tuesday morning.

The meeting room at Mansfield House police station is crowded, because there are people here from the fire service, forensics, organised crime and almost every department in the station.

DI Scabbard's got the role of senior investigating officer, so he's running the briefing.

"Settle down!" he calls. The hubbub in the room ceases immediately. Not just because Scabbard is a hardass, but because this case has shocked everyone.

"We'll run through the headlines and move on to the different strands of investigation."

He signals to someone who's projecting images onto a screen.

"Images of the property shown here, both before the fire and afterwards. Completely gutted internally." The slides change to show detail of the padlocks. "The cellar room which was secured from the outside." He points at the screen. "The commercial kitchen appears to have been separated internally from the other side of the building where more conventional offices and accommodation were located."

There's a view of the property with a thick dotted line drawn to show the separation.

"The property is all owned by the same legal entity Purple Heron Holdings. Tracing that down to a human we can talk to has proven difficult." Scabbard sounds exasperated. "Purple Heron Holdings are registered in the UK, but the only listed director is one Dieter Blass, a company formation agent who manages hundreds of companies. He has no information or personal involvement with the company. Their listed address is an office in London, which exists solely for the purposes of forwarding mail."

Josie rolls her eyes at this. How is this even legal?

"Our colleagues in organised crime might want to expand on the narrative." Scabbard waves to a woman sitting near the front. "DI Bacon."

Josie has seen Abi Bacon before. She has a somewhat hawkish face, as if she suspects everyone of wrongdoing. It's a powerful face, if not conventionally attractive. Nobody would accuse Abi Bacon of using her feminine wiles to climb the ranks.

"This is one of several models that we often associate with gangs and organised crime," says DI Bacon. "Not in itself conclusive proof that this property is owned by a criminal enterprise, but it will take us some time to peel back the layers of obfuscation. We have been made aware of some possible links to the Degutis gang, based on leads uncovered by the major crimes unit, so we're working that hypothesis for now. An individual named Mulholland remains a person of interest. We're not yet sure if he's amongst the victims of the fire, or whether he remains at large."

She turns to the screen. "A commercial kitchen was operating in the building. We believe it was there solely to fulfil deliveries. A so-called 'ghost kitchen'. That, coupled with imprisoned victims, would appear to point at modern day slavery, possibly connected with human trafficking. Again, a hypothesis, but a strong one."

Scabbard takes over again. "Thank you DI Bacon. Now, a focus for us will be to identify those individuals who were associated with this building. We want to know who lived here, who died here, and who went here – in any capacity whatsoever. So far we have anecdotal evidence that suggests students rented rooms in the opposite side of the building from the kitchen. We would like to speak with those students, one of whom was seen walking away during the fire. First name Natasha, according to a witness. We're working with the university to get a shortlist of students by that name. We need to follow up with that witness." Scabbard points at Rob who returns a nod. "We have located a ring doorbell in a nearby house with some partial coverage of the building, but it looks as though we'll be relying mainly on house-to-house. We'll be talking to neighbouring houses and businesses. We've also got an appeal for information going out on local news this evening."

Josie wonders how effective that will be. When something happens that shocks the public, they will get a lot of calls. Not always helpful ones, but something might come of it.

"Post mortems will be spread over a couple of days because we have multiple victims. I'll need someone from my team to cover those."

Scabbard's looking at Detective Sergeant Dean Beaches, but Beaches murmurs something indistinct. Even though Josie can't hear what he's saying, it's clear Beaches is making some sort of bullshit excuse. It's well-known that post mortems for cases like this, where death has been caused by an intense fire, can be overwhelming and traumatic. It's a sensory overload of horror, from the stink of charred flesh to the sound of the pathologist's knife cutting through blackened, crispy skin.

Josie puts her hand up. "I'll go, sir."

Scabbard isn't happy, but he's impatient and wants to move on. "Fine."

"Er, while we're at it, sir," says Walker. "Is the Peckleton Field site being checked out?"

"The what?"

"Peckleton Field, sir."

Rob clears his throat. "Paul Mulholland, the guy who ran the Narborough Road property, he rented out some land near the village of Peckleton. Couple of caravans and that. There might be some useful info there."

Scabbard gives him a dead-eyed look. "Are the officers of Operation Chainlink willing to take a look?"

"Can do."

He gives a dismissive wave. "Fine."

The fire investigation team take the lead for a while. They show slides from inside the gutted building.

"The concrete floor here at ground level shows signs that an accelerant was used to start the fire. Thermal imaging taken while the fire was still active would support this theory, as the fire was most intense at the ground floor level, here towards the centre of the building."

A hand goes up. "With a fire like that, would the people in the cellar have died of smoke inhalation or ... you know?"

"Cooked alive?" says the fire investigator. "That's for the post-mortem to decide."

Josie pulls a face. Either one of those options is horrible.

17

It's nice to have someone else in the house.

I hear Natasha singing as I get ready that morning.

Maybe she doesn't realise how thin the walls are. She's singing what I guess is an old nursery rhyme or something.

"*Falcon flight, cliff so high. Ocean reef, echoes lie.*" The words become hums.

"Morning!" I call, as I walk past her room.

"Morning!" she shouts back.

I drive her into Leicester that morning. The little battery warning light comes on the Jag's dashboard but goes away again.

The local news on the car radio leads with the story about the fire on the Narborough Road. The phrase 'multiple victims' makes me swallow hard as I'm driving. Does it mean they're not yet sure how many people died? I glance at Natasha, and hope she's not taking it too badly. She has her eyes closed. I'm not sure if it's in reaction to the news, or whether she's dozing. She must be as sleep deprived as me.

A full night's sleep has done me the world of good, though. A good deal of what's on my plate still looks crappy in the light of day – Tyrese Jali has still assaulted a man with cerebral palsy, I've still yet to land Todd as my next major client, and the company coffers are still empty – but at least Hannah Douglas-Jones is up, fresh-faced and ready to face whatever the world is ready to throw at her.

My offices are in New Walk. Harvey Kenelm set me up with those. He manages the legal affairs for an old friend who occupies four-fifths of a fine Georgian property on the leafy pedestrianised street, and has arranged for me to have the final fifth for effectively nothing.

The house, the car, the office – it's all giving Natasha the wrong impression of the social level at which I operate. She comes into the office and takes in the battered but beautiful Chesterfield sofas, the stylish furniture I mostly scavenged from charity shops, and the selected pieces of art on the walls (all borrowed) and must think I operate in the lap of luxury. Of course, that's the image I want give clients but it's just giving this poor woman class anxiety.

"Starting to feel less guilty about taking your money," she says.

I laugh it off.

"Grab a seat," I say.

"Sure," she says and sits at the other desk which Karolina sometimes uses. "What would you like me to do?"

"Do?"

I hadn't planned for her to do anything. I want to get her version of the other night's events and maybe start turning her round to the idea that her account, her experiences could work as excellent material for Todd's campaign. But I've got other fires to tackle today as well.

"I can work," she says. "I can do something."

I'm still staring at her.

"You don't have to pay me," she says, with a reassuring smile. "Although I think I'm going to have to get a job if I'm gonna buy replacement..." She blows out her lips. "Like everything."

"You weren't insured?" I say before I realise it's a stupid thing. "Look, do you want to go into town and maybe buy what clothes you need? You still got some of that money? And then maybe I can find something for you to do. It would be really helpful."

"Okay," she says and heads out.

"I don't have your phone number," I blurt as she's halfway out.

"I don't have a phone," she says.

The thought that she's lost her phone seems like madness to me. How can someone exist without their phone? And then I realise that my own thought is the mad one. She came out of a fire with nothing but the shirt on her back – barely even that – and I'm fixating on phones. I dip into a drawer and find one of the cheap phones I put aside for clients. I toss it to her.

"It's got my number in it," I say.

"Burner phone. Cool," she says and heads out.

"You got people you want to call?" I say.

She stares at the phone and then shakes her head. "No one that matters."

18

I tackle the business of the day.

It is approximately forty hours since Tyrese decided that walloping Oliver Chambers at a drunken party was a good move. Nothing has come out in the press yet, but one of my friendly tabloid contacts has sent me a message that the papers have got a sniff of it. It's going to come out soon.

In a situation like this, where celebrity shit is about to hit the fan, one needs to get ahead of the story. Empty apologies are ready to deploy at the push of a button. I've done some research on Oliver Chambers, who works as a DJ in the Midlands club scene. I could work up some character assassination material on him but I'm finding it distasteful. I'm not of the opinion that people with registered disabilities should be forgiven carte blanche for their wrongs – equality cuts both ways – but sticking the knife into the obvious victim in this scenario seems like the wrong move.

I liaise with the football club's media team and we agree

to do an in-house, totally controlled video interview that afternoon. In the meantime, I need to find a scandal to feed to the press that might just deflect the public's attention. It's like Boris Johnson's 'dead cat' strategy – throw something shocking to the press and, like throwing a dead cat onto the table in the middle of dinner, you guarantee that people will talk about it.

I've got some pretty little news stories in reserve. One is drifting to the top of the list. Casper Veenham, TV chef, has been gaining a reputation for behind the scenes 'antics' with female co-stars. His long-standing girlfriend, who works in regional television, had approached me with the frank query of whether coming forward with her own experiences could be leveraged into a positive career move for her. I advised her that a cynical move like that might be too transparent and ultimately backfire. I've still got details she shared and several pertinent voicemail recordings. And Veenham has just been announced as a contestant for this year's *Strictly Come Dancing*. Allegations coming out now could be explosive and the right kind of messy.

I just need to weigh things up and work out the detonation sequence.

When Natasha returns, she's in a change of clothing. I approve. Simple cotton trousers. A smart open-neck top. She looks ready for a day in the office.

"Dress for the job you want, right?" she says.

"You are aware I can't actually pay you," I say.

"Give me stuff to do," she says, making 'gimme' gestures with her hands.

I like her enthusiasm. And I want her on-side if we're going to pivot her as the next focus of Todd's campaign.

"Okay," I say and, with a sigh, gesture her to a desk. "How are you with social media?"

"I'm not on social media."

"No?"

"I've not had good experiences."

"There's a lot of dicks on the internet," I say. "Literally and figuratively."

She nods sagely.

"But you know how social media works?"

"Course. I'm not like one of those Amish people who don't do tech."

I get her logged onto a laptop with my spare work credentials. "Set yourself up on Facebook, Instagram. Even X. I want you to look at celebrity gossip. UK celebrity gossip."

"Really? That's work?"

"I'm particularly interested in Tyrese Jali."

"The footballer?"

"Right. Anything about him, make a note. Start a document of screenshots. Repost anything that's not about him."

"That's it?"

"You're on Jali-watch."

During the day, documents start to appear on my desktop, courtesy of Natasha. Not only do they conform to my existing naming convention, but they bring a sense of order that goes beyond what I'd normally have.

In the Jali folder, there's now an index document for all of the screenshots. I can search through them based on timestamp, source or credibility score.

"Natasha, this is remarkable! How on earth have you done this?"

She gives me a little fake salute. "Common sense really."

"Really?"

"Yep. I can apply this to some of your other projects as well if you want?"

"Please, do what you can to make things function well around here. Obviously I need all the help I can get."

19

When it comes to police investigative work, Walker calibrates his expectations on the low side. He's not a pessimist. He's a realist. Recent years of being sidelined with the Duncans has trained him for this and, in general, his low expectations tend to be proven right.

Paul Mulholland, possibly in the guise of Charlie Bates, seller of knock-off farm equipment and more besides, had organised some of his activities from an encampment in a field near the village of Peckleton maybe five or six miles to the west of the city. The team have come to look at the field where two caravans had stood, along with dozens of tarp-covered trailers that Operation Chainlink had been keeping an eye on.

Walker steps through the gate with Rob and Josie and surveys what remains. One caravan is gone and the other is a burned-out ruin. Piles of rubbish, what looks like a small mountain of building waste and a shed missing its roofing felt complete the scene.

"Another fire?" says Josie.

Rob steps forward and inspects the ruined caravan and the grey-black earth around it.

"This looks old. We can check in with control and see if there were reports of a fire here."

Josie steps aside to check into that.

"I don't suppose there's going to be much to be gleaned here," says Rob.

Walker walks towards the nearest rubbish bag and tips it aside, wondering what's underneath.

"Best thing we can hope for is that we get to work the case in any shape or form."

"Surprised Scabbard has let us lowly worms get this involved," says Rob.

The Duncans are personae non-gratae in Scabbard's eyes, but Walker knows that in truth, decisions about who's involved in working a case of this size is above the detective inspector's head. Multiple teams and agencies will be involved, across the police, and probably the National Crime Agency too, who co-ordinate efforts to look into organised crime and modern slavery. That's as well as the fire service and forensics. There was a total of seven people killed in that fire. This is going to be big.

Walker puts on a pair of gloves and rips open a bag. Food waste and soggy cardboard slops out.

He can hear Rob sigh as the detective sergeant starts to poke around too.

Walker has emptied all the bin bags onto the grass and concluded there's nothing in there. Rob – a brave soul – decides to investigate the shed, which contains a chemical toilet.

"Fire service came to a fire out here a month ago," says Josie. "Arson. Local kids they reckon."

"Not looking at a serial arsonist here then?" says Walker.

"Hey, guys," says Rob. "Come take a look at this."

He's standing by the open door of the shed.

"We've seen a chemical toilet before," says Josie.

He waves away the stink from his nose. "This might be interesting."

Walker grunts as he pushes himself up from his crouch. "I don't suppose it's beyond hope that a family of cute little foxes might have made it their home."

They approach. The stink of human filth hangs around the doorway. It appears at first glance to be exactly what one would expect from a cheap chemical toilet abandoned for months. It's the kind that is little more than a toilet seat on top of a bucket. Human excrement stains the seat.

But Walker sees that the interior is full not just of poop and blue chemicals but also stuffed with matted wads of paper.

"Some of it handwritten, some of it printed," says Rob.

Josie looks in, nose wrinkled.

"It's covered in shit, Rob."

"I think I see a business letterhead in there."

Walker sighs and then coughs at the stench. "Well, we did want to get involved in whatever way we're allowed."

Rob makes a call while Walker considers the best way to tackle this.

"You know, I've got a friend who works with the document conservation department at Leicester Uni. They worked on archival papers from the Greyfriars dig for Richard the Third. They do forensic imaging and suchlike."

"Do they do crap-covered document recovery?"

Walker tilts his head.

Rob ends his conversation with a "Yes, sir."

"Well?" says Walker.

Rob smiles. "Scabbard says – and I quote – that if we want to spend our days sticking our hands in turds then he's not going to stop us."

"Yay for the Duncans," says Josie with zero enthusiasm.

20

Karolina comes into the office later in the afternoon.

She glances over at the desk that she probably thinks of as hers and raises an eyebrow at me.

"I'd like the two of you to meet." I rise to put the kettle on and extend hands out as I pass by. "Karolina, this is Natasha. She's helping me out. And when I say that, it appears that she is *really* helping."

Karolina approaches Natasha to shake her hand.

"And Natasha, this is Karolina. She does research for me."

I see confusion written across Natasha's face. She thinks that she's the one doing research. "When I say research, it's very specialised research. Karolina's an expert at fieldwork."

Natasha smiles at Karolina. "Fieldwork. Sounds like a lot of fun."

I make tea, so I can leave the two of them to get acquainted.

When I return with the tea tray, Karolina is leaning in to see Natasha's screen.

"Your girl here has done some solid work," she says. "I'm showing her how to get a bot score for a social feed. It's really helpful to try and work out if you're dealing with an actual human, or just a bot that's reposting shit. This index thing she's created could be really good for you."

"What a team," I say.

Karolina's right. Tools that can help us deduce whether bots have been used are worth their weight in gold, and nobody's more adept at such things than Karolina.

After a few minutes, Natasha gets up and pours teas for everyone.

"Here you go," she says as she puts a cup down on my desk. Did I already tell her how I take it? She's a remarkably fast learner.

Karolina plonks herself into one of my sofas and waits for me to join her. She has updates for me.

"Want to join us, Natasha?" I ask. "You might as well. You're working on the Jali case too."

Natasha brings her tea across.

"I feel I should bring Natasha up to speed on Tyrese Jali's case." I fetch the biscuits. "He was at a party on Sunday night and he assaulted someone called Oliver Chambers. It turns out that Mr Chambers has cerebral palsy."

Natasha raises her eyebrows. The light's different over here, and I can see that Natasha's eyebrows and hair are badly singed. The ends of all the hairs are blackened and frazzled. I realise with a jolt that it accounts for the smell that lingers. I'd started to believe it was just in my nose. I must find a way to gently raise this.

Karolina's ahead of me.

"Natasha, were you in the fire that Hannah saw?"

Natasha eyes me, as if I might have been gossiping about her.

"It's not Hannah that tipped me off, it's the burnt bits in your hair," says Karolina, cutting off the thought with a jabbing finger. "I will take you for a haircut when we're done here. You need to get rid of the damage."

For a moment, I think that Natasha might take offence, but then her face breaks into a smile. "That would be amazing. Um, thanks."

"Back to Tyrese. How much coverage is he getting today, Natasha?"

"Very little. Mostly it's re-posting of his own activity before Sunday night."

"And Karolina, what's your update?"

Karolina takes up her regular position on the sofa. She calls my lovely Chesterfields "sawn-off" because they only come part-way up a person's back, as if they're not meant to be comfortable. She hooks her arms over the back to make this point, as if she's a bat, draping her wings.

"Lilja Eiríksdóttir is happy to be getting a photoshoot. She will not be a problem. I'm working my way around all attendees at that party."

"And not forgetting friends of friends?" I ask.

She pulls a disbelieving face. "Would I forget that? Friends of friends. Of course."

"What do you mean?" asks Natasha.

"It's natural to focus on the people who witness the event," I tell her, "and to move heaven and earth to track them down and silence them, however we can. What can often happen is that one of those people will have gossiped to someone – a friend or colleague, doesn't matter – and then that is the person who will break the story."

"Oh, then let me revise my earlier statement," Natasha says.

She taps at the laptop she brought over with her.

"There's a TikTok account called VVBrummelz who has promised to spill some tea on Tyrese if their follower account goes over seven thousand. I wasn't sure it was of interest because I don't think this person's even located in the UK."

"Doesn't matter. Let's get onto it."

Karolina nods.

"Hm. That might move my own plans swiftly up the agenda," I say, thinking aloud. "I'm thinking of doing a soft reach out to Oliver Chambers and his family. Test the waters a little."

"Hm, good idea." says Karolina. "Get in there early,"

"And what will you be looking for?" Natasha asks.

I give the mildest of shrugs. "A way in. Gauge the appetite for negotiation. See what's driving them most strongly. For some people it's very much a matter of principle, but it's worth finding out whether money is a driver."

Natasha nods along. "I'll carry on looking."

"Er no. It is time for haircut." Karolina gets up, and looks at both of us, not expecting any contradiction.

"Fine. Go with Karolina. Your hair will thank you." I wave them off with a smile.

21

I decide that I must make that call to the family of Oliver Chambers.

Karolina handed me a dossier, which includes all the details she's found.

Natasha and Karolina are out, so I have the office to myself for this awkward task.

Oliver Chambers lives a relatively independent life, although his flat is within walking distance of his parents' home in Oadby. This suggests that he may lean on them for support from time to time. There's no evidence that he drives, so I wonder how he manages for transport; especially given that the work of a DJ means unpredictable and unsocial working patterns.

I put the call through.

"*Yes?*" The voice is wary.

"Hello? Is that Mrs Chambers? Hannah Douglas-Jones here. Reaching out on behalf of the football club to see how Oliver's doing."

I feel comfortable saying that I'm representing the team.

It's not *exactly* a lie. Well, it is a lie, but it's one I can cover if forced to backtrack later.

"Oliver's in the hospital." She sounds brittle, as if she's teetering on the edge.

"I'm sure he's receiving the best possible care. And are you able to get there to visit him? Any support needed at all with transport?"

"We're fine thank you. My husband's driving us."

"Good. I want you to know that Oliver's well-being, and yours too, is our top priority. So in the coming days, I want you to give me a call if anything comes up that we can help with."

There's a pause. *"I'm sorry, where are you calling from again?"*

"I work for an agency. We'll speak in the coming days a little more about how I can help, moving forward. Just know that there are people here who want to help. To build bridges."

I can almost hear the sound of her working out that I work for Tyrese. The next few seconds will tell me most of what I need to know.

"Build bridges?" I can hear some pent-up anger, but also curiosity. This is good. I can work with this.

"Yes."

I'm saying nothing further at this point. I give her my phone number and end the call.

I reflect on the call and update the dossier with some notes.

- *Oliver's mother did not seek confrontation when I called.*
- *About to send flowers with a personal note attached.*

- *Build relationship through her?*

So much of this business is about building relationships and understanding people.

It's a skill that you can't learn in a classroom.

I've been blessed with a warm smile and an open, guileless face people seem to trust, but that's only part of it. You have to really listen to people, pay attention to the things that they're saying, and the things they're not saying.

It's why I've never thought of having anyone else working with me. If I took on an assistant, where would I even start?

And yet, I glance across at Natasha's desk. She's been here for a few short hours and I feel a rush of gratitude for the difference she's making.

Not only has she worked her indexing magic on the information she's gathered, but I can also see some reminders in my calendar that were not there this morning. She's spotted there are some cases where I haven't yet issued an invoice, or followed up on payment. It's an area where I know I'm lax.

If she can help me improve my cashflow, then that would be incredible.

I start to think that having an assistant could be a positive thing.

22

When I go into work the next day, Natasha comes with me. It seems like the natural thing to do, although Dad's made it clear that he'd very much like her to stay at home and play cards with him.

The local news is now saying there were seven people killed by that fire. Seven! It's horrifying and I feel the need to steer the conversation in a different direction, for Natasha's sake.

"I like your new haircut," I say.

Her hand half goes to it. "I don't really get it cut often."

It's a simple cut that frames her face well. It reminds me of how I used to wear my hair back when I was a holiday rep in Greece. And thinking that makes me wish for the days of my youth again. I mean – Jesus Christ – I'm only thirty, but there's something about Natasha's confident youthfulness that makes me realise how I've changed over the years.

"What do you have on today?" she asks as I open up the office.

"Got a meeting with Todd."

"Ah. *Safe As Houses* campaign," says Natasha. "It's in your calendar as that."

"You're looking at my calendar."

"Keeping on top of things. You've got a thing in your calendar called 'gala dinner' for Thursday evening."

"Ah," I say. "The thrilling LPS gala dinner at Athena."

"LPS?"

"Leicester Professional Services. It's a networking group. Accountants, solicitors, PR. People from Dad's old company come, so even though he's retired, we go along each year. I'm actually sponsoring the keynote speech this year and get to do a bit of an intro." A thought occurs to me. "I ought to see if Todd is coming."

"Yeah?"

"Yes. There's an opportunity there."

"In what way?"

I don't want to leap straight in with the idea that Natasha herself could be the poster child for the *Safe As Houses* campaign. Much as she wants to help, I don't think she'd welcome the idea right now.

"The fire. We don't yet know what caused it. We know that people died."

"Right. Yeah."

I'm glancing at her face, trying to get a read. She's giving nothing away, her expression deadpan, but surely she's put the pieces together by now? "We have a unique perspective. *You* have a unique perspective."

"The survivor?"

"Yes, the survivor!" I bite off any extra words that were about to spill from my own mouth. I want to hear Natasha's own ideas.

"You want words maybe? You want the words of someone

who's felt their eyelids burning while their hair was on fire? You want to hear what it's like when all you can see around you is flames and you don't know where the door is until you walk into it?"

My mouth's dry. I can't even bring myself to respond. This is so raw.

"You want to know what fire tastes like? It tastes like the pain of blisters mixed with barbecued pork." She looks at me with red-rimmed eyes. "Now I know it must have been those poor people in the building. I don't think I'll ever be able to eat barbecue again."

A tear slides down her face.

I realise that I've made a terrible mistake. This is much too soon for Natasha. There's a huge amount of trauma for her to process here.

"Your words will be so valuable," I say. "But there's no rush. No rush at all."

23

I meet Todd for lunch at the cute bakery café down the road. It's mainly an excuse for us to indulge in a fancy coffee and some of their delicious cakes. Todd made some gentle protests about a diet, but when his cinnamon roll arrives in a waft of warm spice, his eyes light up.

"I've got something for you," I tell him.

"Mm." He indicates the cinnamon roll.

"No, not that. If I'd realised you were such a pushover, I'd have broken out the pastries before now. It's the woman from the fire – Natasha."

He leans in, suddenly interested. "You found her?"

"I did." I think about how to phrase the next part. "I need to be sure that we handle her correctly. She's suffered a lot. But she's a remarkable woman. She has real presence and charisma. Coupled with her story of surviving this fire, I think she could be front and centre of your campaign."

Todd absorbs the thought. It's a thought that will forever be associated with the scent of cinnamon and the rich sugary softness of the pastry, and that's no bad thing. Food can be a powerful anchor for emotions.

"When can I meet her?" he asks.

I smile at him. He's drawn to the idea. A meeting with Natasha will seal the deal, I'm sure of it. But I need to make sure it goes well – which means getting Natasha fully on board.

"Have you ever attended one of the Leicester Professional Services events?"

He nods as he takes another bite. "Networking shop, yeah."

"I'm at a gala dinner at Athena on Thursday night."

"Nice building."

The Athena was once an Art Deco cinema. He's not wrong. It's a nice venue.

"Glad you approve," I say. "I'll be bringing Natasha along. We could make subtle introductions."

"You make it sound like you're going to spring a trap on her."

"Not at all. Not how I will play it. I will be upfront and honest. She's re-building her life, and I want to make sure she's on an even keel."

"Fair enough, Hannah," says Todd, meeting my eye. "I trust your judgement."

I dial my smile up to its full wattage and then we settle in to finish our snacks.

As we leave, Todd's driver pulls his car up to the kerb and Todd climbs in. I wave them both off and walk back to the office.

Natasha's back from her errands, and she sets a drink down in front of me moments after my arrival.

"You're spoiling me!"

"Not at all. You've been a lifeline," she says, and then settles back to work at the laptop.

I check on what's been happening while I was with Todd. There have been some notifications from the bank. My heart sinks when I see these, but to my astonishment, they tell me that money has been paid in. There's two thousand pounds from Ribbons and Bows baby shower shop and four thousand from Telepound, the phone services reseller.

Both of those debts have been on the books for over six months and I was utterly convinced that they would never pay me. Both have paid in full. Both within a couple of hours of each other.

"Well I never!"

Natasha looks up.

"Do you know anything about these old bills that have suddenly been paid?" I ask.

"I chased them," she says with a smile. "Sometimes people just need a little reminder. A little steer in the right direction."

"Gosh. Thanks."

I chased those two companies myself, a few times. I tried nice, I tried threatening legal action. I should have done more, but it's not my strongest area. I wonder what superpowers Natasha has?

I must get her to teach me.

24

"This what you pictured us doing, is it Josie?" Rob asks.

He can't see her grin behind the face mask she's wearing, but her eyes are alight. "Working the case, aren't we?"

All of them are dressed in full PPE to protect them against splashback from this particular case.

Scabbard thinks he's inflicted the worst possible punishment on them, and in so many ways he's right.

When it became clear how much documentation needed to be processed and how contaminated it was, Scabbard was extremely keen to lean on the specialist help available at the East Midlands Forensics Network, housed at Leicester university. It's a partnership between the world of academia and forensics practitioners. The only sticking point was staffing. The document conservation lab is tiny, and the work needed is considerable.

And so, the Duncans have been briefed and equipped in

how to process the evidence now known in the office as the Shit Files.

Rob, Walker and Josie are working in the Fielding-Johnson building – a grand old structure – on the university campus. It's a specialist lab where the three of them are helping to process batches of paperwork until they can be transformed into usable evidence. The hope is that they can spot anything relevant, as well as ensuring that the chain of evidence is unbroken.

As far as Rob knows, this lab is more often used for the preservation of historic documents, but now the summer term has ended the university was swift to adapt the lab to get them up and running. He imagines they will be delighted with this collaboration. It looks good to prospective students, even though the smell from the contaminated paperwork is rank.

"Rinse and neutralise," says Walker in a robotic voice as he carefully peels another page from the pile and drops it into a neutral pH water bath.

Rob thinks that Walker is enjoying this. It's certainly different from their usual routine.

"People train for this," says Josie. She's unpacking another bag, another handful of shit-stained documents. "It's their actual dream. But yeah, at least we're working the case."

Rob's at the other end of the production line, loading the rinsed documents one by one onto air-drying racks, so they can go into an airflow cabinet for drying. He thought he'd be able to read the documents as he worked, but some of them are not legible. Apparently there's other equipment that the university has that can help with that. Did they call it multispectral imaging?

He's trying hard not to think about the tiny particles of

shit that will still be present on the finished documents. They will take high resolution scans of each piece of paper, but the physical evidence will still be required, still need to be kept and handled as part of the chain.

Arguably, Walker's got the nastiest part of the process, rinsing visible crud off the paper. He seems unaffected by it. He's had the training with small children – nappies and such like – though his children are adults now.

Rob is the only one who's far from happy to be here.

"You know what makes me mad?" he says. It's bursting out of him. He can't help it.

"What?" Josie and Walker both look surprised.

"Whoever did this, whoever dumped this paperwork in the chemical toilet took a shit on top of it afterwards. They didn't just put it in there, knowing it was already shitty. They saved up their own personal donation, just to make it extra special for us."

"Yeah?" Josie shrugs as if it's a very obvious thing to do.

"Probably thought it gave them an extra layer of protection," says Walker. "The bacteria would get to work faster, too. Break down the paper, destroy the evidence."

Rob shakes his head. The others can see reasons: human foibles, human logic. All he can see is the darkness that some people have within themselves. He hates it, partly because he's afraid that he might also have it within himself.

25

I walk past Natasha's desk a little later and I see some books on the corner.

"May I?"

She nods.

I pick one up. It's the new Lisa Jewell novel. "Nice."

"I went to the library," she says. "Sounds stupid, but it felt like getting a little piece of me back. Took an age to get them to sort me out without ID. But I've got some books to read now."

"You like Lisa Jewell?" I ask.

"Love her stuff. She gets right inside the heads of her characters. I like that she reinvented herself too. Wrote romcoms and then just started on psychological thrillers. I love them all."

I grin at her. "You are never going to believe this, but I have a ton of her books. She's a bit of an obsession for me, too. I've got all her stuff."

"No way."

I nod. "They're a great read."

Natasha nods along. "Right?"

"You know what we should do? We should both read one of her books at the same time and then talk about it as we go."

"I'd really like that," she says.

I'm still smiling when I come back from the kitchen with our drinks. It feels as if I have gained a new best friend, and it's kind of exciting.

I get a call from Tyrese. He's bored, cooped up in the exclusive De Morgan hotel retreat. Of course he's bored. He's in the lap of luxury, with everything a person could want or need.

"I'm afraid you need to stay there until at least the weekend, Tyrese."

A grumbling sound comes down the phone. *"Party on Saturday. I can go to that, right?"*

"Tyrese, I would strongly advise against you being seen at any kind of a party for the next few weeks."

"Nothing's come of Sunday's thing," he says. *"Been all quiet."*

"It's been quiet *because* of the work I've been doing." He has no clue. "If I hadn't bought up all the pictures I could find, they'd be everywhere by now. And it could still happen, Tyrese. You're not out of the woods yet."

He rings off, but I'm a little unhappy with his attitude.

Natasha must have heard all that. I look over at her with a small smile.

"This job is a weird one. When you do it properly, it looks for all the world like you were never needed. I'm like a lighthouse. If no ships have crashed on the rocks for a hundred years, people start to question why they need a lighthouse. When the light goes out, they soon realise, but it's too late by then."

"Tyrese doesn't see the point."

I nod.

"If those lighthouse keepers let a small crash happen, once in a while, people would remember their value," Natasha says.

"That's very true," I say, with a smile. "The analogy breaks down a bit there though. Reputation is something where the value is cumulative. It doesn't take much to bring it all tumbling down."

26

I'm working on a document for Todd's campaign, jotting some thoughts on how we might begin in a small, targeted area. I need to get him properly on board. The news coverage of the fire has been extensive. People are horrified by what's happened, so I think we can use that. We need to tread the line between appearing ghoulish or opportunistic, and genuinely filling a need, but I'm confident we can do that.

I've got a bunch of ideas...

Free fire safety kits. A partnership event with the fire service where they help with practical advice. Natasha telling her survival story. Get local schools involved. Something like a poster competition where Todd gets to judge the entries.

The ideas are coming thick and fast, but I need to take care not to spook Natasha.

The phone rings: Harvey Kenelm. I wonder what accounting quibble he's brought today.

"Harvey."

"Hannah, we have a whiff of good news, my girl."

My girl! I do wish he wouldn't talk to me like that. "Is that right?"

"Yes. The Brascote buildings. The developers are working up some plans, and I think they're fairly credible."

"What does that mean? How far away from making an actual offer would you say they are?"

"We need to keep our cool. Can't afford to look at all desperate or they'll lowball us. Don't you worry though, I can play hard to get. Keep them at arm's length for a few days."

"Right – but Harvey, that's just one possible strategy. There are others. Is it worth setting up a meeting? I often find that it's worth tailoring one's approach depending on who's involved."

"Deary me, Hannah. I think you might have forgotten who you're talking to," says Harvey with a chuckle. *"I've been doing this since you were a twinkle in your father's eye. I know what I'm doing."*

"Harvey. I also know what I'm doing. I work with people every single day. I'm simply suggesting that you might like to take advantage of my expertise."

"I'm sure your touchy-feely people approach works in advertising, but this is the building trade. Things are done differently." He alters his tone. It's austere and cold. *"Now I've made this phone call to you as a courtesy, but if you continue to question my ability to carry out my appointed role as your father's attorney-in-fact then I might have to adjust the nature of our communications. We can keep things as they are, or I can put it all on a much more formal footing."*

I squeeze my fist with frustration. I wish I had something to break. I hate that he can manipulate and infantilise me like this. He even got my job completely wrong. I don't know whether he's being deliberately dismissive or he just doesn't care. But I must swallow this down.

"No, Harvey. You should continue to do what you're doing." It's the best I can force myself to say.

"Very well. I'll let you know how things are in a few days. I'll give you an update at the gala if you're coming."

"I'm presenting," I say.

"Oh, good, good," he says, seeming not to hear. *"Cheerio then."*

He rings off and I stare at my clenched fist for a few long seconds, then I force myself to unfurl my fingers.

It's very good news about the Brascote buildings. Dad and I could really do with the money. I just hope Harvey doesn't blow it with his blunderbuss attempts at negotiating.

27

Rob and the team process the 'shit files' late into the evening. The huge university building is a little eerie when it's mostly empty.

There are now around a hundred sheets that have been dried and scanned.

"We're making good progress," Rob says. He thinks that the smell in the room has subsided a little, too. Either that or he's gone nose blind.

"We should have a chart on the wall. Mark it up every day with how much we've done," says Josie.

Walker's paging through the documents. They will be passed to an analyst, but he wants to cast his eye over them.

"Most of these are receipts for what look like informal cash transactions," he announces. "They're not the sort of paperwork you'd put in front of HMRC."

"Yeah?"

Rob and Josie go across to see what he means.

"Look. There's a format to them. Names are kept brief, the goods for sale are heavily coded."

"Does that mean we can't use them as evidence?" Josie asks. "Even if we work out what they are, it's all deniable."

"Two things to say to that," says Walker. "First of all, these documents go back years. Someone, Mulholland presumably, dumped their whole filing system."

"Well, this is good," says Rob. "We just need to find some names or details that we might recognise."

"You expecting to see the Degutis brothers' names written on here?" smiles Josie. She puts on a blokey voice. "*Dear Arturas, here is the money for the tractors what you stole. All the best, Paul Mulholland.*"

So far, the most promising piece of paper they've come across is a receipt from a letting agent in the city. If they're lucky, it might be to do with the Narborough Road house or some other location where Mulholland was renting out rooms.

"Wait, wait, wait," says Walker, carefully spreading out a piece of paper. "Look at this."

Rob leans in. The written sheet has strings of numbers that could be accounts, or mushed up phone numbers, or something else entirely, and at the top is a nonsense word.

"Bomalley?"

"B O'Malley," says Walker. "Brendan. A nasty piece of work."

The name means nothing to Rob. "You know him?"

"Of old. Like twenty years ago. He'd be in his seventies, easily."

"Links to the Degutis gang?"

Walker tilts his head. "Not now. Not then. He was dealing cannabis mostly on the New Park estate. He was a person of interest during Operation Kilkenny."

Rob has known Walker a long time. Operation Kilkenny

is a thing from Walker's past: his pre-Duncan days. Heck, it was before Rob had even left school. Walker has only spoken about it occasionally, and quite cautiously then. Rob has learned to not ask direct questions about it.

"Operation Kilkenny," says Josie. "Wasn't that the one where a police officer got killed?"

And, just like that, Josie Kaminski blunders in. Rob's got to hand it to Josie. She will always turn over a stone to look underneath. It's an admirable trait in a detective, but less so when it comes to workplace politics.

"Hey Josie, maybe later," Rob says to her, trying to subtly convey that she is on conversational thin ice.

"No, it's fine," says Walker to Rob. "No need for secrecy. It was a long time ago."

He turns to Josie. "I was on that op. There were three of us under deep cover trying to get right inside the emerging gang scene in the Midlands. And yes, a young man lost his life after a sting operation went wrong."

"Shit," says Josie. "Sorry."

"It was awful," says Walker. "But in so many ways, it's our – um, what does my Oscar call it? – our origin story."

Rob smiles at the way Walker uses the terminology, as if he's telling a bedtime story.

"How do you mean?" Josie asks.

"The Duncans. The other person on that op with me was DS Duncan Flanagan. The original Dead End Duncan."

"Fuck," Josie hisses. "What happened to him?"

"He paid dearly for his role in the operation, just like me."

"What?" says Josie. "Paid how?"

Walker waves her question away, not like he doesn't want to answer but because it's water under the bridge.

"Duncan's retired now. Few years older than me."

"There's a real Duncan?" Josie sounds moderately awestruck, as if someone's told her that unicorns are real. "A real person?"

"Yeah," says Walker. "Not seen him for a while. But I tell you what, he got real close to O'Malley. If there's any intel to be gained about this fire via Brendan O'Malley, I ought to have a word with Duncan."

28

At home that evening, it's bright and warm. The farmhouse has a lovely enclosed courtyard, paved in mellow golden stone, so Natasha, Dad and I are all sitting out on the cast iron chairs around the table, enjoying the slanting rays of the sun. Dad's carer, Marissa, has finished her official duties for the evening.

"It's the gala tomorrow night, Dad," I say.

"What's that?" he says.

"The gala. The LPS gala at the Athena."

"Good lord! Has that come round already? My suit will want cleaning."

"I'll sort it out, don't worry." Dad's suit is immaculate, as it only comes out a couple of times a year.

"Gala makes it sound posh," Natasha says to me. She's sitting on another chair, her bare feet brought up beneath her.

"It's just called that," I tell her with a wave of my hand. "I don't know why, really. It's a dinner. A chance for all the professionals to talk shop."

Natasha has made eggy bread. Dad thinks it's the best thing ever.

She has also found a chess set and the two of them are clattering them across the table in a raucous, greasy-fingered game.

My phone goes, so I excuse myself to answer.

"Hello Hannah, it's DS Rob Joseph, we spoke on Monday morning at the site of the fire."

"Oh. Hello." I want to ask how he got my number, but it was there in the details that I filled in.

"Just following up on the statement you provided. I'm especially interested in the woman who you saw emerge from the building. A student called Natasha, you said."

"That's right," I say. I glance back at the student called Natasha who's no more than twenty feet away from where I'm standing.

"We've found some letting agent documents. Natasha Dibello. The only registered resident of that property. We would really like to speak with her. I was wondering if there's anything more that you could tell me about her. Anything at all."

I pause. I'm at a crossroads here, and I need to make a choice. On the one hand, I am a responsible citizen who wants to assist the police, especially when it comes to investigating something as awful as this fire; on the other, I feel protective of Natasha. It's clear that the fire has really shaken her up. If she's compelled to talk about it, then it should be on her own terms. This policeman isn't a complete oaf, but who knows what damage he might inflict with careless questions?

"I will have a good, hard think about that, DS Joseph," I say. "And if I come up with anything at all, I will give you a call, how about that?"

"Fair enough," he says. *"Anything at all, yeah?"*

Dad's got up to have a wander and is now dead-heading some geraniums in a pot. I'm not sure whether he's doing it right, but he looks really happy.

I sit down opposite Natasha. "That was the police."

"Oh?" Natasha looks a little shocked that the police are calling me.

"Nothing bad," I assure her. "They're keen to talk to you, though."

"Me?" Her expression is pure puzzlement.

"Yes. They need information. How do you feel about calling them?"

She gives a shrug. "Sure."

I dig out the card that DS Joseph gave to me. His number's in my phone now, so I don't need it.

Natasha takes it and looks at the name. "And this person. They're ... all right?"

I think about DS Rob Joseph. "He seemed earnest and kind."

She waggles the card. "I'll give him a call."

"Okay. Natasha Dibello."

She looks sharply at me as I say her name.

"It's what the detective called you," I say. "I don't think I ever asked you what your surname was."

"I hate it," she says. "Imagine spending your life telling people how to spell your surname."

I smile. "Point."

"Douglas-Jones," she says. "I'd be much happier with a surname like that."

"You're welcome to it," I say.

29

Middle of Thursday morning.

I'm in the office, fresh off the phone with Tyrese. He wants out of his luxury retreat – what torture! – but I'm not yet confident of the world he's walking into.

Karolina's coming in shortly, so I'll be better equipped to come up with a strategy when I have her report.

Natasha, who is getting more comfortable and indispensable day by day, comes over to my desk. "Some cheques arrived in the post."

She puts them on my desk. I stare at them, dumbfounded. "This one here is a two-year-old debt!" I say. The other one's almost as old.

She shrugs lightly. "Chased down a few more for you. It's wrong when people don't pay their way. Anyways, get them paid in quick, before they change their mind."

"Wow, Natasha, just wow. Listen – can you pay them in? I've got meetings all day and I've honestly got to practise my notes for my one-minute of fame at the gala tomorrow." I sound a bit desperate but she's right, we can't let this money evaporate.

"I could walk into town and deposit them in the bank if you want?"

"That's great." I pull out my notebook, the one I keep all my various account and logon details in. I jot down the bank details.

"Can you read my writing?"

"Yep. I'll get onto that." She takes a photo before carrying the cheques over to her desk and getting to work. "Oh, I gave that policeman a call. He does seem nice, you're right."

"You did? Great news."

I feel some minor relief. I've done my duty as a concerned citizen. Assisted the police with their enquiries, and Natasha has come to no harm. Good result.

When Karolina arrives, she brings Danish pastries for us all.

"These look amazing," says Natasha, taking a maple and pecan twist.

I take an almond croissant and Karolina has one of those apricot pastry things that sort of looks like a fried egg.

The three of us have settled onto the settees to chat about Tyrese.

"Right. Update," Karolina says. "Oliver Chambers is back home. He's cancelled an upcoming gig, but he seems to be functioning."

I jot some notes. "How big a deal is the gig he's cancelled?"

"Small compared to what he normally does. A local party in a park on Friday afternoon."

"Smacks of something he wanted to get out of?"

"I think so," says Karolina.

"How's his face?"

Karolina pulls out her phone and shows some pictures. They are remarkably clear. She has a talent for taking covert pictures better than most people could manage with a studio and fully controllable lighting.

"You can see he has dissolvable stitches on his forehead. Two are visible. There may be another in the hairline."

I tap my pen on the table. "Do we know what pictures exist of him covered in blood, or from the night of the incident?"

"His mum has some. I called her, posing as a journalist who wanted them to run a story."

"Yes?" I'm leaning forward now. This information is crucial. "So what's she after?"

"She said, and I wrote this down, 'I need to speak with Olly. He's making his mind up about how he wants to play this. He's a man with some very strong principles, and I'll stand by his decision on this'."

"Do we know what kind of principles we're talking about?"

Karolina gives me that waggle-headed smile. The one that says she's ahead of me. "His social media has clues to this. He's a big advocate for differently-abled people."

"In what way? Like disability charities?" I ask.

"First of all, he hates the word disabled. It's differently-abled all the way. His big passion is that the world should be naturally accessible to more people. So rather than tacking on a few ramps and lifts as an afterthought, buildings should be designed better in the first place."

"Obviously, he's not a wheelchair user himself?"

"No. Mobility is a big thing for him, just the same. He does a job where he needs flexibility to travel at odd hours and different places, but he says that he's not been able to pass a driving test because he failed the reaction tests."

"Oh – are we looking at an opportunity here?" I think I might sound too gleeful. It's probably not appropriate, given that we're talking about someone's life. But I can smell it.

"We might be. Might." Karolina gives me a warning nod. "He talks a lot about accessible minibus services, and queries why they aren't available twenty-four seven. He wants all differently-abled people to be able to go out where they want, when they want."

Karolina puts a heavy emphasis on the word 'all'.

"Gotcha. So we can't afford to wade in and offer a solution that only benefits him."

"Exactly that."

"This can sharpen our thinking; it's really good information. Thank you, Karolina. I wonder how Tyrese feels about driving a minibus for a while?"

Karolina nods in approval.

An hour or so later, after Karolina's left, Natasha speaks up.

"What's the communication plan between you and Karolina?"

"Hm?" I ask. "What do you mean?"

"Like, you both phoned Oliver Chambers' mum. That could have gone disastrously wrong. But I imagine she'd check in with you before doing something like that."

I ponder the idea briefly. "She does her thing. I do mine. We've never really clashed."

"That's good then," says Natasha. "No harm done, then."

She's got a point though.

30

Rob tries to catch up with DI Scabbard in the morning. The detective inspector is heading up the stairs at speed. He's wearing a suit jacket and a neat tie this morning.

"Sir? Can I catch up with you about the findings from Mulholland's caravan?"

"Got a media briefing and appeal for witnesses, Joseph," says Scabbard, which explains the suit.

DS Dean Beaches, walking beside Scabbard, says, "Which means he doesn't need distractions from the Poo Patrol, Rob."

Beaches' moustache twitches, like he's very proud of that insult. Rob would like to be generous and think that Beaches didn't stay up all night trying to come up with that Poo Patrol line, but Beaches isn't really a guy capable of spontaneous wit.

"You have something to report?" says Scabbard. If there's a press conference, it will be held in the largest meeting room on the second floor. It's one of the few rooms in the Mansfield House nick that doesn't look tired and old.

"Maybe," says Rob. "From documentation we recovered we think that Mulholland, as well as helping the Degutis gang shift stolen goods, had connections with a drug dealer in New Parks."

"Who?"

"A guy called Brendan O'Malley."

"Never heard of him."

"Old school. But the connection remains."

"Any motive to set fire to Mulholland's house?"

"Don't know."

"Hardly newsworthy."

"Sir, I thought we might go over there and, you know, shake a few trees..."

Scabbard pauses at the conference room door and, for the first time that day, actually looks at Rob.

"Any intel goes to the intelligence officers and becomes part of the big picture."

"We've already done that, sir."

Scabbard's face is stony, unfriendly. He dishes out kindly looks sparingly, as though he doesn't want to strain his smile muscles.

"We're dealing with a nasty case where Paul Mulholland had what looks like half a dozen migrant workers locked up in the basement of his illegal kitchen. That's the level I'm dealing with. I'm not particularly interested in which scrotey toerag Mulholland was buying his weed from."

"Yes, sir, but—"

"What you could really do for me," Scabbard says, raising a finger to not quite prod Rob in the chest, "is find that witness you let slip through your fingers on the night of the fire."

"The PR woman?"

"The tenant."

"Never actually met her, sir. She'd gone before I arrived."

"Find her." He turns to the meeting room door and then turns back. "And if you want to send either of your minions to rattle the cages of New Parks drug dealers then I leave that operational matter up to you."

He goes into the meeting room where the police media team are setting up. Beaches, ever the henchman, gives Rob a final sneering look.

"Poo Patrol," he smiles.

"Your mother must be so proud, Dean," says Rob.

31

I've been keeping an eye on events linked to the fire and get a notification when a press conference on the Narborough Road fire goes up on the police website. I take my laptop over to Natasha.

"You want to watch this?" I ask.

She's got browser windows across her screen with all manner of financial and technical information. God knows what it is. I'm just happy for her to keep working her magic.

"What is it?"

"Police press conference about the fire."

A deeply uncomfortable look crosses her face, pained even.

"Sorry," I say. "Is this too much?"

She shakes her head. "I need to know what's going on, don't I?"

I cast the video up onto the display screen in the office.

A woman with the pips of a senior police officer on her shoulder takes the podium. Chief Superintendent Becky Ayres, says the ident at the bottom.

"*Good morning,*" she says to the gathered journalists, just visible in the bottom inches of the screen. "*As you may be aware, emergency services were called to a fire on Narborough Road in the early hours of Monday morning. Units of the Leicestershire Fire and Rescue Service attended the scene and tackled a blaze which had engulfed the property. Once it was under control, fire investigators and Leicestershire Police officers began a thorough investigation into the cause of the fire.*

"*It is with sadness that we have to report that the bodies of seven people were recovered from the fire. Several of those individuals were found in the cellar which was being used to house them.*"

Natasha's breath catches. I reach over and squeeze her hand.

"*Furthermore,*" says the chief superintendent, "*it has become clear that the premises were being used as what is known as a 'ghost kitchen': an unlicensed commercial kitchen, producing food for the takeaway and delivery industry. We are looking into the possibility that some or all of the individuals in the basement were workers in that illegal enterprise.*"

"Did you know anything about that?" I ask Natasha. I don't want to ask, but I have to.

She's shaking her head, numbly. "I knew there was a kitchen," she whispers. "That's all there was downstairs. They used the back door. My key..."

"*Initial conclusions from the Fire and Rescue Service investigation indicate that the fire started in the kitchen area. It is probable that it was started deliberately,*" Chief Superintendent Ayres continues. "*The focus of our investigation at this time will be to ascertain how that fire started and, crucially, who started it. We are not ruling out the possibility that the fire was started by one of the individuals recovered from the property.*"

"This is awful," says Natasha.

I hold onto her hand. If she asks me to turn it off, I will. But only if.

"This sad situation also highlights the real dangers of choosing to operate or work in illegal food kitchens. Those individuals recovered from the fire who have yet to be identified might still be alive if they were living in accommodation that complied with safety regulations."

"Did she just blame the dead people for choosing to be there?" I say.

I'm not even sure myself. *Choosing* to work in illegal food kitchens? *If* they had lived somewhere else? The superintendent skirted close to saying that it was basically their fault.

The press conference ends with an appeal for witnesses or information from the local community and some questions from the members of the press. No, they aren't sharing the identities of the dead. No, there were no children present in the fire. No, the police are not commenting on anyone who might have escaped from the first. No, the police are not saying if the dead people are 'illegal immigrants' or not.

Natasha is still staring numbly. "I had no idea," she says.

"Of course, you didn't," I say.

"I rented the flat through a letting agent. I never met the people there. I used the front doors. They used the back. I..."

She squeezes her eyes shut and tears trickle down. I hold her close. Watching this must be traumatic, a wound re-opened.

"I'm sorry. I didn't mean to put you through that."

"But it's my fault," she snivels. "It's all my fault."

32

I fetch Natasha a glass of water and give her space to calm down.

"I'm that person," she manages to say through the tears. "I'm the kind of person the police are warning about."

I don't know what she's saying. "What do you mean, Natasha?"

She flings a hand at the screen that I've now turned off. "Choosing to stay in illegal accommodation. Turning a blind eye to the glaringly obvious."

"You knew they were operating an illegal business?"

She looks at me, eyes wide.

"I didn't *know*, Hannah. I didn't *know*." She breathes raggedly. "But I *should* have known."

I decide I need to wait for her to make sense all by herself. I sit next to her on the leather settee, hands on my knees and wait.

The words come soon enough.

"I didn't always get on well with my family," she says. "My mum was not always the best mum in the world. She loved me but she just knew how to rub me up the wrong way. I couldn't cope with my mum. I needed to do my own thing." She turns the glass round in her hand. "My mum died when I was sixteen."

"Oh, sweetheart," I say.

There's the rising temptation to share that my own mum died when I was fifteen. I'd be doing it purely to show solidarity, to make a connection, but this is time for Natasha to speak, not me.

She gives a sad smile. "As soon as I was done with school I wanted to just strike out on my own, you know? I didn't want to do the things life expected of me. I wanted to be my own person. Everyone thought I was going to go into work or, if I did something educational, it would be something practical, close to home." She meets my gaze. She's stopped crying but her cheeks are wet. "I had no money, no one to support me. Anything you earn, the world just takes away from you. That's how I ended up renting a single shitty room in a horrid house which—" she sighs heavily "—crooks are using as some sort of illegal kitchen. I should have seen this coming."

I understand now.

"None of that makes this your fault," I say. "Choices in life are limited."

I do want to say something about myself.

"You know, Natasha, I lost my mum at a similar age to you. I definitely reacted badly. Like you, I decided I needed to chart my own course. My family – Dad – expected me to go to university once I'd finished school. I went to a private school. I don't know if you can tell."

Natasha laughs as I dial up the BBC received pronunciation quality in my voice.

"Yeah, you're a bit posh," she says.

"Well, posh or not, Dad wanted me to further my education. I rebelled."

"Yeah?"

"Yep. Took myself off to Greece. Corfu. Zakynthos. I got work as a holiday rep. Eighteen years old and put in charge of looking after coach-loads of drunken British holidaymakers. It was brilliant. It was terrible. It was absolutely the making of me. This..." I gesture around me with outstretched fingers. "This work is being a holiday rep, except it's not a coachload of drunken Brits but one client after another, often hellbent on self-destruction. Fire-fighting day after day."

She nods, wondering where I'm going.

"Point is," I say. "I made big and rash decisions as I struggled to strike out on my own. I stayed in some absolute dives. More than once I was alone in a room with a man who was a bit deaf when it came to the word 'no'. I made some shocking decisions and some bad things happened to me along the way." I reached over and took her hand again. "But at no point was it *my fault*. To hell with that nonsense."

Natasha is nodding in slow agreement. "It's not my fault."

"Not at all. We have to deal with the situation as we find it." I point at the screen. "Those people who died in that fire. Whatever the twats in the police force are saying, it's not their fault. In fact, I'm going to tell them as much."

"You should," she says.

I'm about to stand and then pause. "You're coming to the gala tonight, right?"

"I've bought clothes especially," she says. "I didn't know if I need to get changed here."

"You can. I need to go home and get Dad first. But, listen, there's this man I want you to talk to at the gala. Todd from the *Safe As Houses* thing."

"Look, Hannah. I told you I'm not happy with being in the press..."

"Just talk to him. Tell him your story. All this stuff about our living situations being beyond our control. The lack of choices. It's exactly the stuff he needs to hear. As my assistant, if he can hear that passion from you then he will sign us up to do his PR."

She tilts her head. "Assistant? I'm your assistant?"

"You have definitely been assisting."

"As in, a job?" she asks lightly.

I look at this young woman. The transformation she's undergone in the last few days is enormous. From a soot-streaked wretch to this confident young woman – new clothes, new hair. She clearly has some of the same passion that's driven me through my life. She's soaked up everything I've asked of her, shown some superb initiative. I don't want to start thinking about words like protégé, but the similarities between us are stunning. I like her very, very much.

"Let's see how tonight goes," I say. "But, yes, Natasha Dibello, if you want a job, I'd be happy to take you on."

She grins with delight, any sign of tears now evaporated.

33

The time to get ready for the LPS gala rolls around very swiftly. I leave the office early so that I can go home and organise Dad.

Natasha offered to get him, which was really sweet of her. I had no idea she could drive, but I need to put her on the insurance for the car. Which might be a lot, given how young she is.

And anyway, Dad likes to see that we're making a proper fuss for a night out and, these days, getting a father with dementia properly dressed involves some stopping and starting. Marissa is on hand, wrestling him into his suit. They'll be having fun with the bowtie soon. Dad has always rebelled against clip-on ones, even though they are so much easier.

I get dressed. I've elected for a sleeveless ankle length column dress with clean lines and architectural neckline. I think it allows me to walk that line between formal wear and full-on ballroom glitz. Green heels with bronze accents and a satin clutch bag set things off.

As I select jewellery, my mind can't help but turn over the wording of that police press conference earlier today. There were a lot of weasel words, but the whole thing left me with the feeling that the police were wrapping the whole thing in a bubble of blame. *'Look at these dead people, probably foreigners, shouldn't have been here anyway – they died because they chose to live somewhere they shouldn't'.* It had been cocooned in such a way that the average viewer who might see a snippet of it on the evening news would feel safe, knowing that this was the sort of thing that happened to *'other people'.*

I put on earrings facing the dresser mirror and think about how Todd Streetly's campaign for safer housing has to face this kind of prejudice on an ongoing basis. I start to feel angry on his behalf and then I start to feel angry on Natasha's behalf and then I just start to feel angry.

I told Natasha I was going to give the police a piece of my mind. I haven't done so yet. I've got a few minutes.

DS Rob Joseph's number is in my phone. I stand up – if you're going to be angry at someone, do it standing up – and call him.

It rings and then goes to voicemail. Damn.

I almost end the call there but, what the hell.

"Detective Sergeant Joseph, this is Hannah Douglas-Jones. I've seen the press conference the police have put out today and, frankly, I'm appalled at the stance you're taking on the plight of people in sub-standard and illegal accommodation. I don't know who wrote the script for that shambles, but all it did was reinforce stereotypes about migrant workers and the situation many people face." I recalled Natasha's words from earlier. "People who end up in shitty rooms in horrid houses shouldn't be blamed for their situation. You're better than that. I expect a call back to explain yourself."

I end it there. It was a bit of a rant. I'd made the call and I'd be able to tell Todd about it later. A bit of righteous anger to grease the wheels of our future business. I had a good feeling about me and Todd.

It's six o'clock, the summer sky still light, and we're due at the gala in an hour. Dad complains to Marissa that she's given him the wrong cufflinks. She argues back with equal force that the cufflinks he's got are the only ones in the house. But they're moving. He's dressed. He looks dapper. We're in the car with an hour to spare.

"Have fun," says Marissa. She says it in a pleasant tone, but there's a definite undercurrent of 'he's your problem now!' in her voice. I don't blame her.

We talk about galas of years gone by as we drive into the city. I'm subtly reminding Dad of who will be there and who won't. He seems entirely on the ball this evening. The gala is an annual ritual, and ritual and routine is something that he works well with.

I'm looking forward to the evening on both Dad's behalf and my own and I'm in a positive frame of mind.

That's when the battery warning light comes on the dash again. The car cuts out a moment, restarts and then cuts out completely. We drift to a stop, me battling the dying power steering long enough to get us to the side of the road.

The car is dead.

34

"This isn't the Athena," says Dad unhelpfully as he looks out the window.

I keep my cool. I try to start the car again. It doesn't start. I take the key out, put it back in and try again. Still nothing. Some dashboard lights but nothing from the engine at all. Humming to myself to avoid swearing or other signs of panic, I take the key out, wait a full thirty seconds and try again. Nothing.

"This isn't good."

"What?" says Dad.

"The car won't start," I say, trying not to add an 'obviously' on the end.

He peers ahead. "Where are we?"

We're on the Hinckley Road, a good three miles still from the city centre.

"Not near enough," I say.

I reach over to the glove compartment and take out the manual in the hope that it can somehow both tell me what's gone wrong and how I might be able to fix it.

"Shall we look under the bonnet?" Dad suggests.

I've seen under the bonnet of this car. Like all modern cars it's basically a sealed plastic unit. We don't stand a chance.

"We've got breakdown cover," I say, not overly certain.

I'm sure there was some that came with the car insurance when I last updated it. I don't think I've done anything to activate it. I take out my phone and go to my e-mails. Find the insurance policy confirmation, find who provides our breakdown cover, get in touch with them.

It's six-twenty. I'm meant to be at the venue by seven and delivering our brief sponsorship speech at seven-fifteen. I've put down good money, money I can't afford to waste, on a five-minute slot in which to greet everyone, make an impression, consolidate myself as the number one PR and image consultant in the city and introduce the actual keynote speaker for the evening.

Before I've even found the e-mail I know, just know, that breakdown recovery isn't going to get us there.

"Maybe I should drive," says Dad.

"How is that going to help?" I huff.

I need to forget the car for the moment and maybe just get a taxi for now.

I switch back to the home screen on my phone to open Uber and my phone starts ringing.

DS Joseph.

Not what I need right now but reflex, FOMO and rising annoyance makes me answer it anyway.

"Detective sergeant," I say coldly.

"Ah, is that Hannah? Miss Douglas-Jones. I had a missed call from you."

"I left you a voicemail."

"Did you? I've not checked. I wanted to speak to you, but you called?"

"After seeing that travesty of a press conference the police put out earlier today."

"Why are we talking to the police now?" says Dad. "We need a garage."

I wave him to be quiet.

"I'm actually rather busy right now," I say to DS Joseph.

"You're out and about. I get it. I did want to catch you."

"What for?"

"My DI is breathing down my neck a bit about the woman you helped at the fire, and I wondered if you had any further thoughts as to where she might be?"

That gives me cause to hesitate.

"She didn't call you?" I blurt before I can take proper control of my mouth.

"No..." says Joseph slowly. *"Did you ... have you spoken to her?"*

I think back. Natasha had said she'd spoken to the policeman. And yet clearly she hadn't. She'd lied. Why would she lie?

The answer comes to me immediately. The police are scary. The police only want to talk to you when you're in trouble. There's almost nothing worthwhile to be gained from talking to the police. I can easily see why young Natasha would tell me she had spoken to the detective but, in reality, just simply hadn't bothered.

"I have spoken to her," I say. "We're in touch."

"Oh, great," he says. *"That's good. If you could tell me where she is."*

"I gave her your contact details."

"But she's not called."

"No."

"Look," he says, *"can I come have a chat with you about this?"*

"I'm really busy."

"I'm out and about in the city centre. Wherever you are, I can just drop by for a minute."

A thought occurs to me. It is instantly appealing because it's an unconventional solution to my current transport issues.

"Are you aware of the Leicester Professional Services gala dinner?" I say.

"You may be surprised to hear I am not," he replies.

35

Walker pulls up at Duncan Flanagan's place. It's a modest house, not far from the university.

"Ay up, chuck!" says Duncan as he opens the front door. He pulls Walker in for an embrace. "How you doing?"

Duncan's always had that larger-than-life presence. Partly it's from his girth, which is considerable, but it's also from his gregarious nature. When they both worked at Mansfield House, Duncan would have a small greeting for every single person that he walked past. Nothing showy, no massive conversation-starters, just a tiny check-in to acknowledge each person as he made his way to his desk in the morning.

Walker follows him inside his house.

There's the expected cliché that a single man who's entered retirement might let standards slide in his personal life, but Duncan's house is orderly and clean. Walker has never asked whether he employs someone to clean it for him or whether he does it himself.

"Tea? Or something a little stronger?" asks Duncan.

It's evening, a perfectly acceptable time to have a beer or glass of wine, but Walker is driving and he's expected home for dinner at some point. At least he thinks he is. Off the top of his head he can't remember if Helen is out at one of her clubs or classes this evening. She has plenty of them and it's hard to keep track. Walker would worry that they don't spend enough time together, but even when she's got something on, they tend to find each other sometime around the ten o'clock news, just in time for one of them to drift off on the sofa.

"Tea, please, Duncan," he says.

Walker follows him into the kitchen where Duncan operates on autopilot putting the kettle on, grabbing mugs from the cupboard.

"We've had a blast from the past this week," Walker says.

"Yeah?"

"Someone dumped a load of documents and I saw a name I haven't seen in years."

"Yes?"

"Brendan O'Malley."

Duncan freezes with teabags halfway to the mugs. "*That* Brendan O'Malley?"

"Yep. I assume so."

"Christ."

"Yeah."

Duncan finishes making the tea and carries it through so that they can sit down. The furniture's from a couple of decades ago, but immaculate. Duncan's bookcase contains novels and non-fiction books. History was his thing. Walker remembers how excited Duncan was when they identified the skeleton of Richard the Third. He'd gone to watch the procession when they re-buried his bones at Leicester cathedral in twenty fifteen.

"I still think about Baljit," says Duncan.

"Me too," says Walker.

"He was a stupid idiot."

Walker grins. "He was." Detective Sergeant Baljit Sanghera has been dead for over twenty years, yet Walker can still conjure his face as clear as anything. Round face, wide eyes. He'd come into Operation Kilkenny with a 'my way or the highway' attitude. Something to prove.

Duncan stares at his mug, blowing on his tea. "He didn't deserve to die."

"No." Walker shrugs. "We were all young and stupid back then."

"We were all way too stupid to be doing what we were doing. Fuck, I wouldn't trust twenty-something me as far as I could throw me," says Duncan.

"It's funny, we've got a new recruit on the Duncans," says Walker with a smile. "Josie. She's just like we were. Brash, gobby, over-confident. She's a good copper, but she annoys people."

"Wait." Duncan holds out a hand. "They still call you the Duncans?"

"Of course."

He taps his round chest with meaty fingers. "I was the only Duncan in it. I objected at the time but how can you still be called the Duncans when there's literally no Duncans on the team?"

"You know how nicknames work."

"Sounds fucking unfair."

Walker chuckles and draws a smile from Duncan.

"At least your nickname doesn't come with any negative connotations," says Duncan.

Walker nods. "Most people think Walker is my real name."

"People don't know why you've been called Walker's for the last thirty years?"

"No."

"Fucking unfair. You get named after Walker's crisps because of the boxes your mum nicked from the factory for you to take into work. That's a solid nickname. Me, my name becomes a by-word for crappy, lazy and incompetent coppers."

"If it's any consolation, the current Duncans are some of the finest officers in the force."

Duncan eyes him. "Is that what everyone else thinks?"

Walker shrugs. "The Duncans were never crap, never incompetent."

"Kilkenny wasn't our fault," says Duncan.

Even after a quarter of a century, it's a common conversation between them. Twenty-plus years and the two of them, Walker and Duncan, are the two remnants of Operation Kilkenny who've stuck it out for the longest. The supers and inspectors further up the chain were sidelined when it all went wrong: moved to administrative roles, encouraged to transfer to other forces, or simply hastened to early retirement.

Operation Kilkenny had been mismanaged from the start. Walker and Duncan had been sent into the New Parks area under the guise of young drug dealers from Nottingham who were looking to expand. They made numerous sample buys from Brendan O'Malley and other dealers in the area. Brendan knew everyone in New Parks. He was their gateway into the criminal fraternity in the area. Walker and Duncan had hung around, a lot of the time at the Lion Pub on Park

Rise. They got to know some of the local lads and got friendly with some local girls – more friendly than was strictly professional, especially when the lager was flowing.

All the while they were working their way up to meeting bigger dealers.

Brendan O'Malley had taken a shine to Duncan. Duncan played up his Irish heritage and Brendan liked that. Eventually, this got them into contact with uncle-nephew team, Dean Taylor and Shaun "Shuggy" Taylor. Three months since they'd moved into the area, almost abandoning their whole lives outside, they arranged the big buy. Twelve grand's worth of heroin.

August 2001. Walker and Duncan met with Shuggy and Dean. Sergeant Baljit Sanghera was there as the 'big money guy', the boss who was making the big buy.

The catalogue of failings in the sting were numerous, laughable even.

Police intel had said the sellers might come armed but, for some reason, no police back-up was arranged.

Baljit, the 'money man', was meant to roll up in a prestige car, but all they had was an unmarked police car: a Vauxhall Vectra.

Sightlines on the car park were poor and police surveillance missed most of it.

Most moronic of all, the bundles of cash were held with strips that were faintly marked with the words 'Property of Leicestershire Police'.

It was a shambles.

Before the Taylors turned up, a previously unknown figure, Marty Cole, ran in with a pistol and shot Baljit point blank in the chest before trying to make off with the cash.

Shuggy and Dean were waiting in a stolen Land Rover around the corner, ready to make their getaway.

Baljit Sanghera was pronounced dead at the hospital and all the men involved were rounded up within a couple of days. Everyone from the Taylors down to Brendan O'Malley were handed custodial sentences.

But in an important sense, that didn't matter. An officer had died in an op which fell apart under the investigation that followed. Walker and Duncan told themselves they were the most blameless of all involved – they were the young recruits being directed by the fools above – but it didn't matter. No officer came out of that situation well. And so the Dead End Duncans were born, sidelined for the rest of their careers.

"Kilkenny wasn't our fault," Walker agreed.

Duncan grunted. "You came to ask me about Brendan O'Malley. You know he's dead?"

"What?"

"Earlier this year. Cancer of the oesophagus."

"Shit. That's probably not a nice way to go."

"I doubt it. His wife took over what remained of their businesses."

Walker reaches back into his memory. "Kathleen."

"That's her. Her and their sort of adopted daughter. Ruby Adams."

The name means nothing to Walker.

"I've not seen them in a while," says Duncan.

"I've not seen them at all for decades," says Walker.

"You were very close to that Leanne Church in the New Parks Lion." Duncan chuckles. He's capable of producing a very dirty chuckle.

Walker can feel himself actually blushing with

embarrassment. “Don’t remind me. I was actually engaged to Helen at the time.”

“What happens on the job...”

Duncan sighs deeply and, in that moment, Walker sees that old age is creeping up on his friend. He might still be in his late-fifties but there’s a bone-weariness to the man, a fatigue.

“Kathleen O’Malley still living in the same place?” Walker asks.

Duncan nods. “If you’re dropping in, tell her I said ‘Hi’.”

36

"This is not how I expected to spend my Thursday night," says DS Rob Joseph.

He's driving me and Dad into the city centre. He did not come in a proper police car. There's a very infantile part of me that would have valued a ride in a police vehicle, all lights flashing. My mind however is firmly fixed on the time and how we don't have any at all.

It's five past seven. I'm already late to the venue. I'm meant to be speaking to the assembled diners in less than ten minutes. *'Friends and colleagues, I'm Hannah Douglas-Jones, founder and director of the Douglas-Jones PR and image consultancy. Welcome to tonight's gala dinner...'*

When the lights turn green on the dual carriageway junction, DS Joseph accelerates sharply right into Queen Street.

"Steady on, there!" says Dad in the front seat next to the detective.

"Just want to get you there on time," he says. "And then, Hannah, you and I can talk, right?"

Dad reaches over and points to a dressing poking out the sleeve of DS Joseph's shirt.

"What have you done there?"

"Tattoo removal," says Joseph without looking. "Erasing the follies of youth."

Dad accepts this answer with a grunt.

DS Joseph pulls up on the wide pavement directly outside the Athena. The doors to the former Art Deco cinema are open.

I help Dad out. "Listen, detective."

DS Joseph looks at me.

"I will get Natasha to give you a call, okay?" I say. "I'll make sure it happens."

"It's important we talk to her."

"I know. Just give us time. Come on, Dad," I say. "Let's get you in there."

There's nothing specifically wrong with Dad's mobility, but it does seem to take him a while to get up to speed. We bustle through the reception. The LPS gala is being held in the gallery room, a space that I've seen used for theatre type events, but also laid out for banquets such as tonight.

As we go in, the general lights are down low, a pink and red glow over the dozens of tables and hundreds of guests and, up at the front, the stage area with the hanging presentation screen behind is flooded with golden light. A place like the Athena can put on Oscar ceremony glitz with ease.

Someone is speaking from the lectern on stage. I can hear her and I can see her and still it takes me a good few seconds to realise that the woman talking to this crowd is Natasha.

"Friends and colleagues. Hello! I'm Natasha Dibello, from

the Douglas-Jones PR and image consultancy. Welcome to tonight's gala dinner!"

There is smooth and polite ripple of applause at these opening remarks.

At first glance, I think Natasha is wearing one of my dresses. It's very like the dress I'm wearing now. It's a good choice. It clings to her like mine clings to me.

"In a moment," she continues, "I want to introduce tonight's key speaker, Martin Stimple from Forsyth Legal but, before I do, I just want to say a few short words of my own..."

It's my speech. She's delivering my speech. And she's delivering it well.

She's sending out waves of confidence but at the same time, deliberate or not, she's doing the young and gawky thing. If I was being bitchy, I would even say she's leaning hard into the 'I'm pretty but I don't know it' vibe. If half the men in the audience don't fancy her right now then I don't know people half as well as I think I do.

She carries it through to the end – quick, effective and impactful – and introduces the keynote speaker. The applause is strong.

I don't know if I should be proud of how she's stepped up for me. Or jealous.

37

As Natasha descends the stage, I get Dad over to his table. There's a whole bunch of people from the old solicitors' company, Champion Fellowes, at a table fairly near the front. I made sure Dad and I got put on their table.

Harvey Kenelm is there and Cynthia Fellowes, daughter of one of the original founding partners, and a few other people. The younger ones (all my age and older) are a fairly interchangeable lot. There is such a thing as a stereotypical solicitor. Like accountants, people want their solicitors to be dull and stolid individuals and the legal folk at Champion Fellowes do dull and stolid fairly well. Tailored but unexciting formal wear. Neat and bland-as-hell haircuts.

As the keynote speaker to the Leicester Professional Services gala delivers a warm but essentially empty speech. I get Dad sat down. Harvey, two chair's down, doesn't let Dad's arrival interrupt the conversation he's having with the woman further round, but Cynthia Fellowes reaches over and grips Dad's hand on the table.

"Donald! Lovely to see you!"

"Had a bit of car trouble," he explains. "Ended up with a police escort."

"Really?" she says and her eyes flash to me, like, '*is this true?*'

I shrug and nod. It's close enough.

"You're looking well, Cynth," he says.

"Fat, you mean. Three-week cruise round the Balkans. Terrence says he doesn't like boats but he does like an all-inclusive buffet."

Dad laughs. "Tried one of them once. Arctic cruise. Whales and northern lights. Didn't see a bloody single whale until we docked in Tromsø." He looks back to me. "You remember that?"

"You didn't take me, Dad," I say. "That'd be one of your lady friends."

I say it lightly and it is a matter of joking between us now. Mum died over fifteen years ago and there was a period of seven or eight years when Dad had tried to get back into the dating game. Did I begrudge him that? Maybe a little at first. There were at least four or five of them. None of them lasted very long.

"Which lady friend was that then?" he asks.

"I didn't keep track," I smile.

Cynthia laughs. It's not beyond the realms of possibility that Dad and Cynthia had a thing. If they did, they kept it quiet, and they've managed to maintain a warm regard for each other since. Not that Cynthia has been round to the house since Dad's hasty retirement.

I manage to see across the room to where Natasha is chatting to some men by the bar. I must go and rescue her at some point.

The keynote speaker wraps up to applause. The meal will be served soon. I must find Todd while I'm here.

"You okay with Dad?" I say to Cynthia.

"Of course!"

I stand. As I move round the table, Harvey Kenelm stands with a bit of a totter. Has he been hitting the wine hard and early?

"Hannah, dear," he says. He takes hold of my wrist. I'm not sure whether he's grabbing onto me for support or he went for a handshake and missed. He lets go almost instantly. "Must catch up with you in a bit."

"Yes?"

"Sort out this Brascote buildings thing."

"You've got a potential buyer?"

He taps the side of his fat nose with a finger and winks.

"Right," I say and move on.

I go straight to the bar and find Natasha. She's got a small circle of people around her. One could pretend that the circle isn't focussed on her but it is. I catch what she's saying over the music as I near.

"...really just getting started. We're very passionate about getting what's best for our clients."

A man touches her elbow. "I thought you were a bolt of lightning on that stage, like you'd been doing that for years."

She nods a silent thanks.

I approach and lean round into her line of vision. "Get you a drink?"

She holds up a tall cocktail. A Long Island Iced Tea or something of that sort. "I've had offers!" she says and I can hear a wealth of subtext in her voice, even if the blokes round her can't. "Will you excuse me for a second?" she says to the group. "Just need to chat with my colleague."

We head across to the bar. She looks up at me.

"You're pissed off, aren't you?" she says.

I blink. "What?"

"I'm sorry," she says. "I didn't know what to do. I was here. You weren't. Some knob in a tux kept demanding to know where you were. I tried calling you a couple of times. And then I thought ... I know your speech. I've seen it open on your laptop enough this week."

I grip her shoulder. "You were amazing up there." I shake my head. "No, scratch that. You were fucking amazing up there, Natasha."

"Really?" She looks both shook up and relieved. "I thought you'd be angry with me."

There is a momentary tussle inside me – there is a part that's angry with her. She was presumptuous to take the stage. By doing so she's putting herself up there as my equal. Three days in my office does not make her a professional, a partner, even really a bona fide member of the team. There's an arrogance. But, by Christ, she bloody nailed it. If I'm anything other than pleased right now then that's just churlishness on my part.

"I was stunned."

"First time on a stage," she says. "Unless you count doing ballet recitals as a little girl."

"Ballet?"

"Don't I look like I could do ballet?"

"Oh. I was very much a ballet girl when I was about six or seven."

"Same!"

"No idea what I looked like waddling around the stage with twenty other gangly girls."

She laughs. "Oh, God. I'm so glad you're not angry."

"Well, if you're feeling any sense of guilt or obligation to me then hold onto that. I need you to talk to someone."

"Todd from the building safety campaign," she nods.

"Yeah. And the police."

"Again?"

I try to give her a look that's firm but supportive and non-judgemental. I don't know if I can pull that off.

"They say you never called them," I say.

Her expression closes down.

"It's a free country, isn't it?" she says. Does she sound sullen? Annoyed? She does.

"You don't have to lie to me," I say. "I understand."

"I'm so glad you understand." She swings her drink loosely in her hand. "I'm going to finish talking to these guys. *Maybe* I will find you and Todd later."

"Sure," I say, but she's already turned away.

38

I slide over to Todd Streetly's table. I greet him. He stands to shake my hand. The waiting staff are coming round with the starters.

"You came then?" I said.

"It's amazing. They'll let anyone in willing to pay for a hundred quid ticket."

"I could have got you in for free."

"Not at all. Then I wouldn't have got to sit on a table with Kayleigh, Azar, Chanoch—" he gestures to the people already at the table "—and all the other last minuters and chancers."

"So harsh," says a balding man, amiably enough.

I think I recognise the twenty-something woman at the table as some would-be local journalist. Kayleigh Chandler. That's the name. A pain in the arse.

"Well, I'm glad you are here because I've got that woman, Natasha, we spoke of previously."

"The one who survived the—?"

I bat him into silence, giving a meaningful tilt of the head towards the young journalist at the table. "She is wary about discussing what was ultimately a very personal and traumatic experience."

He begins to nod in understanding, then a frown creases his wide brow. He points at the stage. "*That* Natasha? The one who did the welcoming bit on your behalf?"

"She was good, right? Would do well fronting a *Safe As Houses* promo video, maybe?"

"I knew you'd found her. You didn't say you'd employed her?"

"It was that or have her just lazing about at my house."

He grins. "You let all the waifs and strays in?"

"Only the ones who appeal to me."

"And you say she's shy about speaking to people?"

"On that particular matter," I say, dropping into a more serious tone. "She doesn't want it to define her. I applaud that."

He meets my gaze. He has brown eyes. There's an honest strength in his face. I could totally picture him as a lumberjack or an outdoorsman. And I know that's a really weird thought, even as I'm thinking it. Seal the deal, Hannah, then get Todd to indulge in some lumberjack fantasies later.

A waiter places starters – wafers and prawns, circular terrines – on the table.

"You should meet her," I say to Todd.

"Now?"

"Right now."

39

Once the main courses have been cleared away and there's plenty of time before the desserts, I've coaxed Todd over to a spare seat at the Champion Fellowes table.

The house wine is flowing and it's not bad house wine at that. Natasha is starting to feel more and more relaxed around Todd and somehow we've got round to talking about Tyrese Jali. Long ago I became adept at talking about clients without ever letting a name slip. I've got one eye on Natasha, in case I get an inkling that she might be indiscreet.

"So, this guy," I say, "thinks he's such a big shot. Thinks he can get away with drunken assault on someone with a disability by making a donation to cat charities."

"Why cat charities?" says Todd.

"Because he likes cats, I guess. I told him that wasn't going to cut it."

"But who is it?" asks one of the younger solicitors for the third time.

I ignore her. "So I told him, if he's going to make amends,

he's going to fund twenty-four hour accessible minibus services to enable disabled people who are part of the night-time economy to access work and entertainment. I'm going to make him drive the bloody thing if I have to."

"Is it that Casper Veenham?" asks the solicitor. "You know – the chef guy who's going to be on *Strictly*. I've heard he's a horrible man."

I'm still ignoring her.

"As punishments go," says Todd, "it has a certain sense of ironic justice."

"Thank you," I say.

"But actually, it doesn't really address the problem of accessibility for people with disabilities."

"No?" I say.

"If we have a lift in a building to enable wheelchairs to access upper floors, but only staff can operate it, then that's trying to address the issue but also creating a different sort of burden on the user. If we have to get out special ramps to allow people to access trains then that's drawing attention to the person and creating an inconvenience for everyone. A special minibus service? It's a nice gesture. But in all areas of life, true accessibility and equality should be invisible to the casual on-looker."

"Ah."

"You're so right, Todd," says Natasha. "There's something better to be done."

I'm about to leap in with my own thoughts on the matter, but Dad reaches across and clutches Natasha's hand.

"I need the toilet, Hannah," he says in a low urgent whisper that everyone hears.

I'm about to correct Dad on calling Natasha by the wrong name, but she's already getting up as if she plans to take him.

"No, don't worry Natasha. I'm on it," I say.

I'm not sure if I'm more embarrassed by the idea of her taking my dad to the loo, or that he's got us muddled.

I stand up with Dad.

Todd and Natasha continue discussing the ins and outs of true accessibility. She mentions a module she's been studying for her public services degree and that's all I get before Dad's turning and leading me with what is obvious confidence in the direction of the toilets.

We leave the noise of the venue, go up a flight of curving stairs to a wide corridor where the doors to the toilets are on one side, and the tall, thin, architecturally beautiful windows look out onto the street on the other.

"You good now?" I say.

He gives me a look, both admonishing and playful. "I bloody well hope so," he says and goes inside.

I pace the empty hallway, then sit in one of the narrow alcoves below the windows.

A scuttle of footsteps on the stairs and Harvey Kenelm comes up. He seems simultaneously surprised and relieved to see me.

"Ah, there you are."

There's a languid quality in his voice, halfway between drunk and self-assured.

"We've all got to be somewhere."

"I really did mean to catch up with you. About those buildings?"

"The Brascote buildings?"

I make to get up, but he hurries forward, gesturing for me to stay seated.

"I have a buyer," he says. "One willing to pay market price, and quickly, too."

"That's great."

His heavy hands wave again like he needs me to be quiet or he won't remember the things he needs to tell me.

"But I think we need to get things straight between us two."

"Paperwork?" I say and then realise I'm being stupid.

There's something in his rolling gait and measured manner. He's talking to me like I'm a child, like he has to explain a complicated thing to a little girl.

"I didn't like the way you spoke to me the other day," he says.

"Right."

"I know you're trying to be helpful. Showing us that you're all grown up now."

His hand reaches out and cradles my chin.

40

I flinch at Harvey's touch and push his hand away.

"Harvey. You're drunk."

I'd get up from the chair, but now he's so close that if I do I'll just be right up against him.

"No need to be off with me," he says, cheerily. "I'm only looking after your best interests."

I want to tell him that to serve my best interests – by which we really mean Dad's best interests – then he just needs to sell that property and pass the funds my way. I want to say all of that, but this situation is not right for meaningful discussion.

The bulge of his waist is less than two feet from my chest. I have to look up to address him.

"We can talk about this another time," I say.

"I'm just asking you to be polite," he says.

That's it. I move to stand. He puts a hand on my shoulder and literally holds me in place.

"You understand how this works, don't you?"

I try to appear calm. He wants a response from me. He

wants something he can react to. “This is not appropriate, Harvey,” I say.

“Inappropriate?” he moves an inch closer and looks down. He’s looking right down my dress. “You know what you do to a man, Hannah. I’ve seen you.”

I screw up my face.

“Your dollybird behaviour that you think is some sort of career. I gave you those offices so you can play at being a businesswoman.”

His behaviour is scaring and infuriating me. He’s physically threatening me while verbally goading me. Does he want me to fight him?

“I pay you for those offices.”

“Peppercorn rent!” he spits. “I give you everything. I look after you. And you parade yourself for all to see. You need to think about what you owe me.”

To hell with this. I try to stand again. He doesn’t stop me but, as I rise, his hand cups my breast. A thumb brushes it roughly.

“Get off me!” I hiss. Why aren’t I screaming? For one, and this is the most stupid of reasons, my dad is literally in the toilets just across the way. I feel some sort of embarrassment – for him? for me? – if Dad comes out and sees his oldest friend trying to feel up his daughter.

His hand drops but his other one is coming forward and I am hyper aware of where he thinks that hand’s going.

“I said stop!”

He rocks with a chuckle. I can smell the wine on him. Wine, rich gravy, his cologne.

“You can’t pretend to be a player and then back out when the game gets serious,” he says.

His wandering hand tickles the material at the front of my dress.

"I think she said no," says Natasha.

She's at the top of the stairs, her phone in her hand. She's filming.

"We're just talking," says Harvey, quickly taking a step away from me.

Below the bulge of his gut, I can see his erection deforming his trousers.

I look at Natasha and, for a moment, I feel an acute shame at what my face looks like. What the hell do I look like? Shocked, vulnerable, passive, stupid? But I find myself and I find my anger.

"It's called sexual assault, Harvey," I say. "You go to fucking prison for it."

"How dare you make up such slanders!" he spits.

"I was filming it, you senile cockwomble," says Natasha, venom in her voice. "You ridiculous, ugly, *old*, greasy cunt of a man."

He splutters and blusters.

I'm finding myself more and more with each second.

"YouTube?" I suggest to Natasha.

"YouTube," she nods. "TikTok. All of them. We'll even put it on Facebook so your old fart friends at the golf club can find it, shitface."

"You forget who you're talking to," he snaps, but his tone is wavering. It's a gambit, not a threat.

"I think you're the man who *used to* look after Dad's money," I say.

His eyes widen. "This is a trap. This is deliberate."

I laugh. I laugh at his pitiful behaviour, the fact that he's lost and still pretends he hasn't. The shamefulness of this situation is still present. I'm going to feel some terrible things later. But right now, Harvey Kenelm has been reduced to a joke and he still doesn't know how far he's going to fall.

The toilet doors open and Dad emerges. There's an intent on his face like he's trying to do things methodically. It takes him a moment to see me, Harvey and Natasha arranged in our little tableau.

"Everything okay?" he says.

Harvey is lost for words.

"Perfect," I say. "Harvey's just told me he's sorted out some of your finances so you can still keep living in the lap of luxury."

Dad blows out his lips drily. "Lap of luxury, indeed."

"And Harvey's got to go home now," says Natasha.

"But—" begins Harvey.

"He's not feeling well and he's leaving immediately," she adds.

"Oh, a shame," says Dad.

"Mmmm." I nod.

Harvey taps his belly. "Touch of the ... you know. Have to duck out."

He excuses himself, red-faced, and goes. Natasha and I walk downstairs with Dad.

I keep glancing at Natasha as we walk, hoping to express some thanks to her, not wishing to think of what might have happened if she hadn't turned up when she had.

41

Friday lunchtime, Walker sits in his car outside the Lion pub in New Parks for a long time and just looks at the world around him.

He's had a whole policing career after Operation Kilkenny. More than twenty years of patrolling, investigating, and more form filling than any honest copper ought to face. He's been back to New Parks in that time – he must have been back to New Parks in that time. This was the place where for several months, he was not Walker, he was not DC Smith. Here he was Gary Snow, and he'd lived that role, introduced himself to people in that role, and even made friends of a sort with people as Gary Snow. This was the place where he'd lived a lie, and though time eases all things, it still feels weird to be here.

The Lion has changed. That much is certain. It's still an unattractive flat-roofed pub, but some brave pub chain has moved in, slapped wooden cladding and a logo on the outside and it is now advertising itself as 'the home of the sizzling steak'.

Brendan and Kathleen O'Malley lived in a former council house just across the road. Brendan's perennially broken motorbike has gone from the garden. There are several pots of flowering plants behind the low wooden fence.

Accepting there's nothing to be done by sitting here, Walker gets out and walks across the road to the O'Malley house.

He has no idea what he's going to say to Kathleen when he sees her. Or, more honestly, he knows exactly what he might say, but it all sounds ridiculous in his head.

'Hey Kath. Remember me? That's right. The cop who got your late husband five years inside.'

'Hey, Kath. I know you hate cops, but do you fancy telling me what business Brendan had with Paul Mulholland, the guy who owned the house that burned down in that Narborough Road fire?'

'Hey Kath. It's me ... Gary.'

He walks down the short narrow path to the door, onto the raised block of concrete that's supposed to be like some sort of veranda to the property and raps the door knocker. He turns round as he waits, automatically scanning the street to see if anyone's watching him. He gives it thirty seconds and then knocks again.

"What do you want?"

This comes from a middle-aged woman two doors down. She's wearing joggers and a loose jumper, her hair – dyed red with brown-grey roots showing – pulled back into a ponytail.

"I'm after Kathleen," he says. "She in?"

She sticks her tongue in her cheek and looks at him with wide eyes.

"Fuck me," she whispers, and he realises not only does she recognise him but he recognises her too. Yet he can't put a name to that face. She's smiling, not necessarily in a friendly way. "What do they call you these days?" she says.

"Walker," he says and the name comes to him in that instant. "Jinny. My goodness. How are you doing?"

"Can't complain," she says.

When he last saw Jinny Michaels it was – well, it was over twenty years ago. She and Leanne used to be thick as thieves, and just as Duncan rightly accused Walker of having a thing for Leanne, so Duncan was more than a little sweet on Jinny. Two undercover police officers masquerading as out of town drug buyers, and two local lasses who were happy to let Walker and Duncan buy drinks for them.

Jinny had had a foul mouth on her back then. Not as sharp-tongued as Leanne, but much happier to shout the odds when she had a few Bacardi Breezers inside her.

"You look well," he says.

"Fuck off," says Jinny. "I know what I look like." She nods at him. "You ain't turned to fat like the other one."

He smiles and pats his belly. "Shirt and jacket covers a lot."

"You retired?"

"Not yet. You?"

She snorts. "Between jobs. We had our Liam's PIP until he got sent to prison."

He doesn't know if Liam is a son, a husband or something else. "Sorry to hear that."

"You were a fucking cunt, you know that?"

It's said with feeling, yet oddly without much in the way of anger; as though coppers being cunts was as much a part of the world as wasps stinging and dogs biting.

"It's all a long time ago," he says. "All in the past."

She doesn't agree or disagree. She points at the door in front of him. "Kath died last month."

"Oh, hell. I'm sorry. I heard about Brendan."

"Yeah. Well, she didn't last much longer. She wasn't well. Their Ruby lives there now."

"Ruby?"

Duncan had mentioned a Ruby. Ruby Adams. Some adopted daughter. He got the impression, purely from Duncan's tone, that it wasn't an official adoption. Some families were complicated things. People drifted in and drifted out.

"Know where I can find her?"

Jinny shakes her head. "I've got her phone number."

"Could you give it to me?"

She wrinkles her nose. "No. Don't think so. What do you want them for anyway?"

Walker is strongly tempted to tell her nothing. A separate part of him wants to keep the conversation going. Despite the duplicity and the years, part of him wants to mend part of what was broken, fill in the gaps. That part of him wants to get to know Jinny again. The urge to ask if she's still in touch with Leanne Church is very strong, but that's a part of Walker's guilty past and he just can't do it.

"You heard the news about the house fire on Narborough Road last weekend?"

"Think so," she says.

"People died. It's possible that one of them had some business going on with Brendan and Kathleen."

Jinny sniffs and stretches her back. "You mean Paul whatsisface?"

"You know him?"

"What's the surname?"

"Mulholland."

"That's him. I know he used to handle money for Brendan." She hesitates. "I'm no snitch but, fuck it, they're dead. He used to handle money for them."

"What do you mean?"

"Brendan was still dealing puff, even at the end. More of a hobby than anything. And he'd fence anything. Paul would manage the money side of things."

"You mean launder it?"

It sounds unlikely to Walker even as he says it. Brendan was always small time. Too small to need money laundering services.

"Some people don't like banks," says Jinny. "And Brendan saw himself as a bit of an investor."

"Okay." Walker can't see the pieces yet but this is, at least, something. "Would the daughter, Ruby, know anything about this?"

"She won't want to talk to you."

"She might."

Jinny scoffs. "You always had that air about you, you know?"

He keeps it genial. "What air?"

"The way you talk. You were a smooth bastard back then. What's the word? Smug. A smug twat. You talk like you're a game show host. You know that? Like you're better than the rest of us."

"I'm not better than anyone else. I—"

"I know you're fucking not, Gary," she says and laughs. "At least the other one, Duncan, he'd come round from time to time."

"Round here?"

Jinny nods.

"To see you?" he asks.

"In passing." She nods at the O'Malley house. "He'd drop in. Help 'em out."

He guesses she doesn't mean doing household chores and putting up shelves. "Duncan used to give them money?"

"People show guilt in different ways, I guess," she says. "You... None of it ever crossed your mind, did it?"

"That's not true."

"You ever think about what you did to Leanne?"

He struggles to find an answer. "We were young and stupid."

"Yeah. But some of us have to pay for it."

"You seen Leanne recently?"

Now, at last, her face turns mean to match her words. "You didn't know? She died. Years ago. OD'd."

"Really?"

"I'm not a fucking liar, shitbag. Yeah. Died. Think on that." She pats herself as though looking for something. Maybe cigarettes or a vape. "Think you'd better fuck off now before I decide to call some lads over to sort you out."

It seems an empty threat, but Walker's got nothing to achieve or prove by standing there antagonising her.

"I'm sorry," he says and turns back to his car.

42

The next day, Natasha and I take a taxi into work and I arrange for a garage to collect the Jag.

I feel a strange air between the two of us all through most of the day.

And it feels strange because, for the most part, Thursday night was a success. I introduced Natasha to Todd and they spoke for over an hour. Todd managed to keep it light and about the generalities of renting accommodation, while she reciprocated with some moments of heartfelt emotion about the terror she'd felt at narrowly escaping a devastating house fire. On top of that, Dad had a good night. Utterly oblivious to the sickening behaviour of his old pal, Harvey, he'd spent time with Cynthia and the rest of the crowd from his old company and, in a very small way, had been his old self again.

And if I was reaching for available victories then, after his vile over-bearing sexual advance on me was caught on camera, it seems a given that I will now have the upper hand in any future management of Dad's finances.

But the thing with Harvey. His hand on my chin, my

breast, my dress. The simple and casual way in which an old man – and, for Christ's sake, we're talking about an old man, old enough to be my father! – the manner in which he positioned himself, physically and socially, so that for a time he had me exactly where he wanted me. And I can tell myself repeatedly that I was seconds away from punching him in the nuts or scratching his eyes out. But then those thoughts are immediately followed by the question of why didn't I? When was I going to make that move? When was I going to shove his bloated thrusting body away, huh? When was I going to assert myself as the woman I want to be?

Point is, I didn't.

To my shame, I didn't. And there's no way I should be feeling any bloody shame for what he did.

But I do.

And all of Friday morning, every time Natasha and I speak, that shame seems to blossom anew. And I don't think there's anything Natasha's actually doing. I can't pick her up for it. She's just ... being there. And the shared knowledge of what happened is driving my guilt.

I feel like I don't know how to talk to her all of sudden.

When I walk past her desk and she's browsing the internet, some articles about crypto-currency that can't have anything to do with our work, I feel unable to ask her what she's doing or even show a pleasant interest in her browsing. There's just this disconnect between us.

I'm so distracted all day that when my phone buzzes with a call from Todd, I barely register it.

I almost answer it without thinking. I look at the caller ID, compose myself and answer.

"Todd, hello."

"Let's do it," he says.

"Do what?"

"I'd like your company to do some PR work for the Safe As Houses *campaign. I think we need someone with your understanding of the media landscape. I think you and Natasha speak with such clarity and conviction and we will really be a great fit for each other."*

I'm taken aback a moment. "I'm really glad you think so," I say.

"And, frankly, if you and Natasha don't come on board, then I think I might just have to poach her from you directly. She's dynamite."

"She is, isn't she?"

"Absolutely. Let's get some sort of package together and thrash it out."

"I can put some ideas together for you very soon," I say, knowing we have a full presentation, services and quote ready to go.

He hums. *"I've done this the wrong way round."*

"Done what?" I say.

"Never mind. Forget it."

"I don't know what I'm forgetting."

He *tssks* on the line. *"This. This thing I'm about to say is wholly separate from the previous thing."*

"Separate from the us working with you thing?"

"One's got nothing to do with the other," he says.

"You're getting cryptic now."

"Yeah. Um, Jeez." He's audibly flustered. *"Hannah, could I take you out for dinner next week?"*

I think I had already worked out where this was going, but it's still a surprise of a sort.

"Dinner. You and me. Not a work dinner."

"Is that a terrible idea?" he says.

"I don't think so..." I say slowly. "I'll have to check out your reviews on 'rate my date'."

"That's not a thing, is it?"

I grin, feeling a sort of equilibrium in some area of my life has been restored. "Not a thing. Dinner sounds great."

"Let's sort out the details. Say next Thursday?"

"Sounds ideal," I say.

When I've ended the call, I realise Natasha is standing there, looking at me with a lop-sided smile on her face.

"What?" I say.

"You got a date with Todd?" she asks.

"I might."

Her eyes crease in amusement. An almost wink. "Good for you. I'll pop it in the calendar."

43

The new week arrives and I hit the ground running.

The Jag has – fingers crossed – been working perfectly fine since the garage fiddled around under the bonnet. Modern cars are a mystery and I trust in the spirits of the universe that this one will keep going for a while longer.

"Take a look at this," says Natasha and slides a pad over my desk

There's a scrawl of notes on the lined A4 and I can see *Safe As Houses* mentioned several times.

"You did this at the weekend?" I ask.

"You want to impress Todd," she says. "This is the stuff we can do this coming week."

I glance over it. *Polish Todd's LinkedIn profile with campaign messages. Get Todd to accept and learn three killer talking points about the campaign. Get a joint press event with Leicester Fire and Rescue to talk about the Narborough Road fire.*

"I've got a contact at BBC East Midlands Today," I say. "I

think I know someone who still works at ITV Central News. Todd will need further media training."

"I thought you said he was good," she says.

"He's naturally good, but he needs more. What I'd like to do is get an op-ed piece by Todd, secretly written by us, into one of the national papers. *Times, Guardian*, maybe the *Independent*."

"You can do that?" Natasha's surprise fills with me a superior glow.

"I find," I say, "that just as it's easier to ask for forgiveness than permission, so it's better to assume you can do something without checking to see if you *can* do it."

She nods.

"What I'd really like to do," I say, "is get a press release together for your personal story. I'm thinking survivor-story exclusive in the *Mirror*. Maybe swallow any morals I have and see if the *Sun* are interested."

"I don't want to be splashed all over the newspapers," she says.

"Then, alternatively," I suggest gently, "we do a soft launch on socials with some survivor-story clips. We get photographs and video professionally done. Build it all into a six month social content calendar of clips, infographics, inspirational quotes, et cetera."

She looks less certain. "Um, yeah. Sure."

"You've got nothing to fear," I say.

I'm buoyed by the work that Natasha's done.

Yes, we've got more to do for Todd, but I have something else today that's pressing. Today's the day I told Tyrese he could come out of hiding from the De Morgan retreat. A week of splendid and luxurious isolation. He's been quiet over the weekend, which I didn't expect. It would have been very on-brand for him to start clamouring for the freedom to go to a party or a club.

The footballer-thumps-man-with-cerebral-palsy story has not exploded across the national news, so that's good. But letting Tyrese Jali out into the real world...? That's where chaos might creep into Project Tyrese again. I fear he thinks he's just paid me to make his problems go away and that he can just carry on as normal now.

Obviously, he's a grown man who can make his own decisions, but he's hired me to look after his reputation. He's not the first young hothead to assume that reputation management requires no input from him.

I've told him I'll be over there mid-afternoon. I've got a meeting with Karolina at lunchtime. That gives us the morning to work on Todd's stuff.

I can hear Natasha on the phone to someone, talking money or data or something. With a bit of luck, she's found some more of those older debts to recover. She's a dab hand at that. Her manner is firm and assertive. She's at her desk, phone against her ear, a works laptop open in front of her, and that battered laptop she accidentally brought with her from the house fire open next to her.

I draw up a draft press release for Natasha's story so she can see what that would look like. I get a response from my contact at the *Guardian* about running an opinion piece on building safety 'written' by Todd.

Mid-morning, I set Natasha onto the task of reaching out to *Shelter* and *Which?* to see if they fancy partnering up with *Safe As Houses* on a broader campaign of dealing with sub-standard housing, precarious accommodation, and general fire safety.

We do a bit of brainstorming on where we can take *Safe*

As Houses next and when I discover that they're going to be filming BBC *Question Time* in Leicester in September, I decide to put that on the board as a definite goal. *Question Time, Good Morning Britain, The Rest Is Politics, Channel 4 News*. Nothing is off-limits.

By the time we're done, we've mentally got Todd speaking to Parliamentary committees on housing. Secretly, I'm putting Natasha right by his side, giving her own account too.

It's getting close to twelve. After I've checked in on emails and messages, made sure there's nothing urgent bubbling under, I pick up my keys.

I waggle them and incline my head at Natasha, to let her know that I'm popping out. She nods a small acknowledgement.

Lunch with Karolina. I'm meeting my favourite private investigator at a coffee shop. She likes to mix things up, which I guess is an occupational habit.

The place is a café close to the city market.

It's a place I've not been to before. It has one of those 'living wall' installations, except all of the plants are made from plastic. It's appalling.

Karolina has chosen a table right next to the dusty plastic greenery. It feels as if she's done it on purpose.

"What do you know about Natasha?" Karolina asks, without preamble.

It's Karolina's way to be direct and challenging, so I consider her question. "Um, I know that she's incredibly efficient, charming and a fast learner. There's nothing that's been thrown her way that she's not handled incredibly well."

"Which tells you what?"

I smile at the question. Karolina gets a long way by asking

the sort of questions that a precocious child might ask. Layers and layers of 'but why?' to get to the core of an issue.

"What does it tell me? That she's an undiscovered gem. The assistant I never knew I needed."

"You know what other kind of person is efficient, charming and a fast learner?"

"No, do tell me," I say to her.

"Sociopaths."

She's deadpan, but I laugh. She's funny.

"Yeah, but this isn't that. I threw her a lifeline. She came out of that fire with nothing. She's been incredibly loyal since then. She's really got my back."

She raises her eyebrows in question. "Got your back, how?"

I tell Karolina about the incident with Harvey.

"Fuck," she breathes and then orders coffees and cheese and ham toasties for the pair of us. Carbs, dairy and fat – not exactly my first choice for a quality lunch.

"Eat up, you deserve it," says Karolina. She chews a big bite. "So, this Natasha is a good thing?"

"Yes. She's a real find, honestly. Consider my faith in humanity restored. How about Tyrese? Any updates?"

Karolina dusts her hands onto her empty plate. "He's been toeing the line. Not left the retreat at all."

"Wonders will never cease."

"He's planning an event or something, though. Been on the phone, all excited, ringing round his posse."

How does she know this stuff? I never ask, assuming that she's got the ear of staff, or maybe she's bugged his room. Best that I don't know.

"Well that sounds like a terrible idea."

She nods in agreement. "Got no details on what it might be, but I reckon it's soon."

"Right. Thanks for that."

It would be typical Tyrese to be planning a 'getting out of retreat jail' party. He's impossible, but at least I'm forewarned.

"I'm going to see him this afternoon," I tell Karolina.

"Don't let him fob you off with his lies," she says.

"He can't lie to me. I see straight through liars."

She doesn't exactly snort with derision, but the look she gives me is hardly reassuring.

44

Josie's at a post mortem.

Leicester Royal Infirmary is a couple of hundred years old. Josie's not sure how she feels about that. She's all for tradition, but she wants hospitals to be modern, forward-facing things.

Inside the mortuary, it's all clean lines and stainless steel, which is somehow reassuring in its bleak efficiency.

The smell is unavoidable. There's the background of formaldehyde and chemical cleaner. But she can smell the body that's being prepared. It's an acrid, smoky thing. Like a bonfire, but somehow sweeter, in a way that Josie doesn't want to dwell on.

Three bodies are scheduled for today. Three people who died in a cellar. Three people who remain unidentified.

One of them is out on a trolley, being carefully photographed while the pathologist murmurs instructions.

Josie's observing, and so is Sanjee Baksh, crime scene manager. Josie's pleased to see a familiar face. Sanjee is a relentlessly upbeat character, but his trademark grin is muted today.

"Hey Josie. Happy to have your company."

She glances at him, wondering why he's phrased it so oddly. He's feeling awkward.

"Me too," she says.

"You know that this place is jointly run with Leicester university?" Sanjee asks. "It's very well-regarded."

"Do students come along?" Josie feels herself bristling at the idea. She's protective of these people. They demand respect.

"Sometimes students will attend post-mortems, but not for sensitive and suspicious deaths like these."

"If we're all ready, step over here, will you?" The pathologist is a tall white guy who looks and acts like Josie expects tall white guys to look and act.

"Have you two met?" Sanjee asks.

"No," says Josie.

"Josie Kaminski, Archie Mackintosh." Sanjee grins at them both.

Archie nods at Josie and then beckons them over towards the stainless steel table.

Josie knew this was going to be bad, but she wasn't prepared for this.

When she was around ten, she went to a friend's house. They were having a big party for the parents' silver wedding anniversary, and the centrepiece of the food table was a whole roasted pig. Josie saw it and promptly burst into floods of angry tears, left the party and spent weeks trying to be vegetarian.

She is horrified with her brain for bringing this image forth as she looks down on the body of a woman. It's a person, not a piece of roasted meat. She makes herself pay minute attention. The woman is on her side, curled up, as if she was doing stomach crunches when she died. Josie can't see anything of her hair or skin colour because the entire body is burnt. The flesh is split in multiple places. She glimpses bone on the upper arm. It's exposed and charred. Josie's hand moves to her own upper arm, as if she needs to check in on it.

"You all right?" Sanjee asks.

"Yes."

Archie glances up briefly then he indicates the body. He's talking to the people in the room as well as the voice recorder.

"Victim is an adult female. We don't have much to visually suggest age or ethnicity, due to the extent of the damage to external tissue. The body presents in the classic pugilistic pose – we see this when muscles are exposed to extreme heat. The arms and legs are contracted. The fists are clenched. Very much like a boxer preparing to fight."

Josie doesn't want to play middle-aged white guy bingo, but Archie started it. Using aggressive sporting analogies is something Scabbard would do.

"Clothing fragments remain only where they are tucked into the underarm."

Josie hadn't seen that. She watches as Archie carefully removes a piece with tweezers. He holds up a small piece of patterned fabric. A nightdress or a shirt, perhaps.

"Charring suggests that this is cotton rather than synthetic. Further analysis will help us to determine that."

Archie continues to catalogue the horrific state of the woman's body. Josie clings fiercely to the fact that this was a living, breathing human being.

"We have something here," says Archie. "Fingernails remain on the right side." He's got a tiny scraper, getting something out from underneath. "Looks like paint fragments." He looks up at Sanjee. "Victims were clustered by the door, yes?"

Sanjee nodded. The implications are clear. This woman was desperately scrabbling to leave her cellar prison when she died.

The examination continues. Archie's running commentary mentions the lack of soft tissue as he proceeds with the Y-incision. He talks about the imaging that they captured of the internal organs.

"We'll use data from bone measurements to estimate the victim's height."

Josie has assumed that the woman was fairly short, but she can see that the body she's looking at has probably been shrunk by all the fire damage. She looks smaller in death.

"We now need to focus in on the trachea and the lungs. They will give us the best indication of whether the victim died before or after being burned."

Josie knows it's an important detail, but she swallows as she puts herself into the victim's shoes. She hopes that smoke inhalation made her lose consciousness before the fire reached her.

"We have soot particles in the trachea."

"That means she was alive when the fire was burning, yes?" Sanjee asks.

"It does. She was not placed there post mortem." Archie bends over the body. "We also have heat damage to the airway."

"Fuck." Josie didn't mean to let out the expletive. Her eyes widen. She hopes that she hasn't crossed a line of professionalism.

Archie looks up. "Fuck indeed." There is no condemnation in his eyes. Josie warms to him slightly. "This tells us that the victim inhaled very hot gases."

"So it was the fire that killed her?" Josie asks.

"I can't say that for sure," says Archie. "Toxicology will tell us what her carbon monoxide levels were. It could have been the smoke that caused her death, but I can tell you that her airways were severely restricted by this damage."

Josie permits herself to look away for a few moments, while she steadies her breathing. She needs to pace herself. There are two more bodies to come.

"What's the best bet for identifying the victim?" she asks.

Archie extends a hand to encompass the body. "CT imaging showed no medical implants. We have DNA and dental records to provide a match, but the clues to this woman's identity might need to come from external sources."

Josie nods.

Someone, somewhere is missing this woman. She was a friend, sister, daughter or mother to someone. It's vital that they work out who she was.

45

The drive to Tyrese's retreat takes me right out of the city, through rolling countryside, green and yellow, towards Measham and almost into Derbyshire. I pull off the main road through the gates and up the long drive. It's a converted stately home with a cracking view across the countryside.

I leave the Jag on the gravel drive and get buzzed in by a receptionist with immaculate makeup and a neat clinical uniform. It features the logo for the De Morgan hotel and spa. She walks me through to a gym where Tyrese is doing some one-to-one interval training with a coach. The coach has sportswear with the De Morgan logo at his chest.

"Cheers, coach," says Tyrese, walking over and dismissing the guy with a wave.

I wonder if they were finished?

"Tyrese. How are you doing?"

"Good. I'm out of jail today."

If he's trying to have a pop at me by calling it jail, I can rise above that.

"I'm here to drive you home," I say, in the manner of a cheerful cabbie. "Want to get showered and grab your things?"

"Sure. See you in reception in ten?"

The gym's in a purpose-built extension, but the walk back to reception takes me through the grand rooms, with their high ceilings. Ornate decoration and huge portraits make it feel as though this is still the home of some ancient family. I haven't seen anyone else here, and I wonder if Tyrese is the only person staying here.

It takes him forty minutes to reappear. I'm not sure if he's punishing me by making me wait, or whether he's just thoughtless and hasn't paid any attention to time.

A uniformed attendant appears from nowhere to carry Tyrese's bag to the car, and we're away, driving back towards his place.

"We should talk about what's next for your reputation."

I glance across to see his expression. It's fairly neutral, but he has something to say. He expels a huff of distaste. "Yeah. That minibus thing."

"The minibus thing. Yes? You have some thoughts on that?"

"Yeah. It's a bit ... you know?" he waves his arms.

"No, I don't. It's a bit what?"

"You know. Boring. It's a bit boring." He turns to face me. I can't face him because I'm driving, but a quick look shows me the face of a petulant child.

"Boring," I repeat. "Interesting observation, because that is exactly right. It's a boring and worthy idea. Which is why it's perfect for counteracting the reckless and the stupid."

He recoils mildly at my words. He opens his mouth to argue, but he really can't.

I continue. “Supporting a boring idea doesn’t make you boring. It makes you look responsible and thoughtful.”

“Right, well I had an idea of my own. It’s a good ’un.”

“Oh yes?”

“I’m hiring the guy.” His grin is one of genuine pride. He’s excited by this idea.

“Not sure I follow, Tyrese. You’re hiring who?”

“The cerebral palsy DJ guy. Hiring him for a party at my place.”

I did not see that coming. Karolina warned me about the party, but has this buffoon really invited his victim to work for him?

“How do you see that working?” I ask him. He must have a vision in his mind of how this will play out.

“We move on from all that crap,” says Tyrese, gesturing with his palms up. He thinks this is obvious. “We talk. We hug. We get photos. The world will see that it was all a misunderstanding.”

I have so many responses, crowding to come out. What does that magical conversation look like? Tyrese is no diplomat, and he has nothing in common with Oliver Chambers. The biggest question of all is how on earth he expects to frame assault as a misunderstanding.

I say none of these things.

“You’ve arranged this already?” I ask.

“Sure. He seemed really keen.”

I sigh inwardly. What does that tell me? If Oliver Chambers is really keen to work for Tyrese, then either he wants to bury the hatchet or he has some diabolical plan to take Tyrese down completely.

“Really keen?” I repeat. I could ask more questions about Oliver Chambers and how he seemed keen, but the answers will come through the filter of Tyrese's vanity. "You're sure you want to do this? You know it could go wrong?"

"It won't go wrong. We'll work it out, brother to brother."

I keep my face neutral. It's a terrible idea.

"You know what though?" he says. "You should come along. Then you'll see."

I wasn't expecting an invite, but I smile and try to look delighted. "Let me see. That might be possible. When were you planning to do this?"

"Tomorrow night at the latest," he says, as if anything else would be like waiting for Christmas.

"Sure. I'll be there."

46

Josie returns to Mansfield House police station.

She sniffs her clothes. The smell of the mortuary clings to her. The smoky smell is with her now, like a ghostly presence.

Rob and Walker look up as she plonks herself into her seat.

"You all right?" asks Rob. "Tough day?"

They know where she's been.

Josie nods. She wonders if they can smell the victims. "All three of the victims they examined today were women. All had soot in their trachea and lungs. All three had burns in there too. Toxicology will confirm the cause of death, but they were killed by a fire that burned fast enough to trap them so that they breathed the hot air."

Rob and Walker both grimace in sympathy.

"Two of the victims had paint under their fingernails, suggesting they were fighting to get out," Josie adds.

"That's nasty," says Walker.

"Was there anything to help us ID them?" Rob asks.

Josie heaves a huge sigh. "A large amount of bugger-all. Very little clothing, and their features were gone. It's down to DNA and dental records. One woman had a crown on one of her molars. The pathologist plans to get it examined further."

"Yeah? Dental records are all well and good if we have something to compare them with." Rob shakes his head.

"He said that a forensic odontologist might tell us more about the crown itself."

It feels like the smallest of details.

Rob and Walker clearly think so too. They are no closer to knowing who these women were.

47

On Tuesday morning, I pass by Natasha's bedroom and I can hear her talking to herself again. As I pause, I realise she's not talking but singing that rhyme to herself again.

"*Falcon flight, cliff so high. Ocean reef, echoes lie.* Da-dah, da-dah. *Savage season, hidden child.*"

There's a sudden, almost suppressed exclamation of "Fuck!" from her room. The expletive is violent, beyond annoyed.

I decide to move on quickly. A woman's allowed to be angry in the privacy of her own room. She's probably got plenty to be angry about.

Over breakfast, I convince Natasha to drive with me to the house on Narborough Road.

"We take a look, I take a few photos and, if you feel up to it, we capture some of your thoughts on what happened there," I say.

Natasha is uncertain but doesn't argue. She seems in a distant mood. Despite the summer sun, she has a big coat wrapped around her as though she wants to be cocooned.

The area around the house is back to normal, but the house is still marked by the fire. There are black burn marks around all the windows and the roof is punched with large black holes where the fire burned through. This is how buildings die. Ripped open to the elements. Exposed.

We have the phrase 'safe as houses' for a reason. We build homes and expect them to stay, to be constant, to keep us safe. The idea that buildings are fallible, that they can betray us, is utterly unnerving once you start thinking about it.

I take some photos.

"I've lived in the same house my entire life," I say. "I mean apart from some seriously grotty accommodation when I was working as a holiday rep. What about you?"

Natasha looks to the sky, thinking.

"More houses than I can remember," she says. "My mum had places she rented but all of them we had to move out of eventually. Black mould at one. The boiler went at another and the landlord just refused to repair it. I stayed with family sometimes while mum tried to sort things out."

I lift my hand to the place in front of us. "Did you like this place?"

Natasha laughs. It's a deep laugh like I said something genuinely funny.

"No. God no. Jesus. This was the least worst option at the time."

"I like that line."

"What line?"

"Housing choices as the least worst option."

"It's not a line. It's true."

I swing my phone towards her. "Want to tell us about it?"

She glares at me through the video screen. Her nostrils flare and then she talks.

"I didn't like it here but it was where I ended up staying anyway. Everything was dirty. The wallpaper was peeling in places. It was like being held on by a hundred layers of paint. The shower only trickled."

She's looking straight down the lens.

"I think what most people don't understand is how little choice you have. You're looking for a place to live and if you've got more than one option then you're lucky. But most of us don't. You go for the cheapest place available. Which often means it's in a shitty area. Drug users for neighbours. Gangs in the street. Noises all through the night. And all this to live somewhere where there's no jobs, no easy access to shops or work."

I'm not sure bad-mouthing Leicester in general is the way to go here.

"You're making it sound like the crime-ridden streets of LA or something," I say.

"You don't get it, do you?" she says and there's almost a snarl in her voice. "You have a little story about how rubbish your place was when you worked in Greece. Boo hoo. Whoop-di-do. So you slummed it a little on your holiday job, Hannah. Fact is, at any time you could have caught a plane back home to your daddy and snuggled under the covers of that big bedroom of yours in your warm, clean house. You've played at being poor. You should try it for real some time."

I don't know what to say to that. I leave the video running for a time because what can I do? I wanted Natasha's honest view on things, and these words are at least honest. Not usable, but they're honest.

"Most people don't get to choose where they live," she

says, softer now. "Most people don't get to choose their family or their ... their situation. If we get any choices they're all shit." She pointed to the house. "A bunch of people died in there. You think any of them chose the path that led them there? You think they had any choices at all? Migrant workers or whatever they were. Do you think any of them thought 'Wow, out of all the many fine choices available to me, I think I might just pay thousands of pounds to some crook to smuggle me into the UK where I can work in an illegal kitchen for no money at all'? You think any of them had any real choice in the matter whatsoever?"

I force myself to stay silent. Natasha is exploring her thoughts and feelings right now. There were a couple of snippets there that were just golden.

"People will move into houses they know are unsafe but they have no choice," she says. "The world is full of people who will take advantage of you and know you have no choice but to be taken advantage of. And even if you know people are going to be cruel or nasty or just want to take advantage of you, what else are you going to do? What can you do to change your situation?" She wraps her coat more firmly across her stomach. "What can you do to get out of that situation? That guy who owned that place. He's dead, yeah? I'm glad."

I swallow, feeling my throat gone dry, and decide to stop the video.

"I don't think we can get away with actually being happy about the bloke being dead," I suggest.

"Fuck him," says Natasha simply. She turns around, surveying the area. "I told you I didn't want to come here."

She mostly clams up after that. I can't blame her. I wanted

material from her and I got it, but I can see this has been difficult for her, even traumatic.

We walk back to the car. It's odd how the world has moved on from this fire. The black hollow windows of the house look out on the road where people and traffic pass by, as normal as ever.

Across the road, I see a blond man leaning against a car and looking our way. Not looking at us exactly but just gazing at the house. Just another person looking at the ruins of a place where people once lived.

48

I decide to take Natasha home rather than make her join me at the office. We go back in. I hear the sounds of the TV from the lounge. Natasha and I go into the kitchen where Marissa is sorting out Dad's pill dispenser for the coming week – Donepezil, Amlodipine, statins, aspirin – the list goes on and it seems endless. At least seven pills every morning. Even he jokes that he rattles when he walks.

"You're back early," says Marissa.

She glances specifically at Natasha, perhaps noting the unhappy look I've brought out in her this morning.

"I'm going to get changed," says Natasha and makes her way out.

"I took her back to the scene of the fire," I explain to Marissa. "Bad memories, I think. Perhaps, I shouldn't—"

I'm cut off by a yell of pain. It's Dad.

I run out into the hallway. Natasha is racing down the bottom stairs and gets to the lounge door ahead of me.

Dad is sitting in his armchair, one hand clutched in the other. Blood runs freely from the back of his hand, shining, red like wine. On the floor is a dropped plate, a half-eaten sandwich and a vegetable cutting knife from the kitchen. I can see the blood along its edge.

"Dad!"

Natasha crouches in front of him, her hands cradling his. There's confusion and pain in his teary eyes. He's blinking like he hasn't got a clue what's happening.

"Dad. What happened?" I say.

He looks at me, his gaze empty and for a moment I don't think he even knows who I am.

"Go get a towel or something!" Natasha instructs sharply. I run to obey. Marissa stands dumbly in the doorway, watching.

I grab a tea towel and kitchen roll and dash back. Natasha is holding his injured hand, his blood trickling over her fingers.

"I don't think it's bad," she says and takes the tea towel to gently wrap the wound.

"How the hell did this happen?" I say, hearing my voice rise in concern.

Natasha shushes Dad and tries to calm him.

"Where did he even get the knife from?" I say with a look to Marissa.

"I … I have no idea," she says.

"I think we're going to need to go to A&E," says Natasha.

I drive. Natasha sits in the back with Dad. He keens quietly like a wounded dog all the way and it wrenches my heart to hear it. Marissa offered to come with us and I instinctively refused. I'd need to unpack that decision later.

I drop Natasha and Dad at the entrance to Accident and Emergency and then go off to park the car. Horrible minutes spent circling, looking for a space. I don't want to do this. I want to be with Dad.

I rush inside to find they're not in the waiting room. I go to the counter.

"You can check in over there," she says and points to a row of tablets on stands.

"I'm looking for my dad."

"Name?"

"Donald Douglas-Jones."

She taps. "He's being seen. He's with his daughter."

"I'm his daughter!"

"His other daughter."

"I'm his—" I stop. There's no point arguing. "Where is he? Can I go through?"

"Only one family member allowed with each patient."

I bite my tongue before I launch into arguing that I'm the family. I'm the only family. Instead, I take a step back and call Natasha. She doesn't pick up.

What else can I do? Furious, feeling impotent and lost, I sit down on one of the seats. I'm boiling with anger. But it's anger at myself if anything. I just want to be with Dad. I want to make sure he's okay. By not being with him, by delegating this duty to someone else, however accidentally, I feel I am letting him down.

I try Natasha again but she's not picking up. She's with Dad, attending to him. I understand.

But still I feel awful. Powerless.

49

Over an hour later a door opens and Natasha comes through. There's blood on the cuffs of her top. I stand as she comes over.

"They want to see you," she says.

"I tried calling and they wouldn't let me through."

"I know. They want to talk to you."

We're buzzed through into the wards beyond. Natasha leads the way to a secluded room with glass doors. Dad is sitting upright on the bed, dressings on his hand. There's no staff here.

"They said that Dad managed to cut the back of his hand but there's no damage to the tendons and that," says Natasha.

Dad's hand wobbles as he raises it. There's a bemused look on his face.

"I've no idea what happened," he says.

"It's okay, Dad," I say.

"Not sure if I'll be able to play golf with this."

He hasn't played golf in eighteen months or more.

After all the futile anger, relief washes physically through me – warm and soothing. I sit beside him on the bed and hug him.

I look to Natasha. "Thank you."

She nods like this is all in a day's work.

"Who are we waiting for?" I ask.

"A social worker or something."

I frown. "What?"

"I think they just need to check things out, formally. Got to do things by the book."

"Sure," I say uneasily. That prompts a thought. "Talking of doing things by the book..."

She looks over, wondering why I've paused.

"Want to tell me why you don't want to talk to the police?" I ask.

Her expression hardens a second and then she speaks, slowly at first. "I don't have to talk to the police. I've done nothing wrong."

"They just want to get your version of events, Natasha."

"I have no version to share. I was woken by a smoke alarm. I ran out."

"Then tell them that."

She sniffs and looks away. "You think the police are our friends, Hannah. Really? You think they have our best interests at heart?"

My immediate response would be to say 'yes' but I take care to give it some thought. But my conclusion is still the same.

"Their job is to help people. Sure, they make a hash of it sometimes. That press conference was dreadful. And there's the occasional bad copper. But, yeah, they're there to help us. We should only fear them if we've done something wrong."

"Ha!" She rolls her eyes.

I decide it's time to get a bit tough. I've opened my home to this young woman. I've let her into my office, my home, my world. Surely, in some sense, she owes me the decency of complying with a very straightforward request.

"I want you to speak to the police," I say.

"And I said I don't want to."

I stick to my guns. "I am asking you to speak to the police. I ... I can't instruct you, but you live in my home, you work for me. I put trust and faith in you. And I don't want this hanging over you."

She blinks. "Are you saying I *have* to talk to the police?"

"I'll call DS Joseph. We'll go in tomorrow."

She holds my gaze. "And if I say no."

I don't want her to call my bluff because I don't know which way I'll jump.

"I—"

The glass door opens and a nurse in a hijab walks in.

"Evening," she grins. "I'm Halimah. I'm one of the safeguarding nurses here."

"Er, hi," I say.

"And this is Donald? Hello, Donald. Is it Donald? Don?"

"What's going on?" says Dad.

Nurse Halimah moves specifically into Dad's line of vision.

"Donald. You've got a cut on your hand. Do you know how it happened?"

He looks at his injured hand and sticks out his bottom lip in comedy confusion. "I couldn't properly say."

"He has dementia," I explain, which I'm sure is unnecessary. They must have this stuff on his notes.

"Were you alone when it happened, Donald?" she asks.

"His carer was at home with him," I say.

"His home or your home." She looks between the three of us.

"Our home," I say. "I live with Dad. Natasha's just staying with us for a while."

"And you were there when this happened?"

"We'd just come in," says Natasha.

Halimah nods and gives a supportive smile to Dad. "During your treatment, Donald, the nurse saw some bruising on your arm that caused her concern. I wonder if we could have a look and you tell me how you got those bruises."

"What bruises?" I say.

"Because they're not in usual places for bruises, Donald."

My mind reels. This can't be happening.

50

All the relevant officers are called into a case briefing in the conference room at Mansfield House police station.

Walker was there early and found a corner to tuck himself away in. While he waits for the room to fill, he checks the family WhatsApp group. No new messages. He's used to the idea that the rest of his family have their own orbits, and that they will only occasionally pass through his and spend time with him, but he'd like to have a bit of interaction.

Helen's out with one of her groups this afternoon. He could check the calendar to see whether it's Nordic walking, social gardening or netball. Oscar will be tucked away in his room. If he remembers rightly, Amber's gone into town to meet old school friends.

He puts a suggestion on the family chat group.

Hey, thought I might cook an evening meal for us all. How about Mexican?

He takes a ridiculously long time to find an emoji of a

chilli and adds a couple to the end of the message. The kids speak fluent emoji, maybe it will get them to respond.

By the time the room is full and the briefing is ready to start, there are no replies on the chat. Rob and Josie are some of the last people in. Walker waves them over to the little space he's secured.

Josie squeezes in next to him on the edge of a dusty table.

She glances at his phone. "You cooking tonight?" she says.

"Oh, just trying to get the family to remember I exist," he says and hopes it doesn't sound as pathetic to her ears as it does to his.

DI Scabbard at the front clears his throat.

"If we've all finished chinwagging in the corner," he says with a look at the Duncans.

Scabbard might normally say something more caustic, but he's sharing the briefing with DI Abi Bacon from Organised Crime, and if Walker's any judge of Greg Scabbard's behaviour, Scabbard wants to appear professional in front of the attractive female colleague.

"One week on," Scabbard says, solemnly. "We've been working our backsides off on this case and there's been some solid work done. We know from Fire Investigation Officers that we're looking at arson, started with an accelerant in the ground-floor kitchen. The body of Paul Mulholland, found in the kitchen, had high levels of alcohol in his system and an impact injury to his head. Was he hit on the head and fell or did he fall and hit his head? We don't know. Post-mortems on the six bodies in the cellar – all women – paint a grim picture of death by fire and smoke. They were alive and conscious when the fire reached them."

Next to him, Walker can feel Josie shudder.

"The one survivor of the fire, an upstairs tenant called Natasha Dibello, is still in the wind. DS Joseph, you were tracking her down?"

"I know someone who spoke to her after the fire," says Rob. "I'm following it up."

"Knows someone who knows someone..." Scabbard mutters and shakes his head to cast his annoyance away. "We do however have some leads on the identities of the cellar victims."

He taps his laptop linked to the TV display and a photograph of an open passport with charred edges appears on the screen.

"Found in a not-wholly fireproof security box on the first floor," says Scabbard. "Three passports." He pauses to read out the names with care from a sheet. "Zhou Li, Wu Hong Xia and Liu Mei. We don't know if these three passports match any of the bodies, but they are of three Chinese nationals."

DI Bacon steps forward. "We're waiting to hear back from the Chinese Ministry of Public Security. They may be able to provide us with fingerprints, DNA and, importantly, dental records. If these are trafficked migrant workers we might be granted intel on gangs who could have brought the women here.

"Organised Crime officers have been following up on the ghost kitchen angle at the property," she continues. "Bulk food orders from wholesalers show that this is not the only kitchen being operated by Mulholland or his associates. We're trying to find links to other properties he might have been involved in."

"DS Joseph," says Scabbard, "your team were looking into some Portaloo link, weren't you?"

"Chemical toilet, sir," says Joseph. "Yes. Fascinating work."

This draws sniggers from some, most noticeably DS Dean Beaches. "Poo Patrol," he chortles. The man made one crack last week and he's still trying to milk it.

"We found financial links between Paul Mulholland and a drug dealer in the New Parks area," says Walker.

"Relevant to this incident?" asks Scabbard.

"Not yet known. Two of the people I wanted to speak to have died recently. Natural causes," he adds hurriedly. "They were older people. I might still try to speak to one Ruby Adams who might have known Mulholland."

"Are we looking at an organised crime motive for this fire, sir?" asks a detective constable near the front.

Scabbard and Bacon exchange glances.

"It's a possibility," says Bacon. "Links to drug dealers in the city, evident links to modern slavery. Mulholland is a known associate of the Degutis gang, who were implicated in the attack on the KL group's drugs stash at the Meridian Casino a few months back. Paul Mulholland has his fingers in lots of pies, from drugs to car thefts to stolen combine harvesters."

"Trailers and tractors actually," mutters Rob, but not loud enough for the officers at the front to hear.

"But he was also a thoroughly nasty piece of work on a personal level," adds Scabbard. "In 2020, he was arrested, then unfortunately released without charge, after breaking the jaw of Chelsea Johnson, his then girlfriend. Her brothers were then arrested and successfully convicted on assorted charges of affray and public order offences after seeking revenge. That was not the first time he was arrested for violence against women."

"So being burned alive was too good for him then?" suggests Dean Beaches.

Scabbard's lips are pursed tight, like he wants to agree but can't be seen to do so.

"Whatever he's done, whoever he's offended," he says, "it's still our duty to find the bastards who did this."

51

I'm still reeling as I drive the three of us back home.

Six hours at the hospital. Six hours for Dad to have stitches put in the back of his hand for an injury he can't remember at all. Six hours for us to be told that Dad has 'inconsistent bruising' on his arm and his upper back. Six hours for that safeguarding nurse, Halimah, to do everything but flatly accuse me of abusing and neglecting my dad.

"What are we having for dinner?" says Dad in the seat next to me. There's a lightness in his tone like none of today ever happened. He's patched up and now he's thinking of his stomach.

I don't know whether to laugh or cry. I might do both before the night is through.

Right now there are a few fixed things on my mind and I deal with one of them as soon as we've got Dad inside and settled.

"Marissa!"

"I am upstairs," she calls back.

I stomp up. I don't know if the anger and shame I feel

needs to be unleashed on Marissa. I don't know if I need to do it in this way. But I do know that if I am to do it then I need to do it now, before it ebbs away or softens.

She's in Dad's room, sorting clothes into his drawers.

"How is he?" she asks.

"He's got stitches in his hand," I say bluntly.

"I have no idea how he got that knife. We've not even had it out today."

"You're meant to be watching him."

There's a shift in her eyes, the first realisation that I'm trying to tell her off. Marissa's worked with Dad for many months and I've never felt the need to act like the stern employer at any point. This is a first for both of us.

"I cannot watch him all the time," she says, still aiming to keep things neutral.

"Does he often get hurt?"

"No. This is very out of character for him."

"The hospital showed me the bruises."

"Which bruises?"

"Which—?" The fact that she has to ask me *which* bruises is a punch to the heart. "His arms! His back! When did they happen?"

Marissa is shaking her head. "He is an old man. Slow to heal. He hurts himself and the bruises stay. He has purpura."

"He has what?"

"Purpura. Marks caused by fragile blood vessels. If he has been out in the sun. He has liver spots too."

"The nurses called it bruising. Unexplained bruising! Finger imprints."

She exhales noisily. I can't tell if she's irritated or worried.

"He had a fall after getting showered the other day. I caught him. I held him up. It is probably those."

"And you didn't tell me?"

"He was not hurt. No pain. We came into here. I helped him finish drying and I dressed him." Her hands rest lightly on the clothes she's just put in the drawer. "I care for your father, Hannah. Deeply."

There is an honest emotion in her voice and I almost allow myself to be mollified by it, but I cling onto the shock and horrified embarrassment I felt at the hospital.

"They spoke of them as signs of abuse."

Marissa draws herself up. She's not a tall woman but she stands erect.

"You are not here. I am. But I cannot be everywhere. If you want Donald to have all the care he needs then you need to hire extra carers."

I huff loudly. I'm annoyed, partly because she's right. Maybe I started this conversation with some hot burning expectation that Marissa would break down in front of me, confess to cruelty against my dad and ... and... I don't know what would come after that. But instead we land on the most obvious and banal of realities. My dad needs more care. But until the money comes through from the sale of the Brascote buildings that's not going to happen. The shame I feel is not the shame of being accused of acts of physical abuse, it's the shame of being a daughter incapable of providing my dad with the care he deserves.

"We can't afford that right now," I say. "I will try to arrange it as soon as possible."

Marissa holds my gaze. "It would be for the best."

We're done, but somehow I can't leave without some sort of parting shot.

"And if he has a fall or anything in future, however small, you need to tell me," I say.

"I will."

It still doesn't feel enough, but it will have to do.

I go downstairs. There's laughter from the lounge.

Dad's in his chair. It's gone seven but it's still bright enough outside to not need lights on. Natasha has set up a draughts board on the little table in front of Dad's chair.

It's nice to see him smiling and being entertained by Natasha. Right now, I'd like a large glass of wine and to crash on a comfy seat and sleep.

"I thought I'd order takeaway for Dad and me," says Natasha.

"Not for me?" I ask with a smile.

Natasha gives me a look. "I thought you were off to Tyrese's party."

"That's tonight?"

I'd completely forgotten. Tyrese's ill-thought out party plans. I need to go. I must be there. No wine on the sofa for me.

"Oh, God, I have to go," I say.

Natasha shrugs happily. "We'll be fine. Off you pop."

I rush to get changed.

52

I change in a hurry, jump back in the Jag and drive into the city.

Tyrese lives in the city centre on the top floor of a converted industrial building on Queen Street, barely a hundred metres from the gala dinner venue from last week.

The door to the apartment is open. Caterers are going in and out.

This party isn't starting for another hour or two yet.

It turns out that Tyrese owns the entire top floor of this building. It's a huge apartment that he has, and there's that sense of being above the city. I'm immediately drawn to the window in his lounge. I try to work out what I'm looking at, but the only building I can properly recognise is St George's church.

"What do you reckon?"

Tyrese stands beside me. I'm here well ahead of his friends, because I'm almost certainly going to be needing my bed before they properly get going. But I really want to get a feel for the type of event this will be.

"What a lovely place you have, Tyrese. It must be such a thrill to come home to this." I wave my arm across the city.

"Yeah, it's nice." He gives a small shrug and shows me the rest of the apartment. He has an enormous industrial kitchen. Two chefs are busy in there preparing the fanciest buffet food. It seems as though entertaining is a big part of Tyrese's life. Maybe there is something to be said for his idea of fixing his image using those skills he has.

He has four bedrooms. I glance through the door of the master suite, which occupies a corner of the building with more enviable views. The other three are fitted out like fancy hotel rooms.

"Party space! What do you think?"

I'd assumed he'd have his party in his lounge, but this room is a custom-built party space.

"My goodness, Tyrese. Is that an honest-to-god conversation pit?"

"Oh, you call it that? The architect called it that too. He said it's peak mid-century-modern. I just like the vibe."

The conversation pit's impressive, but this room is lined with seating nooks. It has a dance floor and a performance space. Tables are dotted everywhere, and there's an area where food and drink are being set up.

"What an incredible space."

"We're not done yet!" Tyrese urges me on. He's proud of his place, and I'm an appreciative audience. He must be really glad to be home.

He takes me through to some smaller rooms. "We have some chill space. When you want to take a break from the main event."

I look at him sideways. Is that a euphemism? Does taking

a break mean having sex or doing drugs? His face says none of that.

"Nice," I say. Actually it does look nice. The chairs are comfy and the lighting is soothing. He's even got some of those egg-shaped chairs that are more like a tiny den for grown-ups.

"You know what, I might do exactly that," I say to Tyrese. "You get ready for your party and I'll grab a drink and catch up with some emails in here if you like?"

He makes an expansive 'be my guest' gesture, and leaves me to it.

I wander back into the main room and pour myself a glass of wine.

I scroll aimlessly through my phone for a while. I spend a few minutes wondering how much this place would cost if it went up for sale, but I'm really just being nosy.

The moment the alcohol hits my system, it relaxes me all over and I decide to spend a few moments in one of the egg chairs. It turns out that it's somehow almost soundproof, as well as being incredibly comfortable. The temptation to close my eyes is too much.

And I fall asleep.

53

Walker stands in his kitchen preparing dinner for his family.

He and Helen have lived in this house for nearly a quarter of a century. They bought it as a dilapidated three-bedroomed semi-detached for what seemed like a fortune at the time. You couldn't even buy a one-bedroom flat in Leicester for that amount these days. Amber and Oscar have known no other home.

He rarely pauses to think about this house. It just exists. It's simply there. The mortgage is all paid off and maybe they should have moved on or had an extension built, but this house is the house they've lived their lives in.

Perhaps it was his visit to New Parks on Friday that's made him think about his current existence. Before it all went wrong, he spent several happy months living undercover with Duncan. Was it moderately stressful, living under a false identity? Yes. Did he love it? He really did. Hanging out at the Lion pub had felt like home for a while. Possibly more like home than the house that he now shares with his wife and kids. He feels an odd pang for those times and the people who were part of his life when he wasn't the man he is now.

Walker knows better than to wallow in the past. It's a bad habit.

He forces himself to focus on the meal he said he'd prepare. He pulls out his phone and searches for Mariachi music to get him in the mood.

Walker's making guacamole when Helen returns. She's got Amber with her. Oscar hasn't appeared downstairs yet. Not since he fetched a bowl of cereal this morning.

Walker's phone has shuffled on from Mariachi now and it's playing the Spice Girls, but that surely doesn't matter. He shimmies round the counter to raise a smile, but neither Helen nor Amber are paying attention.

"Glad you're both back. Making a Mexican feast," he announces.

He half expects to hear that everyone's got other plans, but they both turn to see what he's doing.

"Did you get Mexican beer?" Amber asks. She's moved on from being simply a fan of alcohol to being something of a self-appointed expert. Walker's not sure how this is possible for an unwaged student.

Walker silently scolds himself for not thinking of Mexican beer. "No. We might have to make do with Fosters."

"Shame." Amber's about to walk away, but then she checks herself, realising that she's being rude. She glances back at him. "It will be great, I'm sure."

She disappears upstairs and Walker calls after her. "Tell your brother. Half an hour."

He plans to make margaritas, but he'll let that be a surprise for later.

"Be lovely to get us all round the table," he says to Helen. "Have you seen the cactus theme?"

He indicates six tiny cactus plants. He also found some napkins with cartoon cactuses on them. Tea lights are ready to light in little glass holders.

She smiles. "Yes, it will." She glances at the table. "This is nice."

She drifts off into the lounge, looking at her phone.

Walker looks at the table.

He thinks of Jinny Michaels and her caustic, foul language. She would never call it nice.

They're thoughts that belong to another time, another place. That version of Walker is long gone.

54

I wake up very disorientated.

It's hours later, almost full dark outside, and as I lever myself up out of the egg chair, I can hear the muted sounds of a party that's in full swing.

I stand up and smooth my clothes, then I pat my face, wondering what state my makeup's in. When I'm satisfied that I'm in a fit state to be seen, I enter the large party space.

If I expected large-scale debauchery, I needn't have worried. There are a lot of people here, but most of them are younger, in their twenties. A good number of them are drinking soft drinks. There's a large group who are dancing wildly on the dancefloor, but an even larger group is in the conversation pit. I can see why Tyrese is fond of this feature. He can be the centre of attention for a lot of people.

I look across to the DJ in the performance area. He's sitting at a small console, headphones on, but I can see him quite clearly.

I look across at Tyrese and wonder how I can speak to him privately.

I walk across to the conversation pit and kneel down so that I can tap him on the shoulder, as he's directly below me. I feel a little ridiculous, but it's the fastest way.

"Tyrese. I need to speak with you. It's quite urgent. About the DJ," I hiss.

He jumps up. "Yeah! My bad, I should have done this before."

He's in the centre of the pit, walking away from me towards the steps. I hurry round to intercept him, but he's faster than me.

"No! Come here Tyrese. I need to talk to you."

He's at the console, speaking in the ear of the DJ.

The music's cut off and Tyrese has a microphone in his hand.

"Hey everyone. Thanks for coming. We have a very special person here tonight, and I'm so glad he agreed to come." He hugs the DJ awkwardly around the shoulders. Tyrese needs to bend down because the DJ is still seated. "I – you all know I'm an idiot, right?" A ragged cheer erupts around the room. "I misunderstood his condition a couple of weeks ago and we had a – we knocked heads a bit." He looks at the DJ. "Hey, is it OK to say that to someone with cerebral palsy? Sorry mate. Anyway, we're here together to show that we're over that now. We stand together as – oh wait no. We stand and sit together as one. We are brothers."

The crowd in the room know that they're expected to cheer this moment, so they do. There are hoots of approval, and someone yells "Speech!"

Tyrese hands the microphone to the DJ.

I gesture to Tyrese to take it back. I consider running over there and batting it from the DJ's hand, but it's too late now.

"Yeah mate," says the DJ, eyeing Tyrese. "I think you

might have me mistaken for someone else. I never met you before."

Tyrese frowns. "No. That's not right. You're—"

"Oh, I know," says the DJ. "You got me mixed up with the other DJ with cerebral palsy, didn't you? Oliver Chambers."

I bury my head in my hands as the awful truth comes out of the DJ's mouth and even Tyrese realises the mistake he's made.

"Think we all look the same, do ya?" says the DJ, grinning.

Could this bloody night get any worse?

55

I need to be in work mode now. I scan the room for people who are recording this moment. I need to get that footage. All of it.

I go round to all of the people in the room who were holding up phones and recording Tyrese and that DJ. It's a terrible, humiliating moment for Tyrese. I can't let it get posted on social media.

Sadly, it's also a highlight for some of the people who are here, so I have a bit of a fight on my hands. I call Karolina to come and give me a hand.

She arrives just after midnight, much quicker than I expected. I wonder if she was already in the city. She helps me talk to everyone.

Together, we check everyone present for footage they might have taken. Tyrese doesn't know it yet, but he's going to be planning a mini-break with exclusive photo-opportunities for four up-and-coming influencers. A weekend in Ibiza is my placeholder idea.

I've got nothing nice to say to Tyrese. He's got nothing

nice to say to me. The stone cold moron can't see that he's done anything wrong.

Karolina and I leave the apartment at two in the morning.

"Tyrese is a loose fucking cannon," says Karolina.

I shake my head. "If this is what he does when he's allowed out in public then I need him on permanent lockdown."

I wave her off with profuse thanks for her help.

I get home a bit before three and collapse into bed.

I wake to the sounds of activity downstairs. It's nearly nine. I know I'm the boss but I feel like I'm late for work. I have a pounding headache. I am in a foul mood. I'm brimming with anger.

I'm angry with Tyrese Jali because he's a moron who can't see the damage he's constantly doing to his reputation.

I'm angry with Marissa for keeping information about Dad's various trips and slips to herself so that I look like a negligent daughter.

I'm angry with myself more than anyone else. I'm the one who let the moron off the leash. I'm the one who hasn't given my dad enough attention. I'm the one trying to slice myself into too many pieces and keep too many people happy.

I go downstairs and find Dad eating his cereal and raspberries in the kitchen. Natasha sits opposite him, a cup of steaming coffee in her hand.

"Dad and I didn't think you'd ever get up," she says cheerfully.

Dad looks at me. I swear that for a good few seconds he has no idea who I am. He then grunts and continues slurping at his cereal.

"You didn't think to wake me?" I say.

"You came in very late. A good party?"

I feel emotions rise in me. My anger and exhaustion at what happened last night might come out in any number of ways. I turn to the coffee pod machine and stick a cup under it.

My phone rings.

"Something's going buzz-buzz," says Dad.

It's Detective Sergeant Rob Joseph. Another unshakeable presence in my life. I answer.

"Yes?"

"Ah. Miss Douglas-Jones. Hannah. It's Rob Joseph. Listen, I hate to be persistent but I really must—"

Something gives inside me. I'm tired. I'm angry. I'm like King bloody Canute or whatever, trying to hold back the tide. Everything is rushing in at me and I've had enough. I decide in an instant that I'm going to kill two irritating birds with one stone.

"Yes, absolutely, detective," I say, turning to Natasha. "I have Natasha Dibello with me right now."

Natasha's eyes widen.

"You do?" he says.

"I do. And you would like to speak to her to get her witness statement regarding the fire on the twenty-ninth."

Natasha mouths "I don't want to" but apparently, today, I don't give a shit.

"We would. If we could see her at Mansfield House police station that would be ideal."

"I will drive her to meet you today. Should we ask for you at reception?"

"That would be great."

Natasha's now mouthing "what the fuck". Maybe it's the headache and the residual foul mood in control now, but I'm of the opinion that this woman has been living rent free in my house for over a week and, frankly, she owes me. She's been a great help and a cornerstone of our work with Todd's campaign, but she owes me.

"We'll be there this morning," I say. "See you later, detective."

I end the call.

"I didn't agree to that," says Natasha.

"Time to put on your big girl pants, I'm afraid," I say.

"I don't have to do that."

There's an urge to trot out some "you're living in my house so you do what I say" parental nonsense, but I'm not her mum. She's a grown woman.

"We're not discussing it," I say. I take my coffee from under the machine. "I'm drinking this. I'm getting dressed. And then we're going."

56

In Rob's experience, people get immediately defensive around police officers. Even in everyday situations, the moment people discover you're a copper they become wary, the fences go up. This might be the inherent guilt that lies in all people. It might be because, in the modern world, people feel they have good reason to distrust the police. Rob also thinks it might be because people assume that the police are always watching, that coppers are always trying to peer into your soul and winkle out those dark, hidden secrets.

Rob tends to see and accept people as they present themselves. He has no special lie-detecting skills, but that's okay because most people are terrible liars. He doesn't need to see into people's inner thoughts because, in time, the facts tend to make themselves known.

Natasha Dibello looks at him across the interview room table with something like suspicion, but there's nothing special to be read into that. When Hannah Douglas-Jones dropped Natasha at reception he tried not to smile at the school drop-off energy between them.

Hannah seemed hesitant to leave Natasha. Natasha glared daggers at Hannah.

"I'm Detective Sergeant Rob Joseph," says Rob. "You can call me Rob. This is my colleague Detective Constable Josie Kaminski," he says, nodding to Josie at his side.

"Hey," says Josie.

Rob tries to give Natasha a welcoming smile. "I won't take up much of your time. You've been a hard person to track down."

"I didn't know I was wanted by the police," says Natasha.

"Not wanted," he assures her, "except to give your account of what happened at that house. First up, how are you doing?"

"Doing?"

"You were in a house fire, Natasha. You went off before you could be given medical attention. Are you okay? Were you hurt?"

She pulls a face and inspects her arms. Are there marks she's looking at?

"My hair got singed."

"You were that close to the fire?"

"The smoke alarm went off on the landing. It woke me up."

"So you were asleep when it happened?" The interview is being recorded but Josie is also making notes.

"I was asleep," Natasha confirms.

"Are you aware that there were people hurt in the fire?"

"The dead people in the cellar," she says.

"Yes. Tragic stuff. Did you know the other people who lived there?"

She frowns as she thinks. "Honestly, I didn't realise..." She shakes her head, abandoning that sentence. "I feel really stupid."

"How so?"

"I spent three terms living in that place. I had no idea anyone else was living there. That's how stupid I am."

"Not stupid at all, Natasha. We all live our own lives. So you didn't have any contact with the people who lived or worked in the rest of the building?"

She shakes her head again. "There were some women. I think they might have been Chinese. Or Korean or Malaysian or something. I thought they worked there. Were they the...?" Her face tightens. "Were they the people they found? The bodies in the basement?"

"We're working to identifying everyone. It's a slow process, I'm afraid."

"And I suppose I saw the landlord guy occasionally. I think he was the landlord. I booked the place through a letting agent."

"Which one?"

"I don't remember. But this guy was doing odd jobs and I saw his vehicle in the driveway at times."

"You know his name."

"Paul something. I want to say his surname began with an M."

Paul Mulholland. Rob doesn't say it out loud.

"Tell me about him," he says.

"What's to tell? He was like a... He was a bloke. Maybe your age. Bit of a beer gut. Always unshaven. Looked like he should be a plumber or an electrician. Looked like the kind of man who works all day and stinks of BO."

Rob smiles.

"What?" she says and then checks herself. "I'm not saying all plumbers stink."

"I know what you mean," he assures her. "It's a colourful description. So – you. It'd be good to get some details in case we need to contact you. Do you have a current address?"

She smiles for the first time since he's met her.

"No permanent address. No phone. Not even got any ID. Lost it all in the fire."

"I'm really sorry."

"Hannah's been really helpful."

"I bet she has."

57

Josie studies the young woman across the interview room table. There's something in her eyes, a glittering intelligence. Josie's not sure if she finds it fascinating or disturbing.

"Honestly," says Natasha. "That's really all I can remember."

"You've been very helpful," says Rob.

Josie looks at her sarge and wonders if he's really going to leave it at that. The young woman looks ready to move as though she thinks they're done with her.

Josie shifts in her chair. "If I may leap in with a couple of questions."

Rob gestures for her to go ahead.

"Miss Dibello, you mentioned that you lost your phone and ID in the fire."

"I did," says Natasha.

"Bank cards, phone. Everything."

She nods.

"Have you got new cards and a new phone sorted?"

"Not yet."

"Oh." Josie pretends to be surprised. "But you told your phone company?"

Natasha shrugs and shakes her head at the same time.

"Should be easy to sort out," says Josie. "What's your phone number?"

"Sorry?"

"Your phone number?"

"I don't know."

"Really?"

"I don't think I've ever known. It's in my phone."

"But who are you with? Which company?"

"Er, EE."

"You could log onto your account and find your details there. Get a new phone sorted."

Natasha gives her a smile like Josie's made a mistake. "But I've no phone. Can't log on without internet access. I'm not sure what my account details are."

"Probably could get a password reset sent to your e-mail address on any computer. You have an e-mail address, don't you?"

Natasha frowns. "I do. I don't use it."

"Can you tell me what it is?"

"What? My e-mail address? You want my e-mail address?"

"I'm just curious."

"About what?"

Josie smiles. "Everything. Police habit. Um, obviously, you were paying rent on your room at the house."

"I was."

"Direct debit or standing order?"

"Yes. I think so."

"It would be really helpful to us if you could show us

what account that was being paid into. We're struggling to get to grips with who owned the property and managed it. That would be really useful."

"Again, I don't have access to my accounts. I lost everything."

"Who did you bank with?"

"Monzo, I think."

"You think?"

"Monzo."

"Maybe you could log onto your account. Again, you could probably get a password reset. We might even be able to let you use a computer here. That bank information would be really handy and might help us find the people who were responsible for the ... living conditions in that house."

"I'm not sure I can help."

"You can try," said Josie and she smiles again. She's smiling because Natasha is looking increasingly nervous. Josie's digging. She doesn't know what she's digging for but she's digging anyway. "Can I ask about the night of the fire?"

"I thought you already had."

"Just to clarify. You said you heard the smoke alarm go off."

"I did."

"Where was that?"

"I was in bed."

"I meant where was the smoke alarm?"

Natasha thinks for a moment and then shakes her head. "I don't remember. On the landing somewhere."

"You were on the first floor? Or was it the attic room?"

She closes her eyes to think.

"Not a difficult question," says Josie.

"You confused me. There is no attic room."

"Right. Right. Obviously. So you ran straight downstairs and… Can you remind me how many doors you needed to go through to get outside?"

"The front door?"

"There was the front door, but I'm asking was there a door at the top of the stairs? At the bottom?"

Natasha looks to Rob as though he is the voice of reason and can save her from these questions.

"What's this got to do with anything?"

Rob stays quiet. Even if it requires virtually zero effort to stay quiet, Josie feels a warmth in that silence. Rob trusts her. He trusts her instincts. For the moment at least.

"I'm just trying to build up a mental picture," Josie says to Natasha. She keeps her tone light, overtly friendly, so friendly that, for the wise, the undertone of "I'm onto you, bitch" is perfectly obvious. "You are our only witness in this case, Natasha. Literally our only witness to this fire. Think of that."

Natasha pinches her mouth. "This is…"

"It is upsetting, I know," says Josie.

"Perhaps," says Rob with an emphasis just for Josie, "we could take a break and get Natasha a drink."

"Oh, absolutely," says Josie, "But let me just ask you quickly about the six women in the cellar."

"Don't remind me…"

Josie shuffles through the papers in front of her and Rob.

"Er, Zhou Li. Wu Hong Xia. Liu Mei. We don't yet have the names of the others. But there were six of them."

A tear trickles from Natasha's eye.

"Did you hear them trying to get out on the night of the fire?"

A sob bursts from Natasha. She tries to speak but her crying wipes everything except the shape of the word "Why?"

"We're sorry this is upsetting," says Rob and puts a silent hand out when Josie opens her mouth to speak.

"It's not my fault," Natasha manages to say. "You think I haven't thought that? You think I'm responsible?"

"Of course you're not responsible," says Rob.

Natasha manages to draw in a breath though the tears are still flowing. "I just wanted to get out. That's all I could think of. I just needed to get out."

"We understand."

"If I'd had time to think. I mean – if I'd even known – then of course I'd have done something different. I would. I would!"

Josie has a pack of tissues in her jacket pocket. She offers them to Natasha.

"Let's stop for a coffee, yeah?" says Rob.

"I'm done. I'm done," says Natasha and Josie knows they can try to persuade her otherwise, but they can't legally compel her to stay and answer their questions.

"Well, let's get some coffees in," says Rob, "and then we'll wrap things up as quickly as possible. DC Kaminski."

Josie follows him outside. Rob draws her a distance down the corridor. His expression is terse – not exactly angry but he seems low on patience.

"Happy with that?"

Josie waggles her jaw from side to side, considering things. "I think she's lying."

"About what?"

"I don't know." She studies his face. "What do you think?"

"I don't think we're getting the whole truth from her."

"No, sirree," says Josie.

58

I sit in my office and try to focus on work, but my head is entirely in the wrong place today. I'm in no mood for creativity and there's only so much admin one can do.

I take a look at the work Natasha's been doing for me lately.

Everything's organised to within an inch of its life. My calendar has all of my appointments – that dinner with Todd's marked in for Friday night – but the calendar also bristles with reminders about upcoming commitments and things I should be chasing. The accounts are up to date, and looking a damn sight healthier since Natasha chased down those aged debts. It's the first time in ages that admin has been properly up to date. I love running my business, but I know that I tend to focus heavily on my favourite parts, which is the client work.

I think about Natasha and wonder if the police are done with her now. I expected her to give me a call when she came out, so I could pick her up.

Her speaking to the police was inevitable. It had to

happen. By taking her I was only doing what ultimately had to be done.

That's what I tell myself.

My phone lights up, a message from Natasha.

Call me when you can.

I call her straight back. "Hey, how's things?"

She ignores my question. *"That party at Tyrese's last night..."*

"Yeah?"

"There's a really bad video of Tyrese."

"What?"

"Did he really hire the wrong DJ?"

"He did. I thought..."

There's a notification on my phone. It's a link to a TikTok video.

The video is exactly the thing that I thought I'd prevented. A clear recording of Tyrese digging himself into the worst possible hole where he manages to look both stupid and bigoted.

The user name is *ggfruitshake.* The name given is Georgia Byron.

"I went round the room," I say. "I thought I'd got all the footage. Can't believe I missed one." I groan. "You finished with the police?"

"I'm back home."

"You are?"

"I Ubered. The police ... I didn't exactly ... it wasn't easy."

"I know. But you've done it now." My phone's going. I look at it. "Got another call coming through from Tyrese."

"Answer it. Find out what he knows about this Georgia Byron."

"Sure," I say and switch calls.

I put up with Tyrese's angry panic. Apparently, it's all my

fault. I don't mention that the entire thing was caused by his stupidity and that I cautioned against the idea in the first place.

Tyrese tells me that Georgia is a receptionist at an estate agent.

I switch back to Natasha and give her the lowdown.

"I might be able to deal with that," she says.

"How?"

"Just have a quiet word with her. Anyway, I have something else to report."

"What?" I ask.

"Marissa's gone."

My mind is clanging in alarm. "Gone? What do you mean, 'gone'?"

"I mean she's gone. She's left and she's never coming back."

"I don't understand," I say.

"We can discuss later when you come home."

"Um..." I have no idea what to say.

"It's okay," Natasha says in a light and breezy tone. *"I'm with your dad. He's perfectly fine with me."*

I don't understand, but clearly I have to go home.

What's happened now?

59

I drive home quickly. The gravel slides beneath the Jag's skidding wheels as I pull up outside our house. The sun high and painfully bright in a cloudless sky.

I rush inside.

I hear noises from the lounge and find dad there, giving answers – right or wrong I've no idea – to the quiz show on the TV.

"Natasha!" I call.

"In the kitchen," she replies.

"Oh, it's you?" says Dad, realising I'm there for the first time.

"Yes, Dad."

"Have you made me that sandwich?"

"What sandwich?"

I wave away my own question and go to the kitchen.

Natasha stands there, making a cheese and pickle sandwich on the kitchen table.

"You didn't need to rush back," she says.

"But Marissa—"

"She's gone. I know."

She cuts the sandwich in half and lays the bread knife on the table.

"But what actually happened?" I say.

"She gathered her things and went."

This is a gut punch. I didn't expect this, and I can barely breathe. My head's swimming.

"That can't be it. I mean, that can't be all. That's..."

Natasha has a thoughtful, but stern expression. "She made some very personal remarks on her way out. All the swear words."

She can't possibly be talking about mild-mannered Marissa. She is the gentlest of souls. Marissa is capable of a pointed sigh at most. I don't think I've ever even seen her roll her eyes at any of the many, many liberties I've taken with her good nature.

"I think whatever she'd done, she realised she was about to be found out," says Natasha.

"Whatever she'd done...?"

"Your dad is almost certainly better off without her. I can sort out a replacement."

"I still don't understand."

But she's already walking out, a sandwich on a plate to deliver to Dad.

I half follow, but my phone is ringing.

It's Harvey. I really don't want to talk to him, but the Brascote buildings thing is a pressing matter. My dad needs care. More care. His one carer has now gone for some unfathomable reason. And we need cash to sort things out.

I answer. "Harvey. Hello."

"Ah, I'm glad you're there, Hannah. I really did want to talk to you."

"The Brascote buildings. You—"

"Oh, no. I meant we need to talk about last week. I assume a few days has given you time to cool your jets, eh? Hot heads and all that. I don't want to rake over the ashes. You and I are closer than that, eh?"

He's not calling about the sale of the Brascote buildings. Suddenly, I don't want to be talking to him at all.

"We need that money, Harvey."

"All in good time. You and I seem to have fallen out of step with one another. That thing last Thursday. The things said."

"I've nothing new to say."

"You know, I was rather hurt by those wild accusations. The disrespect."

I can't believe it. I can't believe he's calling me, calling me now, and he's trying to spin what happened at the gala dinner into something where he's the victim. It was *his* hands on me.

Abruptly, Natasha is standing in front of me in the hallway.

"Is that Harvey?" she says.

"It is."

She snatches the phone from me. "What the fuck are you phoning Hannah for?" she says forcefully.

I don't hear his reply. He possibly doesn't even get chance to make one. She launches into him with a tirade of abuse. He's a bastard. He's an arsehole. He's an abuser. He's a worm.

Her words power her into the kitchen and out through the back into the rear garden and she's still going.

"You want to communicate anything to Hannah, you go through me, ya hear?" she yells.

She goes on for a full two minutes. I don't know if he's even hung up by this point. Or is he listening in completely stunned silence. He's probably never been spoken to with such venomous hatred in sixty-plus years.

I stand in the kitchen and watch Natasha – she's a bloody force of nature, that young woman – as she strides back and forth shouting the odds at him.

I've seen angry people. Anger is an energy that builds up inside you, and the very nature of anger is that it wants to build and build, but ultimately, you just run out of it; it wears out. I know full well that the best tactic with angry people is to wait for them to expend all that energy and come down from that hot, high level of fury they're in.

But Natasha doesn't let her fury diminish. She ends that call on a high, with a great snarling "Fuck off!" before she walks back to the house.

I'm a mess of confusion and anger and sheer sense of loss at what's happened in the last twenty-four hours.

Natasha holds out my phone to me. I take it numbly.

"Cup of tea?" she says.

I blink. "What?"

"Tea."

"Um, yes." I think of how relieved I am to have her here with me right now. "And thanks."

She fills the kettle and then gives me a big smile.

"What would you do without me, Hannah?"

60

Thursday morning, Rob stands at the conference room table in Mansfield House. It's covered with plastic pouches. Each pouch holds a piece of paper. Many are torn. Most are marked with unpleasant stains. But they've all been catalogued, cleaned, dried and sealed into these clean little pouches.

Detective Inspectors Scabbard and Bacon have been considering them for several minutes.

"You've waded through a lot of shit," says Scabbard eventually.

Josie and Walker stand at a respectful distance while Rob goes over the material.

"It's all being entered into the Holmes system, and we can get the force intelligence team to make further analysis, but this is a snapshot of what Paul Mulholland's business empire looked like a short while ago."

"Is it going to tell us who killed him and those Chinese girls?" says Scabbard.

DI Bacon twitches, possibly at the word 'girls'. The

women so far identified from the cellar were in their late twenties and early thirties. Hardly girls at all.

"It shows the people he's worked with and therefore potentially some people who he's crossed," says Rob.

DI Bacon circles the table. She casts a hand over a section of notes. "These here are all to do with sales of machinery to the continent."

"Specifically, Lithuania," Rob agrees.

"So, that's work for the Degutis crime gang?"

Rob tilts his head. "Probably. But that's a natural direction for those kinds of goods to travel in. Once machinery has reached the end of its useful life in Western Europe, it might still be seen as a fine investment further east. That's just the way of things."

"And we can tell what stuff he's sent that way?"

"Not necessarily easy. Tractors and the like don't have log books. They're only on the DVLA databases here if they're licensed to drive on the road. So it's a trail of invoices and serial numbers we have to follow. But to export legally, Mulholland needed to raise commercial invoices that show the buyers and sellers."

"And we don't have those commercial invoices?" says Bacon.

"We could ask the hauliers he uses, ma'am," says Walker, stepping forward.

"You know who they are?"

Rob taps one of the hundreds of laminates. "This guy, Jamie Priest, gets mentioned a bit. He's mentioned by name because he's a one-man operator. He's known to us."

"A young guy too," adds Walker. "Probably only drives for Mulholland."

"Is he going to have kept the paperwork?" says Scabbard sceptically.

"No knowing," says Rob. "Again, we're building up a picture here. I don't know if any of this will lead us directly to those responsible."

Bacon and Scabbard glance at one another. Rob can read them perfectly. They're lacking leads. It's been ten days since the fire and the police haven't made any arrests. Cases can go cold very quickly.

"If you know this haulier, Priest, go speak to him," says Bacon, her face grim. "Any information. Any leads."

"On it, ma'am," says Rob.

61

I slept like the dead last night and I feel at least a bit more refreshed the following morning. But my head is still a whirl of things that I need to do, professional and personal. I go downstairs and I'm surprised by the sight of Natasha standing at the front door with a stranger.

"Hello?"

"Ah Hannah," says Natasha. "This is Dolores."

"Dolores?"

"She's here for a day's trial as Marissa's replacement. She's about to get your dad out of bed and ready for the day, but I thought you'd want to meet her first."

"You ... you arranged this?" I say.

"I thought it best. We need someone."

I'm not happy about this and that's probably evident on my face as I go down the final steps.

"Of course." I force on my game face and stride forward to give Dolores a warm handshake and a wide smile. She looks very wary after seeing my initial reaction.

"Many thanks for stepping in, Dolores. You'll love my

dad. He's a complete sweetie. Perhaps when he's up, you might join us and we can get to know each other a little better."

I'm concerned now that Dad might be awake and trying to get himself up. He's got himself into a pickle in the past when he's done that.

I go into the kitchen and pour coffee while I wait for them all to come back.

The coffee's somehow bitter on my tongue as I think about Dad railing against the idea of someone new helping him. I'm concerned for Marissa as well.

I fetch some extra cups, and pour everyone a coffee when they emerge.

"Morning, Dad."

His face says that he's unhappy. A sideways glance at Dolores underlines this. He doesn't know what's happening. He's not the only one.

I go over to him and lean in to whisper gently. "You know what you should do, don't you? Dolores is new, and a bit nervous. Why don't you take her on a little tour of the garden. See if you can put her at ease?"

He rallies then. He has a sense of purpose and he turns to Dolores, inviting her to look at the geraniums with him.

I glance over at Dad, who's now quite animated, talking about geraniums to Dolores. At least his needs are taken care of.

I suppose it was really thoughtful of Natasha to get straight onto the agency to sort that out.

Once we're at the office, Natasha goes straight to work at her desk. I'm not completely certain what she's doing, but her hands fly over the keyboard, and there's intense concentration on her face.

"I've sent you those video files I recorded outside the house on Narborough Road," I tell her. "Maybe take a look. See what we could use as part of material we send to Todd."

Natasha gives me a look. It's not exactly piercing, but we both know I'm talking about the videos in which I pressed her to confront the scene and revisit her trauma.

"Just take a look," I say. "*You* decide what is okay for us to use and not to use."

"Okay," she says and then, "Oh, I've put a bit more pressure on Mr Harvey Kenelm."

"More?"

"I reminded him that he's a dirty old bastard and, although the Brascote buildings sale is going to take weeks still, he's going to hand control of your dad's investments over to you this week."

I think back to the language she blasted Harvey with last night.

"Excellent," I say.

I don't know exactly how much Dad has in investments. Harvey would let me look over the accounts about four times a year. There's at least a quarter of million in various ISAs, stocks and other accounts. It's not free money. It's got to see Dad through the rest of his days, but we can definitely use it to shake up his level of care.

Things might be looking up.

Despite Tyrese's actions. Despite the gut-wrenching business with Marissa and Dad. Despite the upset that the fire and the police have caused to Natasha. Things might indeed be looking up.

I get a text from Karolina.

Need to talk to you. Take a walk towards the Tesco Express. Will meet you.

This is different. I wonder if Karolina has discovered a coffee shop that she wants to show me.

I let her know I'm on my way.

"Natasha, I'm just off out to see Karolina. Back in a bit."

"You don't have a meeting in the diary."

"She probably has an update on something. No idea what."

She gives me a nod as I leave.

62

I'm not far down the road when Karolina appears. I'm not even sure where she was waiting, but she's suddenly there, walking beside me.

"Hello again."

She fixes me with a level stare. I gather from this that there will be no small talk.

"I spoke with Marissa," she says.

"You what?"

"I spoke with your dad's carer."

"What? When?"

"This morning."

"Why? I didn't ask you to do that."

"I was..." She makes a noise. "I was keeping an eye out for you. Marissa was sacked by Natasha."

"Er, no. Marissa just walked out."

Her face twitches. "Not what Marissa says. Says Natasha gave her the boot. The old heave ho. That's what they say, yes?"

"That is not how Natasha told the story."

"How did Miss Natasha Dibello tell the story?"

I try to think straight as we walk. I put the ideas in order and then put those thoughts into words. Her telling me that Marissa had left. The fact that Marissa had a few choice parting words for Natasha. Natasha's hint that Marissa jumped before she was pushed.

"But what did Marissa have to say?" I ask.

We stop at this point. We're near the benches at the bottom of New Walk. It's an open area in front of a curved apartment building. We take a seat.

"You will find this hard to believe," says Karolina.

"It's that bad."

"No. It just doesn't make sense."

"So tell me," I say.

Karolina looks me in the eye. "She asked Natasha if she was pregnant."

"What?"

"Marissa asked Natasha if she was pregnant."

"Really? What a strange thing to ask. Any idea why?"

Karolina shrugs. "Marissa says that she can often tell that a woman is pregnant by the way she stands."

"Bollocks."

"Apparently it's a thing. Something to do with hormones softening ligaments. Alters the posture."

"So Marissa asks the question. What happened then?"

Karolina shrugs. "Apparently Natasha flew off the handle. Yells at her that she's out of line. Tells her that she's violated her privacy. Tells her that she's fired."

It all sounds very unlike Natasha.

"How sure are you that Marissa was telling the truth?" I ask.

Karolina does a head-exploding mime. "Are you listening

to yourself? You're doubting the person you've known and trusted for ages, while you continue to believe the person you only just met. Seriously?"

I should think about what Karolina's saying to me. Her instincts are generally very good, but surely she's wrong.

I give her a nod. "I should check it out."

"Check it out? Like how?"

"I think I need to have a heart-to-heart with Natasha. Uncover a few truths."

Karolina gives me a look. "She will tell you what you want to hear."

Now she's just being unkind. I give a mild huff of displeasure, wondering how to phrase my rebuttal, but she puts a hand on my arm.

"What was that?" She twists in the seat.

"What?"

"I heard a noise."

This is a wide open area. There are other people here, but they are yards away, sitting on the other benches or walking along the pavement by the road.

"What? There's nobody."

"There."

Karolina stands and looks behind our bench, where a low wall borders the ramp that goes up to the building's entrance.

She walks round and looks up the ramp. "Gone."

I stand and watch what she's doing.

"You think that someone was behind this wall listening to our conversation? Then that person ran away, crouched down below the level of this wall?"

"Yes."

I'm a little worried about Karolina. She has always been so reliable, but she's starting to sound a little paranoid.

"Come on. We need a cuppa. We can find a coffee shop, or head back to the office."

Karolina shakes her head. "You go back. I have some things I need to do."

I walk back to the office, trying to remember the last time Karolina had a holiday. I might suggest that she's due a break.

63

It takes Josie and Walker the best part of the morning to track down the haulier, Jamie Priest.

The address they'd had for him on the system was two addresses out of date, and a phone call early afternoon confirms that he's currently staying with his mum in the Netherhall area of the city.

Her home is a neatly painted former council house. The road itself is poured concrete, dug up and repaired so often with tarmac that it looks like a patchwork. Mummy Priest is at the door before Josie and Walker even reach it.

Josie can see a hard-nosed no-nonsense attitude in the woman, like she's taken her full quota of shit in this life and has no fucks left to give.

"He's round the back," she says and leads them through the side gate.

Jamie Priest is at the little patio table set in the neatly managed rear garden. The guy looks unpleasantly thin, stubble growing in the hollows of his cheeks. He has rings round his eyes like he hasn't slept in weeks. If he's not addicted to something bad for his health, Josie would be surprised.

He's got a vape broken open on the little table, a spent cartridge removed, a replacement not yet put in.

"Here they are," says his mum, like she'd warned him the cops were coming. "Talk to them." She makes to step into the rear of the house.

Jamie looks from one detective to the other with grey eyes. "So, what do you want?"

Walker tugs at his trouser knees as he sits at one of the other chairs.

"Afternoon, Jamie. This is DC Kaminski. I'm DC Smith. We wondered if we could pick your brain."

"About what?"

Josie sits on the low brick wall that edges the raised lawn. "Paul Mulholland."

"He's dead, isn't it?" Jamie says without any emotion or emphasis.

"He is. The house fire. We're trying to find the person or persons who might have started the fire."

"I don't know." He picks up the pieces of the vape, not because he intends to do anything but for something to hold.

"You worked for Paul," says Josie.

"And?"

"We're trying to build up a picture of his business, people he knew."

"You think I know something? You want me to snitch?"

Walker is shaking his head in a slow, kindly manner. "Not at all. Literally, we just want to understand his business, maybe speak to other people who worked with him. You drove for him?"

"I did."

"You own a lorry?"

"I rent a unit whenever I need one."

"Right. And then Paul paid you maybe cash when you did a job?" He offers Jamie a smile. "We're not interested in your tax situation. Was it cash in hand?"

Jamie jiggles his head. A nod without being a nod.

"And who paid him? He was doing this for other people, right?"

Jamie doesn't answer.

"Tractors, trailers, machine parts," says Josie. "We know the stuff he was selling. But he was acting for others."

"You know I can't tell you that," Jamie replies.

"Did he owe people? Did he have money trouble?"

Jamie coughs and laughs at the same time. "He was always moaning about money."

"Yeah?" says Walker.

"Never happy."

"Yeah?"

"People he owed. People who owed him. It's all he ever talked about."

"You met any of these other people?"

"Who?"

"The people he dealt with?"

"I saw faces."

"Come on," says Josie. "You can do better than that."

"He was always bitching about contractors. If he was having work done on property or getting something repaired. Brickies, joiners, fuckin' plasterers. He liked to moan."

"And did he get any blowback from that?"

"What?"

"Did he get any trouble from anyone?"

Jamie shakes his head, frowning. "You know Paul?"

"After a fashion," says Walker.

"He was a bloke with a bit of money and big mouth who acted like he was big wheeler-dealer. You ever seen him do his sales videos? His Charlie Bates sales pitch?"

"Sound as a pound!" says Josie, putting on her best cockney geezer voice.

Jamie laughs. "That's him. Them's the ones."

"I've watched every single bloody one of them," she says.

"He had the gift of the gab," says Walker. "He was a charming guy."

Jamie finally snaps the new vape capsule in the vape. "Always had some girl or other he did. For a fat ugly bloke, he somehow worked his magic."

"You met any of the girlfriends?" says Josie.

Another head shake. "Some of them didn't hang around long. And he moaned about them an' all. The last one. He did nothing but moan about her. She was costing him an arm and a leg."

"What? Why?"

Jamie shrugs. "Expensive tastes."

"What was her name?"

"Dunno. I didn't think I'd need to remember." He turned the vape on and toked on it. "Was it the fire that killed him?"

"Why?"

Jamie shakes his head, draws back. "I was in a … not the same but similar situation."

"How so?" says Josie.

"I had my own place. Well, a room in a shared house thing. Carbon monoxide leak killed half the people in the building."

"Oakleaf Road?" says Walker. "That place?"

"That's the one. Some of us had to be dragged out. Fuck. You go to sleep and, next thing, everyone's dead. You know?"

Walker's voice is low. "I can't even imagine."

"But fire..." Jamie takes a mouthful of vape and expels big white clouds. "That's a fucking awful way to go."

"It is," says Josie.

64

I get back to the office to find Natasha not there.

In one sense, it's a relief. After the things Karolina has told me, I've got no idea what I was going to say. But I do need to speak to her.

Natasha arrives back in the office fifteen minutes later.

"Sorted," she declares. Her face is grim. There's something in her demeanour that's mildly unsettling but I can't put my finger on it.

"What's sorted?"

"Georgia Byron." She throws a phone down onto her desk. It has a cover studded with pink rhinestones and a long tassel hangs down.

She can't possibly mean Georgia Byron who recorded Tyrese's party has been sorted.

"Is that her phone?"

"Yes. She's deleted her video and I've reported the reposts as AI manipulated."

I stare at Natasha, then stare at the phone.

So many questions.

"What does she want in exchange for the video?" I ask.

"Nothing. We're all square."

This isn't adding up at all.

"So why do you still have her phone?"

"I'm going to give it back to her. I told her I needed to do a proper clean-up of the video. It takes a bit of time."

"What do you mean?"

"It was something that Karolina mentioned. I plan to ask her advice on how to make sure there isn't a backup anywhere."

That does sound like something Karolina would know about. I wish she was here to ask.

"And Georgia is fine with you having her phone?"

"Yes she is. I think she really wants to help. She's a diamond, really."

I briefly wonder what it would take for me to give up my phone to someone – a stranger! – for any length of time. I can't imagine it at all.

This has thrown my intention to talk to her about Marissa a bit askew but I decide then to persevere.

"We need to talk."

"Yeah?"

"About Marissa."

"Dolores seems good, doesn't she?"

That's not the aspect I want to talk about at all. I wonder if Natasha knows that.

"You fired my dad's carer."

"What?"

"You fired Marissa."

"Yeah. You know that."

"No. You said she walked out."

She shrugs like she's going to say they're the same thing but she doesn't.

"I ... put certain facts to her and she didn't stick around to hear them."

"Certain facts? I was her employer. That's my home situation. You are a guest. You don't get to fire my dad's carer."

"You think we should have kept her on?"

I bristle at the use of the word 'we'. I've heard it out of Natasha's mouth quite a bit of late. I wasn't lying to Karolina when I've said that Natasha is an absolute find, a godsend even, but she has become very comfortable in my world, in my life over the last two weeks.

"Did Marissa say something to you to make you think you needed to fire her?" I say.

"We could see she wasn't offering the right level of care to Dad. The nurse said someone had hurt him."

"But something made you take that decision to fire her." I don't want to literally state that Marissa had asked Natasha if she was pregnant. I don't want to make it clear that Karolina has spoken to Marissa. And it doesn't make sense. It's not a thing. No one flies off the handle because someone suggests they're pregnant. "Did she say something to you?"

"Probably best if you don't know, eh?" There's an undercurrent to Natasha's voice there. A warning.

"Know what? I think if there's some aspect of your situation—"

Before I can go any further, Natasha has her phone out and is opening something.

"What's this?" I say.

It's a video.

65

It's a phone video, presumably from Natasha's own phone.

A door opens and I realise it's the door to the study in our house. The door swings wide and Marissa is there by the desk against the wall. The drawer is open. Marissa looks up at the camera and there's something in her hand. Cash.

"What are you doing?" says Natasha from behind the camera.

"I was looking for the key."

"What key?"

"The gas meter key."

"That's not your money."

Marissa is both confused and alarmed. *"I just found it."*

"What the hell?" says Natasha. *"Is this what you do? You think you can just help yourself? You're meant to be in a position of trust."* She takes a step forward and the video ends.

Natasha gives me a tight-lipped "I told you so" look. "You saw it. She's been hurting your dad. She's been stealing from you."

"I can't believe it," I whisper.

This puts a fresh context on the frankly nonsensical story Karolina was giving me about pregnancy.

I don't have a chance to explore further, because there's a buzzing from the front door – Tyrese.

I feel like life is throwing everything at me all at once. But Tyrese is my main client right now. I have to deal with him.

He's come over here in a panic, having finally learned there's a video out there of his party gaffe and throwing his arms around the shoulders of the wrong DJ with cerebral palsy.

I ask Natasha to escort him in and once he's in the room, I sit him down on the Chesterfield.

"This is all effed up," he says.

"It's okay," I say. "Let's get some tea brewing and open the best biscuits. We can sort this out."

"Sure. Whatever, man."

I go to make the tea.

When I come back with the tray and set it down on the table, I see that Georgia's phone is already there on the table, and that Natasha and Tyrese are deep into the conversation already.

"That is such good news," Tyrese says to Natasha. "Good for you, jumping on it like that." He glances up at me. "I see Natasha here's fixed things."

"We get the job done," I say. "Now, about that cup of tea..."

With an indifferent *pff* he waves the tray away, his attention on Natasha. "So tell me how you did it. You just, like, asked for the phone and she gave it you?"

"Well..." Natasha begins.

Tyrese is entirely focused on Natasha.

While I'm grateful that she's somehow managed to do this, I feel mildly aggrieved that she's jumped in and commandeered the conversation while I was still in the kitchen. I feel like the hired help.

I keep my game face on. My smile is wide and genuine, but nobody's looking at me. This is now a conversation between Tyrese and Natasha. Somehow, they are the grown-ups in the room, and I am not included.

66

Walker's phone rings as Josie turns into Sandacre Street behind the Mansfield House station.

Unknown number.

He answers. "Hello?"

"DC Smith, we need to talk."

Walker recognises the voice, mostly by the light Lithuanian accent. "Arturus?"

Josie glances at him.

Walker has never had a direct phone call from Arturus Degutis before. He wasn't aware that Arturus had his number. It's not an everyday occurrence to receive a phone call from one of the brothers at the head of the Degutis crime gang.

"We need to talk," Arturus repeats. *"Things to straighten out."*

"I'm happy to talk. Where would you like to meet?"

Josie's slowing. Arturus Degutis is standing next to the police car park gate on Mansfield Street, phone to his ear.

He gives a satisfied smile to the two of them and ends the call.

"We inviting him in for a nice little chat?" says Josie.

"Drop me off and get parked up," says Walker. "I'll see what he wants."

Josie gives him a look, as though this might not be the wisest idea. Walker smiles. Arturus Degutis is hardly likely to cause any aggro on the doorstep of a police station.

She pauses so Walker can get out and then waves her card to open the gate.

Walker steps over to Arturus. Walker is a tall man but Arturus is taller. He's got a round belly and the grey stubble on his jowly face is always as long as the hair on his head. He's a bear of a man, looks like he could have spent a lifetime doing manual work like trawler fishing or animal butchery.

Arturus doesn't offer a hand to shake. Walker decides he's not going to be the one to extend the hand of friendship.

"This is a surprise," he says.

"Can we walk?"

"Sure."

They turn to go up towards the main road.

"And to what do I owe this pleasure?" says Walker.

"You are investigating the death of Paul Mulholland," says Arturus. "You have been asking people questions."

Ah. Jamie Priest called the Degutis gang as soon as Walker and Josie left.

"Do you have information you'd like to share with us?" Walker asks coolly.

"You know who started the fire?"

"It is still an open investigation."

Arturus rocks his large head and then looks directly at Walker. "You should know we had nothing to do with this."

"We? As in...?"

Arturus's look turns sly, like he expects Walker to play the game better than this.

"My brother, Darius, and I own a number of legitimate business interests. You know this. The racist British police keep trying to pin various crimes on us. We know this."

Arturus's nephew, Lukas, was arrested for an attempted armed robbery earlier in the year. He'd been caught red-handed with gang members, weapons and cash. A woman died. There was no need for the police to 'pin' crimes on the Degutis gang.

"And Paul Mulholland was one of the people who worked for you."

"A business associate," Arturus corrected. "He had his own business interests. He provided services for us."

"Farm machinery sales and transportation to Lithuanian."

Arturus inclined his head, a slight agreement. "All above board and legal."

It takes an effort of will not to snort with laughter.

Their walk takes them round Abbey Street and onto Belgrave Gate. Movement in the corner of his vision makes Walker glance back. Josie is following on foot ten metres behind.

"So, what have you got to tell me about Paul's death?" says Walker.

"It was not us."

"Okay. Hardly dynamite."

"It does not serve our business interests to have one of our associates dead."

"You think rivals did it?"

Arturus mushes his lips thoughtfully. "I don't think so."

"So what? This was just an accidental fire?"

"No. Paul was a man who could rub off people the wrong way."

"Rub people up the wrong way," Walker corrects automatically.

"Yes. He had a temper. He was handy with his fists." Arturus makes two fists. He has big ham hands. Walker hopes never to be on the receiving ends of hands like those.

"He broke an old girlfriend's jaw," says Walker.

"A man should never hit a woman. And if he must, he must know his own strength."

"Is that so?"

"Chelsea's brothers were convicted for attempting a, er, retaliation."

"I gather. You think they did it?"

Arturus sucks his teeth irritably. "I am not saying that. I am saying that Paul's troubles are of his own making and you shouldn't poke your nose into the legitimate dealings of local businessmen."

"Basically, back off. Right?"

Arturus shrugs.

"And what would you do if you found out who was responsible for that fire. There were six women who died in that fire. Trafficked women."

"It is a sad situation."

Walker has no knowledge that the Arturus gang are directly involved in trafficking migrants, but if it turns out to be true, he won't be surprised.

"So, you have no information to offer us at all?" says Walker.

"I am offering my help by telling you where to focus your investigation."

"Sure. Well, thanks for that." Walker is about to say

goodbye when a thought crosses his mind. "You wouldn't happen to know about Paul Mulholland's latest girlfriend?"

Arturus raises his chin, an acknowledgement. "A girl named Ruby something. I think maybe half his age."

"Ruby?"

Arturus nods again. "Ruby. Ruby Adams."

With that, he gives a nod of farewell to Walker and crosses the street to where a waiting car is parked on the double yellow lines. The driver, a lean man with blond hair, watches Walker through narrowed eyes. Walker meets his gaze and stands there until Arturus is in the car and the car has gone.

Josie catches up with Walker.

"An interesting chat?"

Walker strokes his chin. "Maybe. I think we'd better catch up with whoever started that fire before the Degutis gang do."

67

Rob is sitting in the Dead End Duncans' little corner of the CID office when Josie and Walker come in. He's been reviewing the shit files. A civilian analyst has given them an interim report, and Rob's reviewing it for possible leads.

Rob glances across at Walker as he approaches and sees the concerned look on the DC's face. "You all right, mate?"

"Of course." Walker smiles, but his actions are a little wooden. Something's bothering him. "We've just spoken to Arturus Degutis," he says.

Rob sits up straight in surprise and straightens his folded tie. "What?"

"*He's* been talking to Arturus Degutis," says Josie.

"And?"

"Basically told us to back off," says Walker.

"He's scared."

"Don't think so. Irritated perhaps."

Josie looks over Rob's shoulder at the financial reports based on the shit files.

"All the data uploaded."

"It's a good report," Rob says.

"Yeah?"

"An organised mind has applied logic to the chaotic mess."

Josie grunts. "Hopefully, all put together by someone who understands all those shell company references."

"Right."

"I mean, I get that shell companies are a way of hiding who owns things, but actually following a trail is something else. And you saw the stuff where Mulholland appears to have diverted half his funds into crypto-currency."

"Yeah," says Rob.

Robs finds it interesting that people think crypto-currency like Bitcoin and Doge Coin can be easily hidden from the authorities. Every transaction is permanently recorded on a public blockchain, creating a transparent trail that can be traced with forensic tools. The only problem is that it requires resources and expertise that need to be allocated to the investigation.

"Did you see the note about recent transfers?" says Rob, pointing to a node of data on the screen. "And there's a link with setting up a trust fund, yeah."

"Paul Mulholland setting up trust funds?" says Walker.. "Have they offered thoughts on what's going on there?"

Rob taps the screen. "It's an unusual pattern, apparently. The bloke in Force Intelligence says it might point to some sort of life event. Like Paul Mulholland was getting married."

"Or becoming a father," says Walker.

Rob catches a fleeting, faraway expression on Walker's face.

Walker inhales sharply through his nose. "Arturus did mention Mulholland's girlfriend."

"Yeah?"

"Ruby Adams."

Rob thinks. "The one who had links to Brendan and Kathleen O'Malley?"

"Their adopted daughter."

"So we need to speak to her, then." Rob glances at the data on the screen. "She and Mulholland had a baby together?"

"Or are having."

"Do we know where she is?" says Josie.

"No," says Walker. "But I know someone I can ask."

68

I'm still not properly dressed on Friday morning when my phone buzzes with a message from Todd.

Disappointed, Hannah. Did something come up?

What on earth can he mean?

I call him. "Todd? What's wrong?"

"Dinner? Last night?"

"No. It's in my calendar for tonight. I was very much looking forward to it."

"I sent you a calendar invite."

He's being terse with me. Not only is he annoyed at being stood up, he thinks I'm incompetent. Who wants a business partner who can't even organise their calendar?

"I really don't understand how that's happened, Todd. I'm so very sorry. Can you make tonight?"

"No. I'm afraid I'm not available."

He hangs up.

I stare at my phone. What just happened?

Dad's in the kitchen. I can hear the back and forth between him and the new carer, Dolores. I'm not sure if they've settled into a routine yet. Most of the time he doesn't know who she is.

I switch to my calendar. There it is, *Dinner with Todd.* It's this evening.

How did it get onto my calendar? Was it something where my phone picked it up out of an email or did I add it manually?

I search for messages and emails from Todd.

Shit.

He sent me an email with a reservation and it was for last night. How could I be so stupid?

I'm normally so good with dates and meetings, even before Natasha showed up and started organising me.

I text Todd, explaining my calendar error, but he ignores the message.

I really hope that I haven't damaged our business relationship, and I'm stung that I might have damaged our personal one.

69

Walker is back at Duncan Flanagan's place. Time to find out what he recalls about the O'Malleys and this adopted daughter of theirs, who might have been Paul Mulholland's latest girlfriend.

"That's you," says Duncan, passing him a tea.

Walker gives Duncan a small salute with his mug.

The wall next to his chair is nothing but bookcases. He's sat here before, but it occurs to him for the first time that this space is more study than living room, and he wonders for a brief moment if he'd like to spend his later years sitting in quiet reflection, surrounded by books, newspapers and puzzles. It seems enticing, but Walker doesn't know if he'd survive with the relative hurly burly of family life. His kids and wife might all be busy doing their own thing but he think he would die from lack of purpose if they were gone entirely.

"You're back soon," Duncan asks. "Suddenly remembered how charming my company is?"

"Obviously." He sips the tea. It's hot. "Just admiring the trappings of retired life."

Duncan's eyes flick to the shelves. "Staving off boredom more like."

Duncan had been married once but it did not last. If Walker remembered correctly, she'd left him for a mobile DJ in Melton Mowbray within five years. Duncan hadn't seemed bothered. Walker guessed that some people were more invested in the idea of marriage than others and Duncan Flanagan was the sort who had tried it out, seen it hadn't worked and decided not to bother again.

"Did you catch up with Kathleen O'Malley?" Duncan asks.

Walker sighs. "That's one of the reasons I came round here. She died last month. Thought you should know."

Duncan pauses with his cup part way to his mouth. "Oh." He puts it down. "I had no idea."

Walker doesn't respond. He needs to let Duncan take on this piece of news for a moment.

"Last month," Duncan responds eventually. He's talking more to himself than anything. "I must have seen her not long before that."

Walker nods. "You were giving them money. The O'Malleys."

Duncan lifts his gaze and stares at Walker. He stares long enough for Walker to start to feel a little uncomfortable. Was he going to deny it?

"Yeah," says Duncan. "Yeah, I was."

Walker doesn't look away. There's more, clearly. He doesn't want to derail Duncan.

"They had Ruby to look after. Seemed only right."

Walker's missing some piece of this jigsaw. "Why's that then?"

Duncan heaves a sigh. "You don't know about Ruby. Who she is."

It's a statement. Walker can't understand why Duncan's being so cryptic.

"She was Leanne Church's daughter," says Duncan. "Leanne died years ago, so the O'Malleys brought her up. Like she was their own."

"Sorry? Leanne had a daughter?"

"Yes. She'd be twenty-two, twenty-three now."

"So...?"

"Around the time of Operation Kilkenny, yes."

Walker's had minor tinnitus for years. It's a ringing in his ears that can't be cured. Mostly he can tune it out. It's just another tiny symptom of him getting older. He's trained himself to ignore it.

Right now, it's almost all he can hear. An overwhelming, high-pitched tone that threatens to block out all other sounds. He tries hard to concentrate.

"Nine months after Operation Kilkenny, I should say," says Duncan.

The pieces are falling together, but they are making something much bigger than he might have expected. Something that he can't quite bring himself to comprehend.

He hears Duncan's speak, but it seems muffled and distant.

"Leanne Church had a daughter. From back then, when we were all hanging out. She's your kid, Walker."

Walker manages to get his mug onto the side table before his suddenly numb fingers drop it.

"You sure?" he mumbles.

Duncan nods. "Ruby Adam's your daughter, mate."

70

In the office that morning there's plenty of work to be done but I'm just not feeling it.

Natasha has gone out to chase more of those outstanding client fees I thought were never going to be paid. That leaves me in the quiet of the office with my own thoughts.

And, for whatever reasons, this morning those thoughts are not my friends.

I've not been able to keep my dad safe and secure from uncaring hands and thieving fingers. Tyrese Jali is a walking dumpster fire, causing fresh issues continuously. And my potential new client, Todd, is possibly lost to me because I can't remember a simple bloody dinner date.

I'm sitting in an office which, however you look at it, I only have because bloody Harvey gave me a mates rates deal on the rent. And he clearly thought that was a mates-with-benefits deal. I shudder at the thought of him, the feel of his hands on me.

My sense of worth is very low at the moment.

I'm feeling very anxious, and I need to give myself a bit of a breather. I need a good talking-to.

I message Karolina, asking if she's free to talk. I want to talk about the Marissa stealing thing. She video calls me straight back.

"Hey Hannah."

She's walking. She's wearing loose exercise gear but I don't think Karolina ever partakes in deliberate exercise. I can see tall buildings around her. She might be in the city centre somewhere.

"I can call you back if you're in the middle of things," I say.

"You know me," she says. *"Always in the middle of things. I need to talk to you anyway."*

"Ah good. Me too. I spoke to Natasha about her sacking Marissa."

She doesn't respond for a long second. I wonder for a moment if the call has frozen.

"What did she say to you?" Karolina asks.

"I know you said that she'd say what I wanted to hear. But she showed me a video. A video that very clearly shows Marissa stealing money."

Karolina grunts. *"It showed what, exactly?"*

"The video? It showed Natasha walking in on Marissa taking money from a drawer."

"Yeah." Karolina's face is raised to scan the pavement or road ahead but she sounds sceptical.

"What?" I say.

She shrugs. *"Easy to set up a thing like that. I can think of several ways. Tell me this – do you see Marissa's reaction to the situation?"*

"Hm. No." I think back to what Natasha said. "Her finger hit the button at that point, and the video gets cut off."

"You know why? Because the next words out of Marissa's mouth are something like 'Hey you just told me to come to this exact drawer and take out what's inside, what are you talking about? Why are you filming me?'"

I emit a short bark of laughter. Not that this is funny, but simply because I can't handle the ideas that are coming from Karolina.

"There's something important you need to know about Natasha," says Karolina. *"Ah shit!"* She steps back suddenly, the picture wobbly. *"Drivers!"*

She says something but I don't catch it.

"Sorry?"

There's the sound of a horn and swearing. *"Natasha. It's not her real name – I—"*

There's a thump. The screen is suddenly a flicker of light and dark. With a clatter it lands and I'm looking at the sky.

There's a shout, not Karolina. *"Did you see that?"*

"Karolina!" I call. "Karolina!"

"No, I saw it," a man shouts. *"She's—"*

And then the call ends. Dead.

My hands are shaking so much that I can barely work my phone.

Was Karolina just in an accident? What happened?

I need to know that she's all right. I also need to know what she was saying to me. Natasha is not really Natasha? What on earth can that be all about?

71

Walker sits numbly and still in Duncan's living room.

The bookcases around him suddenly seem to loom over him, threatening to fall. He cannot process what Duncan's saying, even though it seems so obvious now that it's been said.

"Ruby's mine?"

Duncan nods slowly and stands. "I think this calls for something stronger."

He goes to a little upright furniture unit, old-fashioned, the kind no one makes anymore, and pulls down the tray door of a drinks cabinet to reveal rows of bottles inside.

Walker really doesn't drink a great deal. Right now, he'd swallow it all down.

"How long have you known?"

"Pretty much since always," says Duncan.

"How?" Walker knows it's a dumb question but it's about all he can manage.

Duncan pours a pair of whiskies from a bottle that looks like it's been in the cupboard for years. He passes one to Walker.

"You know how babies are made, right?" he grins. "You and Leanne were messing about. You in your alter-ego of drug-dealer Gary Snow. We both enjoyed playing the part. And I don't know what passed between you and Leanne, emotionally like."

"Shit," Walker whispers. "It was so long ago."

"Yeah, well, that's kids for you. One accident twenty-odd years ago and..." He sips his whisky and winces.

"But how long have you known?"

"Pretty much since the beginning. Jinny and I were close at the time. I saw her a year or so later, when I was back on regular duties. She did not have many nice things to say to me."

"I bet." Walker wants to smile but he can't.

"But she told me Leanne had had a kid and that you were the dad."

"You've known *all* this time?"

Duncan is nodding.

"Why the hell didn't you tell me?" Walker demands angrily.

Duncan isn't cowed. "Because I knew it wouldn't do any good. You were married to Helen. I think she was probably pregnant by that time, too. Leanne didn't want anything to do with you. She'd hooked up with this guy, Adams, by then. You know how these things are. She had a baby. She needed support and protection. This, um, Sam Adams guy. He was there. He had convictions and shitty prospects, but he didn't hit Leanne and he was good to Ruby. They didn't want you."

Walker still can't believe Duncan has never told him. "You kept it secret."

"I didn't want to do anything that might risk the truth getting out. You think your police career was in the toilet after Operation Kilkenny. What would have happened to you if they discovered you'd had sex while undercover? Technically, that'd be Misconduct in Public Office. Up to ten years in prison. I looked it up."

"Shit." Walker takes a gulp of whisky. He needs it.

"And it would have destroyed your own marriage too," Duncan points out. "What happened was wrong, but it could have been so much worse."

He sits back in his chair.

"The guy, Adams, didn't last long. He just moved on. I was still in touch with Jinny and I decided that it was the right thing to pass Leanne a bit of money now and then for little Ruby. It was the least we could do."

"You did that? You paid for my..." He doesn't know what word comes next. Daughter? Mistake? Sins? "For twenty years..."

Duncan nods slowly. "If you want to pay me back, I can give you my bank details." He laughs.

Walker doesn't think there's anything to laugh about here but he laughs too.

"You've been a better friend than I deserve."

"I think I have," says Duncan.

"But you should have told me."

Another sigh. "People move on. Leanne went off the rails before she died. Gave up her daughter for drugs. Ruby moved in with the O'Malleys. I saw her still from time to time. I was just that old copper who used to be friends with her mum. And that's how it was."

Walker downs the rest of the whisky.

"The big question," says Duncan, "is what are you going to do about this now that you know?"

72

Karolina has not been reachable, but I keep trying her number.

I've been trying constantly, compulsively for hours. What else can I do?

Her phone rings out again, but then – finally! – at something like one in the afternoon it's picked up.

"Hello?"

The voice that answers isn't Karolina.

"Oh hi. I was looking for Karolina."

"She is not available."

The voice has an accent that could be Latvian. I'm gripped with sudden fear.

"Is Karolina all right?"

There's a pause. *"You employ my daughter, yes?"*

"I do."

"You should know she's been in accident."

"Oh no."

I say 'Oh, no' but my mind is running through far

stronger language. Oh, shit. Oh, fuck. Oh, please don't let this be true...

It takes me less than half an hour to make the trip to Leicester Royal Infirmary, but it feels like forever.

I find Karolina's mother in a small waiting area. Her name is Roze. She is a small woman with a sharp little face and a severely short haircut. She looks like a distilled version of Karolina – a version of Karolina pickled in time and weariness.

She takes my hands as I sit.

"Can I see Karolina?" I ask.

"She is on a high dependency ward. They let me in sometimes to sit with her."

Roze Ozols tells me everything.

Karolina's in a coma.

That's impossible. That's mind-blowing. Karolina, in my head, is indestructible.

I don't need proof that Karolina is in a coma – that's absurd – but my mind swerves away from the idea of Karolina being incapacitated. Maybe it's selfish of me, because I feel as if I need her more than ever.

I should be thinking about what she needs. And her poor mum.

"And how are you doing?" I ask.

"I am a survivor. So is Karolina."

She presents this as fact, but I see a tremble in her hand that I don't think is age-related.

"What can you tell me about the accident?" I ask.

"Police say it was hit and run." Roze purses her lips. "She was hit hard. Someone said she stepped into the road. A policeman was here and said some people thought there was someone with her when it happened. She has rib fractures, broken leg and what they are calling a traumatic brain injury."

I don't know this woman but we share a deep affection for Karolina. I squeeze her hand.

"And what have the doctors said about—?" I run out of words. My hand sketches a wavy pattern of possible future outcomes.

"They do not know."

I nod and sit silently with Roze for a while.

I rely heavily on Karolina. Yes, her work is an essential part of my business, but she's always been the closest thing I've had to a friend. At least before Natasha came along.

The timing of this couldn't be worse. There are so many things that I wanted Karolina's thoughts on.

But, like Roze, all I can do is wait and hope.

73

When I get back to the office, it's late in the afternoon.

If I felt rubbish first thing this morning, I feel terrible now.

As I'm heading from the car park to New Walk, I pass by a car parked on Museum Square opposite my place. I wouldn't really have noticed it all except the number plate contains HDJ – and those are the three initials of my name. A ridiculous moment of coincidence of which life is full, and if things weren't so awful, it might have even raised a smile. And that might have been it, but the car drew my attention enough for me to look at the man sitting behind the wheel.

He's not an exceptionally distinctive man, but that lean face and, particularly, that thick blond hair, make me think I've seen him before. And I have. He was on the other side of the road when Natasha and I went to look at the burned house on Tuesday. Odd. But it's just another one of life's coincidences.

I thank the stars that I had no appointments, but as I

come in through the front door, I pass someone coming the other way.

"Who was that?" I ask Natasha as I settle in at my desk.

She does a tiny drum roll on the desk. "I'm delighted to say that it's a new client!" she says with a broad smile. "You were indisposed, so I took the meeting."

I feel the smile fall from my face. "What meeting? My calendar was empty."

"Oh no. No it wasn't. I wonder if you were looking at the right day? You've missed three appointments."

I look at my calendar and she's right. How on earth has that happened?

"Oh, I'm so very sorry Natasha, I don't know what on earth I was thinking."

"It's fine, really. To be honest, these were new business enquiries that have come in since the gala dinner. Most of the people who came along expected to talk to me anyway."

Natasha smiles broadly to make me feel better.

I really ought to feel better, so why don't I?

"Our rating on Trustpilot is up. It's good news all round."

I don't tell her about Karolina.

I go and look at Trustpilot, hoping that it can do something for my own mood.

We've got a score of four point eight, which is just marvellous, but I see one of the new reviews.

Ask for Natasha. Gets things done. All-round superstar

I close my laptop.

Natasha looks up.

I'm being mildly ridiculous – I don't know what I was actually planning to do next. I open it again and make myself look at the screen.

I spend much of the next hour doing that. My

productivity has nosedived, because I'm unable to concentrate.

I don't understand how I've managed to miss appointments – and miss a dinner date with Todd. I'm beginning to think that I should reset some of my passwords. I might have been hacked. It couldn't hurt.

I rootle through my bag, looking for my notebook with the passwords in the back. It's not here. Maybe I took it out at home. I'll look for it later.

My mind won't settle at all. For someone who's watchword is poise, I feel like a mess. Karolina's accident has knocked me for six, but there are so many small things that have rattled me over the past few days.

Losing Marissa for the most peculiar of reasons. Accidentally standing Todd up on what could have been a really nice date. That horrible business with Harvey. The feeling that clients (including Tyrese) value Natasha more than me.

And what was Karolina about to tell me before the accident? Something about Natasha? I want to ask her about that, but how would I do that?

I'm no stranger to mental illness. I need to carefully look at myself and ask whether my anxiety has come from these incidents, or vice-versa. I wouldn't be the first person with anxiety to create a whole load of spin-off dramas.

I'm contemplating what to do as I drive us back home after work. There's comfort to be gained there. I breathe. I can meditate. I might book some time with a therapist. Those are all things I can do to regain perspective on things.

It's a relief to go home.

When we get back, I park the Jag and Natasha jumps out to unlatch the gate to the drive.

She takes longer than usual. She's struggling with the latch, so I get out to help her with it.

"Must get some oil on this," she says as we loosen it together.

"Christ, Natasha, you do enough! Leave something for me."

I'm only half joking.

I drive the car inside and grab my handbag.

As I'm locking the car, I reach for my phone inside the bag. It's not there.

"Huh."

I open the car again and look inside, patting down seats and looking in the footwells.

"What's wrong?"

Natasha bends over to see what I'm doing.

"My phone. I can't find it anywhere."

She helps me to look. We scour the entire car. I even pop the boot, knowing full well that it's not in there. It is not in the car.

"It's not in a pocket?" Natasha suggests.

"Nope." Today's outfit is a shift dress and a cropped jacket. The only pocket is in the jacket, and it would accommodate nothing larger than a USB stick.

Natasha's looking on the ground. "Has it dropped out while we've been looking?"

She looks towards the gate. "Oh." She points.

I can see where she's looking. Near where I got out to help with the latch.

I hurry over. "Oh fuck, no."

I must have dropped it when I got out. I then promptly drove over it. My phone is destroyed.

74

It's Saturday and I crave a bit of quiet time – some reflection. I need to get my head in order. There are not many things that might have budged me from that plan, but being without a phone is one of them.

How strange that we used to manage without mobile phones. I know that it's theoretically possible. I know that there are people who reject the idea of being available all the time and who just don't have mobile phones. I am not one of those people. My career is built upon my responsiveness, and my communication skills.

I cannot be without a phone.

I have spare phones in the office. I keep some handsets in case I need to take over a client's phone when something needs careful handling. Mostly I would opt to give them a dumb phone – dumb being the opposite of smart. I don't want them logging back into all of their socials, I just want them to be contactable. You can still buy handsets that do nothing but make phone calls.

I don't want one of those. I need a smart phone, so I need to go shopping for a new one in the city

It takes up more of my day than I'd imagined.

Highcross is busy, but the sales staff talk me through my options with well-trained patience.

Suki, the assistant, helps me retrieve the sim card from the mangled remains of my old phone. I'd assumed that it would be impossible, but with some wiggling it comes out in two pieces.

"This will need to be replaced," says Suki. "You can contact your provider and they should send you a new one."

All I can see is another delay, but I force a smile at Suki, who is only trying to help.

"But you can use your new phone on Wi-Fi in the meantime."

Then of course there's the business of getting my new phone hooked up to everything. I'm not a complete doofus when it comes to technology, but I'm missing my little notepad that has all of my passwords written on the inside cover. I can't understand how I've misplaced it.

Still, with the never-ending patience of Suki, who has promised to sit with me until I can walk out of the store with my phone set up, I eventually manage to connect to my email and most of the important accounts. It takes a very long time. I feel as if Suki and I ought to be toasting some sort of friendship anniversary by the time I get out of there.

I hunger to access my life again. There were dozens of things in my various inboxes, when I got them fixed, but I haven't had an opportunity to see what they all are. And so I decide to pop into the office where my new phone can feast upon Wi-Fi.

As soon as I sit down and open up my email I can see that something is badly wrong.

There's a chain of emails with Todd. They follow on very swiftly from each other. It's the sort of pattern I'd expect to see in a crisis.

I look for the first email and it's from me, earlier today. I haven't emailed Todd today. I really really haven't. The subject of the email is *Some initial ideas for the campaign.*

I mean, I was going to send some edited video files over to Todd, so perhaps Natasha has stepped in and done it. I'll be annoyed if I find out she did it from my account, but fair enough, we can all make mistakes.

But then I see Todd's reply. It's come less than an hour later, and he's not happy.

What the hell is this, Hannah? I genuinely have no idea whether you think this is funny. I can assure you that it's not.

Oh no. I feel a dull squeezing in the pit of my stomach.

I click on one of the video files. Maybe he thinks this footage is too raw. I wanted Natasha to edit the files, so that she was happy with them, but obviously I should have had final sign-off on what got sent to Todd. We can't hit him with anything that's genuinely upsetting.

The video starts, and that dull ache in my stomach blossoms into suffocating horror.

I can't believe what I'm seeing.

On screen, Harvey is pressed up against me. His hand is on my breast. There's no sound with this video, and my expression is not visible.

"Oh my God!"

It's footage of Harvey assaulting me.

My expensive new phone slides to the floor. I don't really

want to pick it up again. That video is appalling. I can't bear that it exists in the world, although it was useful leverage against Harvey. But to have it sent to Todd? I can't process the idea, it's too huge and horrible. And the fact that it looks almost as if it could be a consensual act ... that is intolerable.

75

I feel physically sick. I have to take myself over to the kitchenette and splash myself with water.

What the actual fuck is going on?

I do some breathing exercises and retrieve my phone.

I'm nowhere near caught up with this email trail.

All of the replies to Todd have come from me. From my account.

I could understand doing it one time, but surely – surely you'd notice what had happened?

But no, there's a reply, from 'me'.

Sorry. My bad. Little too much vino last night and not wearing my glasses, lol

I would never write anything like that. Vino? Good grief.

Todd comes back. As you might imagine.

Wholly unprofessional attitude, Hannah. You can do better than this. I need some time to think about what's needed here.

I sigh with relief. It's not over. I can salvage this. I'm not yet sure what it will take, but I've pulled things out of the fire before.

My mind starts whirling with tasks and actions. The things I need to do, and the order in which I should do them – oh—

It's not the end of the exchange.

It seems as though 'I' responded again.

Sure. Take your time. Files attached for when you want to take a look

I scroll down to the attachment. It's a zip file, and I don't even need to click on it to see the problem. The zip file is called *FFS – he is doing my head in*

Why? I don't understand why this is happening.

Predictably, Todd has not taken this well.

Enough Hannah. I'm blocking you now. We will not be working together.

White hot anger surges through me and I grab my car keys. I need to go and get to the bottom of this.

As I'm preparing to leave, the bell rings. Someone's here at the office, on a Saturday afternoon, when nobody even knows I'm here.

My mind flits to that blond guy I'd seen both outside here and the house on Narborough Road.

"Hello?" I ask over the intercom.

"It's DS Rob Joseph."

"Oh."

My bingo card did not contain a visit from the police. Although it's par for the course on a day when it feels as though the sky is falling in.

"And what can I do for you?"

"Can I come in?"

I stare at the car keys in my hand. It seems urgent that I get home and kick up a storm until I understand what's going on here. But DS Joseph has been nothing but even-tempered and patient in our interactions. The man has kind eyes.

"Yes. Fine."

He comes in and gives me a look. "I'm really glad I caught you. Just stopped in on the off-chance. You're not answering your phone."

I take a huge inhale. I briefly consider telling him every shitty thing that's going on, because I think I might just burst if I don't.

"My phone is broken. Sorry." I shake my head. I'm pretty sure I look like a crazy person right now. "Tea?"

"Love one."

He's still not walked fully into the room.

I whirl past on my way to make tea.

"Am I interrupting?" he asks. "You seem ... distracted."

I was doing so well.

I make it to the kitchenette, my hand on the kettle, but then I turn and his kind eyes are on me, and his head is inclined with concern.

I give a slow nod. "Yes. Yes I am distracted. It's been a hell of a day. A hell of week."

"Come on," he says. "Let me help. I can make tea you know. You don't have to wait on me."

He comes over, picks up the tray and starts setting things out.

I feel weirdly overwhelmed. Such a small kindness, but sometimes, a tiny act of compassion feels like a balm. I stand there and watch him. I should tell him where the teabags are, but he's found them. He has the biscuits too. Moments later, he's got the tea tray all ready to go and he smiles at me.

"Shall we?" he says. "Maybe you want to tell me all about it?"

76

In my office, we take one of the battered Chesterfield sofas each, and I catch his look of concern again.

"Lot going on?" he asks.

"Like you wouldn't believe. I've got enough trouble trying to look after my dad."

He nods. "Dementia must be very difficult."

"Yeah. Care's expensive and..." I sigh. "You have family?"

He pulls a tight expression. "Most of them don't talk to me."

"Oh?"

He shakes his head. "Over the past few years. I was in a relationship. Veronica was her name. But while we were together, my family and I... Ugh. Let's just say I burned a lot of bridges that I don't think will ever be repaired."

"You still ... in that relationship?"

"No," he says and grins. "And I was very much the dumpee in that situation. But glad to be out of it. But we were talking about you."

"You don't want to hear all my woes," I say.

"I do," he says and he says it like he means it.

"Well, care for my dad is expensive. The guy who's meant to be looking after Dad's finance, Harvey Kenelm, is being an arse. He lives in this huge pile in Houghton on the Hill, out beyond Thurnby. You know it?"

"I do."

"Right. So super posh area. And he thinks everyone has the kinds of funds he has and can't see we're struggling. Oh, God. I'm rambling, aren't I?"

I stuff a biscuit in my mouth whole. No idea why – am I trying to prevent myself spilling everything? I regret it immediately. Hamster cheeks is not a good look.

Rob pretends not to notice my gluttonous weirdness as he settles back with his cup of tea. "Natasha's been staying with you since the fire?"

I nod.

"Good of you to put her up."

I force a smile onto my face. "She's earned her keep."

"Yeah?"

I recognise the technique. He's leaving gaps so I will fill them. "You came here with some questions, DS Joseph?"

"Rob, please."

"Rob. What would you like to ask me?"

I spot the briefest glint in his expression. He's professional to the end, but my question must have sounded flirtatious.

Was it flirtatious? Surely I'm better than that?

Apparently not.

He coughs lightly. "When we spoke to Natasha, we were a little surprised that she's not picked up many of the pieces from her old life."

"Yes?"

"Things like getting in touch with her bank. The sort of thing you'd normally get straight onto." He pauses. "I wondered whether you could shed any light on that. How's she been?"

I give the question some thought. How has she been, really?

"She's been very busy..." I try.

I pull a face at myself. Nobody's too busy learning about reputation management to regain access to their bank.

Rob can see my doubt. He nods encouragement.

"She's been taking on new things. She's learning the ropes with the business, dealing with things at the house. Got her feet properly under the table."

That last part came out more harshly than I'd intended. Rob spots it immediately.

"You mean, feathering her nest, that kind of thing?"

"You could call it that, I guess."

I hesitate, but Rob continues to sit patiently, those kind eyes urging me to continue.

"But things have got a bit strange." My gaze falls to my lap. Where am I going with this? He's not here for therapy.

"Go on, tell me," says Rob gently. "Might be unrelated to anything, but I'm a good listener."

I laugh at that. "You certainly are! Honestly, can I book you by the hour?"

As soon as I've said it, I recognise another remark that sounds vaguely flirtatious. It's as if my mouth has a mind of its own.

"Forgive me," I say. "I'm a bit all over the place today."

"Nothing to forgive."

I take a deep breath. "The strangeness. Well. It sounds bizarre, but it's as if she's taking over my life. Literally. I should be flattered – I mean I *was* flattered – that she wants to be like me but younger and better. Now though? It's starting to feel a bit threatening."

I stir my tea for something to do. I feel slightly ridiculous saying this stuff out loud.

"She's got all the clients asking for her, now. Just now I saw an email chain where I've been sacked by a new client. Of course, that client would be only too delighted if he heard from Natasha."

That thought was hovering in the back of my mind. Now I've said it out loud it seems much more solid and very possible.

"My dad loves her. He thinks she's me, I swear." I shake my head. "She sacked his carer. Sacked her without even checking with me. Said she caught her stealing. Showed me a video."

"And was she? Stealing?"

I blow a noisy exhale through my lips, thinking about the video. "I don't know. It could have been a setup. The funny thing about all that is that word got back to me from Marissa, the carer. She says that the real reason Natasha sacked her was that Marissa asked Natasha if she was pregnant."

Rob's very still. His cup was part way to his mouth, but he's frozen in place.

Eventually he speaks. "Pregnant?"

77

Josie is in the CID office, following up on the wealth of information their team have to work on. That Natasha Dibello character makes her feel uneasy. There's something just not right about the young woman and her story.

It's Saturday and Josie doesn't need to be at work, but this is an itch that she can't seem to scratch.

Paul Mulholland's bank records have now been made available and that's where she starts. There are lots of transactions. Some of them go places she can't identify immediately. Mulholland had put a lot of funds in cryptocurrency and that will account for some of these records.

But in terms of normal transactions, if this lodger Natasha has been paying rent to Mulholland, she'll surely show up there, unless she's been paying cash.

Josie finds Natasha's payments. A monthly deposit of four hundred and eighty pounds from a NatWest account. Not Monzo, like Natasha had said.

Why would she lie about that?

Josie could put this to Scabbard. If there's reason enough to do it, they could request Natasha's bank details too, but she's not sure she has enough evidence of wrongdoing. Yet.

Natasha Dibello came in for an interview. She was vague, evasive and told some lies. She's certainly not unique in that regard, but it's the nature of her lies that Josie can't get a grip on. Most people will lie routinely to the police about what they said, what they saw and what they did. Josie's puzzled why a person would lie about which bank they are with.

"Someone's keen," says a voice behind her.

Walker drops into his chair and gives her a grin.

"You too, eh?" she smiles.

"Oh no. I'm here because I had nothing much to do at home. Thought I'd catch up in here."

Something about Walker's tone is off, but he goes to the kitchen to make a round of drinks, and Josie's grateful for the company.

He hands her a mug.

"I don't know what to make of Natasha Dibello," Josie says. "Rob and I interviewed her. She was not telling the truth."

"About what?" Walker asks.

"Everything." Josie screws up her face as she tries to remember. "Can't be sure, but I reckon she was lying about every single thing she said to us."

Walker shrugs. "It's a thing. Lie to the police on principle. Some people just do that."

"She lied about which bank she's with," Josie says. "But it was more than that. It was like she didn't know."

"Have you checked her out online? Get a feel for the sort of person she is, maybe?"

"I could take a look. She claimed that she didn't even use

her email address, so I can't see her being all over social media."

"Name like that, you'll soon find out," says Walker.

"Yeah."

Josie starts searching.

Walker's right. Natasha Dibello is a fairly uncommon name. Josie finds a few hits. She discounts the one that's in Italy and scrolls through the two that are left.

She's not sure either of them are right. One's in Scotland, the other in Oxfordshire. She'll take a look at both, to be sure.

"What are you working on?" she asks Walker while she's waiting for a profile to load.

"I was following up on Ruby Adams."

She raises her mug to him. "We're both looking for invisible women."

He grins at her, but it's a weak facsimile of Walker's regular smile. She wonders if he's having a hard time at home.

Josie finds that the Natasha Dibello in Scotland is co-owner of a bed and breakfast business in Skye. She finds photos, but it's a much older woman. She can't see any family resemblance.

She moves on to the woman in Oxfordshire. This is someone who posts a lot on Instagram, which is good, although she is clearly not the woman she and Rob interviewed. She's in Oxfordshire at her parents' house for the summer, and has been spending time at local music festivals. Josie scrolls back to June and sees that Natasha was at *Summer of Soul* in Victoria Park, in Leicester.

"Huh."

It could be a coincidence, but Josie decides to keep digging.

78

I'm on the way home.

Driving west from the city, the summer evening sky is yellow and orange.

I have a great many thoughts clamouring in my mind, but for the first time in days, I'm starting to get an inkling of what could be happening here.

Rob's questions made me pause and examine some of the facts as I told them to him. It's a useful thing, sometimes. When you describe a situation out loud to another person, it gives you a different perspective.

He never came out and said it, but I could tell that he was thinking that Natasha might be carving out a new life for herself. Whatever life she was leaving behind, she likes the look of mine better. I can't blame her for that, in fact I'm sure that I very much encouraged it.

Trouble is, she's gone too far. Where's the line between imitation being the most sincere form of flattery and something that borders on just plain creepy and invasive?

When I pull up at home, I park the car and stand tall for

a moment as I get out. It's a useful exercise for me sometimes. When I've gathered myself together I go inside, and find Natasha and Dad playing chess on the kitchen table.

I stand just inside the doorway.

"Natasha, can I have a word please?"

"Sure." She doesn't move from the table.

"Now. It's important."

She gets up, giving Dad a look. It might have been an eye roll. She reaches across and puts a hand on his. "Back in a minute. Take your pills and we'll carry on the game when I'm done."

She slides some pills across the table and puts them by his glass of water.

"Where's Dolores?" I ask.

"Gone home for the evening. But we've been fine," says Natasha.

I lead her into the lounge, and gesture to the settee. I sit across from her in a chair.

"Natasha, you've been using my credentials to email Todd."

She hesitates for a moment that feels like it could stretch on forever.

"I did."

"I saw the e-mails you sent him. I don't understand."

She presses her lips together tightly. "You know, I really don't think you do, Hannah."

My voice is cold. "He's lost to us now as a client."

She tilts her head. "Evidently."

I shake my head. "I still don't understand. Are you literally trying to make me look bad? Do you think you can take my clients from me?"

"That was what I was aiming for," she admits. She says it with such casual indifference.

A chill runs through me. I'd suspected that she might be manipulating the situation for her own gain, but to hear her come out and say it is shocking.

"You've been stealing my business from under my nose," I whisper.

She gives me a light nod. "That was the plan, Hannah. Competitors emerge. Smarter, younger, brighter professionals take business away from the complacent old guard."

I shake my head. "That's not what this is. You're making it sound like business manoeuvring. This is much more personal than that."

"Personal?" She tastes the word and paces the lounge. "You made it personal."

"Sorry?"

I curse myself for sounding apologetic. What I mean is that I don't follow her train of thought, but as a polite English person, I make it sound as if it's somehow my fault.

"You started this. You made it personal."

"I what?"

She gestures to herself and then the room around us.

"All of this. It's your doing. It was you that found me. Remember? I didn't need rescuing from that fire."

"I just—"

"I got myself out. By myself. I didn't need help. But you came blundering in. 'Here. Sit in my car. Have some clothes. Drink this water'."

"I was being kind."

"I just wanted to get away. And I did. But then—" she

laughs "—you tracked me down. You all but dragged me into your home."

"I was trying to be kind."

Her laugh is loud now, scoffing. "You were trying to be something. For a woman whose job is relationships, you are a completely selfish bitch. I didn't want you. I didn't need you and then you brought me here." She stabs a finger at the bookshelf. "Right here."

"I let you into my home..."

"Damn right," she says. "You gave me a glimpse, didn't you? And so I decided I could make use of that. You brought me into your life, even gave me a little job at your office. Do you know how many office jobs I've had before?"

"No, I—"

"None! None, Hannah. People like me don't get to work in posh offices. Two days after a fire and I'm staying in your big old mansion and working in your classy office and I thought to myself, I could get used to this. I could enjoy this new life while I dealt with my other business."

"What other business?"

She stands and goes to the side of the sofa and lifts out that old, scuff-edged laptop, I've seen her working on.

"This," she says. "This has been driving me insane."

"Your old laptop?"

She jiggles her head. "Well, not mine. Not exactly. You know how Bitcoin works, Hannah."

I open my mouth to answer and then close it. I don't know; and I don't want to be talking about bitcoin when I still need to unpick Natasha's inexcusable behaviour.

"I've been learning fast," she says. "The Bitcoin itself, the money, sits on the blockchain, right? It's out there in the cloud.

And a Bitcoin wallet—" she taps the laptop "—is the thing that lets you get it off the cloud." She shakes the laptop. "Six million pounds in Bitcoin here. Owed to me and mine. But in order to unlock the wallet, you need what's called a seed phrase. That's like a string of words. I heard Paul say it more than once."

"Paul? Paul Mullholland?"

"He just kept it memorised. Never wrote it down."

In my confusion of trying to follow her, something suddenly leaps into my mind.

"That rhyme? The one you keep muttering to yourself."

Her smile turns bitter. "*Falcon flight, cliff so high. Ocean reef, echoes lie.* Something, something, something *tide. Savage season, hidden child.* Falcon, cliff, reef, echoes. Twelve words I need to unlock the money."

"You knew Paul Mulholland?" I say.

"Keep up, Hannah. I thought why not enjoy a bit of your middle-class life while I try to remember it. Play at being normal for a while. And it required work. I couldn't be the real me. You wouldn't like the real me."

"I thought we got on really well."

"Well, you would," she grins. "Something I've learned. People like people who are a reflection of themselves."

She throws the laptop onto the sofa and walks over to the bookcase.

"You're always keen to find connections," she says and picks up two photos in frames, the one of me as a holiday rep in Zakynthos, the other of me at a ballet recital as a child. "Little things," she says. "You know, how we both were awkward little ballet dancers as children." She holds the Corfu one to the side of her head. "And how much did you like the haircut I got the other week?"

Oh, God. I'd thought that her haircut reminded me of my

Corfu days. She'd literally copied it from the picture. I look past her at the books on the bookshelf and a realisation slams into my brain.

I've been such an idiot.

Everything was right under my nose in here.

This room contains the Beginners Guide to the life of Hannah Douglas-Jones. The photo of me repping in Corfu. The well-thumbed row of Lisa Jewell books.

"Have you even read any Lisa Jewell?" I whisper.

"Never even bloody heard of her," says Natasha. "But a bit of Wikipedia and some talking points from Google and you're suddenly ready to start a fucking book club. Pathetic really."

I can't believe it. "You did all that in order to ingratiate yourself with me, get cosy in my house."

"And you would have been none the wiser, mate. But you wouldn't let me enjoy it. You forced me to revisit the past. That business of filming me outside the burned out house. That really hurt. Poking a fucking open wound, Hannah. It's traumatic. You might have pretended to be my friend but you were a user, an abuser, like so many others. So I thought, fuck it. She's not going to let me enjoy this life unless I take it from her. So that's what I decided to do."

"Take my life...?"

"If Hannah Douglas-double-fucking-barrelled-Jones wasn't going to let me be part of her life like a normal person then I'd take it from her. Todd ... a dozen other clients. Your job's not difficult really. A bit of charm, some clever ideas. I decided I would just take them from you. A few handy fuck-ups from you along the way, to speed up the process."

"So, you want a leg up in business," I say. I try to say it lightly, as though it doesn't matter. "You've achieved that. You could walk away now and take a bunch of my clients. Leave us alone, huh?"

"Would have been nice," she says. "But then you spoke to the police. You forced me to speak to the police. I think I threw them off well enough, but now, it's a race against time." She looks to the clock above the mantelpiece. "Yeah, I should think I've kept you busy for long enough now."

"Busy?" I frown. "What?"

"Just needed time enough."

"Time enough for what?"

Her gaze is piercing, callous, hateful.

"Time enough for those pills I gave Dad to work."

The bottom drops out of my world.

I run for the doorway. "Dad!"

79

Walker's still looking for traces of Ruby Adams, but he's turned up very little. He's not sure what he expecting to find. He needs to acknowledge this extra presence in his life – a daughter he never knew he had – but he's not sure how.

He has a daughter he's never met. His daughter is Ruby Adams. His daughter was dating Paul Mulholland.

He wonders what she's like. Does she resemble him at all?

Every parent wonders which of their attributes their child might inherit. Will it be looks? Temperament? Taste in food?

Walker sits back from his keyboard. He's overlooked the most obvious source of information. He was in a daze when he left Duncan, or he'd have done it before.

He texts Duncan.

Have you by any chance got a picture of Ruby?

He gets a reply after a few moments.

Gawd. Now you're asking. I'll have a look, see if there's some photos in the bureau.

He sighs heavily.

"Hey, Walker." Josie's staring at him. "You all right?"

Walker stares at the ceiling for a long moment before answering in a calm and measured voice. "I am well."

"*Pfft!*" Josie wheels her chair round to be closer to him. She stares into his face. "What does that mean? You're acting weird."

Walker wants to share his news. It's a secret that he just can't sit on.

He's aware that there is probably a correct way to do this. A correct order to inform people. It's the same when someone dies. You tell the inner circle – close family – before you tell more casual acquaintances.

He should tell Helen and the kids first; of course he should. If they found out in some other way, it would be devastating. Even more devastating than it already is.

"Oh fuck," he says, to himself. "Fuck."

Josie says nothing. She can see that something is overwhelming her colleague. She's there, waiting for him to speak.

There's a clatter from the doorway.

The office – empty apart from Josie and Walker – has a full complement of Dead End Duncans now. Rob's arrived.

"Glad you're both here," he says. "Something interesting's happening and I don't quite know what to make of it."

Josie doesn't take her eyes off Walker, but she lifts her head to acknowledge Rob. "You're not wrong."

Rob walks over and stares at the two of them. He's registered the odd dynamic. "What's going on?"

Walker makes a small, nervous patting gesture. "There's something I need to share with the two of you."

"Right?" Rob drags a chair across. The three of them are now in a tight huddle.

Walker gives a small shake of his head. "Tell us your thing first. I could do with the breathing space."

"I have an update, too," says Josie. "And it's a doozie."

"Me first," says Rob. His face is filled with concern for Walker, but he sits back and pulls out his notebook. "Guys, I popped in on Hannah Douglas-Jones."

Josie leans in, her face amused. "You know that you say her name in a certain tone of voice, don't you?"

"Do I?"

"Yes. It's as if you like saying it. Like it's a tasty treat."

Rob's cheeks flush a little red. "Er, right. Good to know. As I was saying. I went to see our witness. Follow up on our interview with Natasha Dibello."

Josie straightens with interest.

"She was telling me all about the way that Natasha's been acting," Rob says. "I mean, it's a side issue, but it sounds to me as though Natasha has been manipulating Hannah."

Rob reels off some details from his notes. He lists how Natasha's been sidelining clients, inserting herself into Hannah's life in ways that seemed helpful initially, but that now seem more sinister.

"Right. That's horrible and all that," says Josie. "But it's not exactly related to the case, is it?"

"Right. There's this other thing—"

"Nah. Wait. Because I think you need to look at this." She's reached across to grab her laptop. It's open on Instagram. A young woman smiles into the camera. She's holding up a key and standing near to a door.

"Who's that?" asks Rob.

"This is the Instagram account of one Natasha Dibello."

"Not our Natasha."

"Ah, well. She's been in Oxfordshire for a few weeks,

staying with her parents for the summer, but this picture is from last September, when she moved into her accommodation for the start of her second year at university. Recognise the front door?"

Walker nods. "Front door of the property that was destroyed in the fire. Good work, Josie. It's our girl."

Walker sees a look pass between Rob and Josie.

"Yeah. Except it's not our girl," says Rob. "This is not the woman we interviewed."

"What?" says Walker. He didn't see the young woman when she came in to give her statement. He doesn't understand.

"This is not the woman we interviewed," says Josie, "the one who said she was Natasha Dibello."

Walker frowns. "Then who was that?"

Rob taps the bottom of the notebook page he's just been reading from. "Well. That's the other thing I was trying to tell you about what Hannah said. The woman who's staying with Hannah, the one calling herself Natasha... She might be pregnant."

Walker tries to process this.

Josie says what they're all thinking. "Fuck. Could this woman at the Douglas-Jones house be Paul Mulholland's girlfriend? Ruby Adams? That trust fund he was setting up for a new arrival..."

"It's a decent hypothesis," says Rob, pushing his glasses up his nose.

Walker picks up his phone. A photo's come through from Duncan. He clicks on it and holds it up.

"Could this be the woman that you interviewed?" he asks. He hears the tremor in his own voice and wonders if they hear it too.

"Yep. That's her," says Josie.

Rob nods in agreement.

"That's a photo of Ruby Adams," says Walker, jabbing a finger at his phone. "Sent to me by Duncan Flanagan."

He licks his lips. It's time.

"That thing that I wanted to tell you about?" he says.

"Is this really important?" Rob asks, pulling his phone out. "I'm suddenly worried for Hannah."

Walker hesitates and then chooses the cowardly option. "It can wait. Let's do what we need to do."

"You sure?"

"Totally sure."

Rob's jigging his leg with frustration. His call is not being answered. He tries again but gets no result. "She's gone home to confront this woman." He shakes his head, a grim expression on his face. "She has no idea who she's dealing with. It's not some uni student who's overstepped the mark. It's a woman who's part of a criminal network, who escaped from an unexplained fire."

"Yes." Walker can't process this right now. "Of course."

"I'm heading over there," says Rob. "Who's coming with me?"

Josie picks up her jacket. "Yeah. I have questions for that slippery bitch."

Rob looks to Walker. "You okay holding the fort?"

Walker's mind is a whirl of thoughts. "Yeah, yeah. I'm going to see what else I can find out. Call me if you need anything."

80

In the kitchen, Dad's slumped against the arms of the dining chair, unconscious.

I put my hands to his face, his neck.

He murmurs and raises his head.

"Dad! Dad!"

He mumbles something, but he's away with the fairies.

"If you've hurt him..." I snarl at Natasha.

"I didn't want to," she says, breezily. "I was planning on making him my dad at one point."

"Making...?"

"He doesn't know the difference between us. You know that?"

"Fucking psycho!" I hiss and take out my phone. "I'm calling an ambulance!"

"Then you won't know what he's taken. Neither will the paramedics."

I've punched in two of the nines, but I stop before hitting the third.

She wanders over to the units by the sink, opens the top drawer, hums to herself as she decides and then with an 'Ah!' of recognition, takes out the sharp short-bladed vegetable knife.

She flexes her hand around its grip in satisfaction.

"You cut Dad?" I say.

"You made me do it. The police questioned me for hours. I was so angry with you."

"You..." I close my eyes in disgust and fury. "And the thing with Marissa? You fired her. The money she stole."

"The money I put in the drawer before asking her to go get ... I can't even remember what I asked her to get. But you lapped it up without question."

She puts her free hand to her stomach. That business about her being pregnant flits across my mind.

"What have you given Dad?" I demand.

"All in good time. Now, are you calling the ambulance and putting his life at risk, Hannah?"

I hesitate. I back out of the dialling screen. There's my recent calls list. It's a new phone. Hardly any numbers called at all.

"What is it you want from me?"

"What do I want?" Natasha laughs at me. "I want to make some choices in my own life for once."

I must look confused because she nods. She expected this.

"You have no clue how privileged you are, do you? That's the thing about privilege. You think you're having a bad day when you're late for some posh dinner gala. Boo fucking hoo."

She does a little sing-song voice as she mocks me. I've been verbally attacked many times. It's much easier to shrug off a full-on assault than the insidious sense of doubt that Natasha has brought to my life.

"I was going to unlock this fucking Bitcoin, get what's mine and then be out of your hair," she says. "But you decided to be a bitch about it. So I thought, fuck it, might as well take your life."

"What? And become me?"

"Become the daughter Dad deserves," she says. "This house. This business."

"You didn't need to do that. You had other options."

"No. No, I fucking didn't. It's so easy to stand there in your designer heels and believe that the world can be fixed with your sweet talk, your minor bribery, or your slick manoeuvring. It's not like that. Some of us do live in fucking awful situations. The only thing you and I truly have in common is that our mums are dead. Except mine was a sodding addict who killed herself and then I lost the two people who were the only real parents I've known. No family, no home, and the man who should have looked after my interests..." A miserable darkness clouds her face and now both hands go to her stomach.

"You are pregnant then?" I say.

She looks up, angry tears in her eyes. "I have a ticking bomb inside me. I've got needs. And there are certain situations that need someone with the balls to take things further."

"Please," I say, still cradling Dad's head. "Whatever it is, can we get my dad to hospital?"

"I can't remember the Bitcoin seed phrase," she says. "I need to move on. You want rid of me. So we're going to get me some cash and then I'm gone."

"Fine. Fine. Good. How ... how much?"

She wipes the tears away. "I know that your creepy financial guy, Harvey, has received the buyer's deposit for the Brascote buildings."

"Right?"

"We're going to get that."

"That's over fifty thousand pounds. We need that. I need that for Dad's care."

"Yeah, well, me and this bundle of joy need it more. Remember, this is all your doing. I've already messaged him, reminded him of his star turn in that little video."

"You've messaged him?"

"Well, you messaged him. I do have access to your e-mails, as you know."

"He's not going to give you the money."

"I can be persuasive," she says, with a flick of the knife in her hand.

"You've hurt people before?"

She laughs loud now.

"Your debts, Hannah!" she says. "Those people were never going to pay you. Not until they had no choice. That's what I'm talking about. I come from a world where you don't get a choice unless you fight for it."

"Wait, what?" Did she just say what I thought she said? "Are you saying that you threatened violence to get those bills paid?"

She smiles. She huffs on her fingernails and rubs them to a shine on an imaginary lapel. "You're most welcome."

I'm reeling at the idea that she would go round and threaten my clients. Then another penny drops.

"Is that why Georgia Byron gave up her phone with that video of Tyrese?"

I don't even need to see her acknowledgement to know I'm right. Nobody gives up their phone.

Another piece falls into place.

"Karolina," I whisper. "That was you."

Natasha's eyes gleam in the evening light.

"I didn't want to, but she's almost as bad as you. Poking, poking. It hurts. That bitch couldn't just leave me alone, could she?"

"You nearly killed her!"

"I tried to kill her. One shove. Some people stand too close to the road, you know."

I can't believe what I'm hearing. I can't believe I doubted Karolina. The woman who's had my back for years was completely right about what was going on here. The guilt and shame threaten to overwhelm me.

And fear.

Natasha has it all sewn up. I'm almost out of options. I still have my phone in my hand, open at recent calls.

"Sure, sure," I hear myself say. "We'll drive over to Harvey's."

I surreptitiously hit the top number. It's a brand new phone. There's only one person I've had a chance to give this temporary number to, and I hope it was him who just tried to call me. Either that or I'm putting my dad's life on the line with a cold caller.

I blindly call DS Rob Joseph.

81

The traffic on the Hinckley Road is not quite gridlocked, but it's slow going.

Rob's phone is mounted on the dash and it lights up with a call.

"Your girlfriend," says Josie as it the ID comes up as Hannah Douglas-Jones. Rob hits the answer button.

Hannah starts talking as the call is connected.

"How do you see this working Natasha?"

Rob opens his mouth and starts to say something about Hannah being on loudspeaker when another voice is heard.

"It's very simple, Hannah. Less than an hour from now I can be gone and you can get the help you need— Are you on the phone with someone?"

The call is ended abruptly, and there's a brief, surprised silence.

"That was Natasha's voice," says Josie.

"Ruby," says Rob.

"Did that sound like a ... situation to you?" Josie says.

"A situation?"

"Like a hostage thing?"

"It was half a conversation." Rob exhales, thinking.

"I'm not sure it was that," Josie says.

"One way to find out." Rob taps his phone to call Hannah back.

It rings out. No one's answering.

"What do we make of it all?" he says.

"Well," says Josie. "Either something dodgy is going on, or they are trying hard to have a proper conversation without being interrupted."

"What kind of conversation?" Rob asks.

"I reckon you need to put your foot down so we can get there," says Josie. "We debate this too long, then Natasha or Ruby or whoever will be gone."

Rob inclines his head and then huffs at the traffic. "Fair point. It's times like these we could do with one of the unmarked motorway cars. Get the blue lights going."

"Yeah," says Josie.

She looks at the traffic ahead and then reaches over and pushes Rob's horn for him.

"Come on, you lot!" she yells. "Get out of the way."

Meanwhile, Rob takes the more practical option and radios control. "Control, from Tango four-two-four, message."

"*Go ahead, four-two-four.*"

"Four-two-four and four-two-seven are attending a possible domestic incident at the home of Hannah Douglas-Jones on the Hinckley Road near Stanholme. We've just received a disconnected call suggesting a possible disturbance involving a second female, Ruby Adams. We're en route now, ETA ten minutes. Requesting possible back-up on stand-by."

"*Received four-two-four.*"
The traffic starts to move.

82

Natasha insists we take Dad and then refuses to help me carry him to the car.

I get his arm over my shoulder and force him to stand.

He's groggy – like ten pints drunk groggy – but forcing him to move draws a groan from him and he stands.

I don't know if getting him moving and keeping him awake is a good thing, or if we're just speeding the drugs she gave him through his system. Is it sleeping pills? I don't know if Dad had some of them. Or maybe it's some of the powerful painkillers he was taking when he did his back in a few years back. Or has this woman just got a bunch of illegal drugs stashed in her pocket?

Who the hell is she?

The painful facts of the matter are like stabbing wounds in my soul and the knives are still there. She's a woman who painted herself as precisely the individual I wanted her to be. Natasha Dibello – university student, doing a safe and boring degree – polite, intelligent, but with a spark of confidence – a burning desire to learn, to become a newer and better version of me. I never even scratched the surface of who she was. She was just that reflection of me I craved and I didn't look any deeper.

Dad and I make our way down the hallway to the front door. I'm a strong woman and Dad has lost a bit of weight in the last year, but he's not easy to move at all.

"Quicker," says Natasha behind me, the knife in her hand.

I let this woman into my home. I didn't even stop to think. There wasn't a moment's hesitation. I am an idiot.

We struggle with the front door and then Dad and I go out onto the driveway beneath a red sky.

I let her into my workplace. I thought I was keeping her under my watchful eye when, in fact, she was moving in. Systems, passwords, clients – she learned it all. Two weeks. That's all it's been. Two weeks and she soaked it all up like a sponge.

It's crazy.

I hate this young woman now; I hate her with all my heart. For her betrayal, for what she did to me, to Marissa, to my clients, but most of all, for what she's done right now to Dad. I hate her but just as I can't shake the agonising shame and my stupidity, I can't help but admire her for the cunning monster she is.

She's an amazing woman. I truly admire her. And I'm certain that, once Dad is safe, I'm going to kill her. Even if I have to hunt her down to the ends of the earth. I think I'm going to kill her for what she's done.

83

Walker calls Duncan Flanagan. The handset is tight against his ear as it rings.

The rest of his body seems a million miles away. He's still reeling from one shock after another.

"Ey up, Walker," says Duncan.

"Tell me about her," says Walker. He doesn't trust himself to form long, nuanced sentences right now.

Duncan's sigh is long and loud. It's an old man's sigh.

"Huh. What do you want to know, mate?"

"Everything." He knows that's not helpful and immediately adds, "You've known Ruby in recent years."

"I suppose so."

"What's she like?"

"Like?"

Walker's looking at the information on his office computer screen. The details of the fire on Narborough Road, the financial transactions linked to Paul Mulholland, crime intelligence maps linking Mulholland to the Degutis gang and others.

"As a person," he says. "As an adult. What's she like?"

Duncan pauses before answering.

"She had less time for me in recent years, I guess. You know how it is. When you're younger you have all these people who you call 'aunt' or 'uncle' but you eventually realise they're just people your parents knew. I went from being Uncle Duncan to that bloke who knew her mum before she died to ... to that weird ex-copper who showed too much interest. Me and her new life, they weren't exactly compatible."

"She knew Paul Mulholland, right?"

Duncan makes a thinking noise. *"Brendan O'Malley was using Mulholland to handle some of his so-called business dealings, I guess. As Brendan and Kath got older, Ruby was handling more things for them."*

"She a drug-dealer?"

"I think she had bigger ambitions than that. She—" Duncan goes silent.

"What?" says Walker.

"It's tempting to say she had a chip on her shoulder."

"Right? So did she?"

"She's an angry young woman. She's very angry. Life has dealt her the shittiest of hands. She never knew her real dad. Her pretend dad, Adams, walked out on them. Her mum, Leanne, chose heroin over her daughter. It's not a happy story. She had a lot of resentment inside her."

Walker thinks about what the Duncans uncovered about Mulholland.

"Any chance she had a relationship with Mulholland?"

"A relationship? Like...?" Duncan blows out breath noisily on the line. *"I'd say no, but you and I both know how easy it is to make bad decisions."*

It's a grim thought.

"Mulholland had convictions for violence against women," says Walker.

"Hmmm. I think Leanne Church's girl's the kind to give as good as she gets. Like I say, a chip on her shoulder; resentment. Hate to think what she might be like when backed into a corner."

Walker thinks of Mulholland, dead in a house fire. The pathologist said it had been a massive head injury that had killed him though, not the fire.

"Right," says Walker. "Good to know."

84

On the driveway, I unlock the Jag remotely.

"Put him in front," says Natasha.

I look at her.

"Him in the front. You drive. I'll sit behind you. And then we go to Harvey's."

Dad is a dead weight.

"Get the door then," I grunt.

She hesitates a moment, then, never turning her back on me, moves round and opens the front passenger door. Dad and I nearly fall in. I have to drop low to avoid cracking his head on the door frame.

"Where we goin'?" he mumbles.

"Taking you to the hospital, Dad," I say, trying my best to conceal the mix of horror and delight at hearing him still speaking. "You've had a reaction to your tablets."

I let him slide off my arm. He's at an odd angle but he's safely in. I turn on Natasha.

"What is it? The, um, Donepezil? Tramadol?"

"When we're done."

I look at the knife held low in her hands.

With her canvas bag containing her laptop, my phone and not much else, she gets into the back, directly behind Dad.

It's just me on the driveway. I could run back inside right now if I wanted. I could lock the door. I could go to the landline phone and dial 999.

The fact that she thinks I won't – the fact she *knows* I won't – is both gut-wrenching and chilling. I feel powerless.

I go round and get in. Seatbelt on, I reach over and do Dad's too. I put my hand to his face. Does he feel cool to the touch? I can't trust myself to be sure.

"Harvey's house," Natasha reminds me.

"Yes, I'm doing it," I say.

I start the engine. The warning light flickers on the dashboard and I have a momentary panic that it's just going to die on me. After a moment's hesitation, the engine rumbles into life.

"Drive sensibly," says Natasha. "No speeding. Put it on the satnav so I can see where we're going."

"Of course," I say.

I force fresh confidence I don't feel into my words. I've been brought low, embarrassed and degraded. I try to take control of myself at least.

I'm Hannah Douglas-Jones. I've spent the last decade working in one customer-facing role or another. I know how people work. I know how people think. I know how to project a personality that people respond to.

Natasha Dibello – or whoever this woman really is – is perhaps the toughest customer I've ever faced, but in a sense, that's all she is. I need to massage her ego, make her feel like she's in charge and that I'm someone she can trust. And then

I steer her, like any client. If I've ever had the skill to nudge people towards doing the things I want, then I really need to employ that skill now.

Harvey Kenelm, lives in Houghton on the Hill. It's a village as close to Leicester as our house but way over on the other side. The satnav says it's a forty minute journey.

Forty minutes. Every moment that Dad is in a groggy, insensible state is torture.

Natasha sees the journey time on the satnav screen but says nothing.

I set off. I pull out onto the lane and turn towards the city.

Natasha immediately winds down her window to toss something out. That'll be my phone.

A hundred yards down the road, we pass a car in a lay-by. I've got enough on my mind and wouldn't notice it normally but that registration number. *HDJ*. My initials. It's the same car I saw next to near my office yesterday. The one with the man inside.

Coincidence?

I look in the rearview mirror once we've driven past.

The HDJ car lets another car go past, then pulls out and follows us towards the city.

85

Rob accelerates hard once they're free of the city traffic.

Josie has been getting to know Rob better since she's been made one of the Duncans. He doesn't seem to be the kind of bloke who gets over-excited by prestige cars and motorsports. He seems to want to paint himself as a man of culture and high-brow interests. However, she's noticed that, given the chance to drive at reckless speeds along country roads, he absolutely will.

He overtakes several vehicles along the A-road out of town. The road has few bends but the traffic offers limited opportunities for overtaking.

The last mile, he's nudging seventy-five miles an hour at times.

"There," he says.

Josie lets out a low whistle. Hannah Douglas-Jones's place is *nice*. Or, at least, it's large. It's not a mansion, but it's the kind of big old house that would have had servants when it was first built, in Victorian times or whatever. It's the kind of house that Josie will never ever own, never ever live in. It's a rich person's house.

"This Hannah is way out of your league, sarge," she says.

"Mind on the job, Josie," he says as he pulls into the driveway.

He's worried. Josie can hear it in his voice.

"There's no cars here," she notes.

"She drives a big Jaguar X351," says Rob. "Technically belongs to her dad."

Josie casts her mind back and wonders if they might have passed one on the way here.

"How are we playing this?" says Josie.

Rob's just staring.

"Rob," she says.

He comes back to the moment.

"We arrest Natasha Dibello – Ruby Adams, whatever name she's going by. She lied in the police interview. That's wasting police time as a bare minimum. We don't arrest her on any larger charges yet."

"Got it." Josie looks at lights that are on in some upper windows. "And if something bad has gone down."

"Dynamic assessment. Call for back-up at the very first sign of trouble."

Josie nods curtly and gets out.

They approach the house together, but at enough distance apart to give them space. Josie consciously holds her hand near her radio button.

She scans the windows for signs of movement.

"Well, that's not good," says Rob.

"Huh?"

He points. The front door is slightly ajar.

Rob steps ahead and places a hand on the door to push it slowly open.

"This is the police! Is anyone home?"

There's no reply.

"We're coming in! If anyone's inside, make yourself known!"

Rob steps into the gloomy hallway. Josie follows.

86

It might be a Saturday, but there's still an evening rush hour traffic in Leicester. We're moving slowly down Uppingham Road, heading east out of the city, when Dad stirs suddenly with a snort.

"Where are we going?" he mumbles.

My heart leaps. He's still with us.

"We're off to Harvey's, Dad," says Natasha from the back, putting a hand on his shoulder.

I want to snap that he's not her dad, that she doesn't get to talk to him with any warmth. But I hold my tongue. I'm going to stay in control now.

"We're ten minutes away," I say. "Come on, Natasha, why don't you tell me what you gave him?"

"I will. When we're done."

Done. I still can't believe that we're going to walk into Harvey's house and he's going to hand over cash or a cheque or whatever Natasha thinks she's going to get. She's got the bag with the laptop inside it on her knee.

"That Bitcoin on the laptop," I say. "It belonged to the man in the house? Paul Mulholland."

"It belonged to me."

I look at her in the rear view mirror, try to read her face.

"You weren't just a student living in that house, were you?"

She shakes her head tersely. "*She* went home for the summer or whatever. I needed an identity for a while."

"Natasha Dibello is a real person, huh. Studying tourism and stuff."

"I've no idea. Never spoke to her. Only saw her once."

"But you lived there too? Or didn't live there?"

Natasha grunts, a forced laugh. "I was living anywhere. I wasn't living. Paul thought we had something."

"You're pregnant with his child."

"Shut up. Just cos he got me pregnant, doesn't make it his." She mutters something I don't properly hear, then makes some angry noises. "I had no choice."

There's always choice, I think. Even when things are terrible and rotten, there's always a choice. But I'm not going to tell her that.

"No choice, in what way?" I ask gently.

She inhales sharply. I can almost hear her thought processes. She's angry. She's in the middle of angry deeds. She's drugged my dad and she's taking me at knife point to steal tens of thousands of pounds from us. We're not friends any longer. She doesn't want pleasant chit-chat with me. And yet. She's carrying all manner of inner turmoil around with her. Who else is she going to confide in? How else will she get it off her chest?

"You never gone with a guy because you needed to?" she says. "Safety? Protection? A roof over your head?"

"I guess I've been lucky," I say.

"Yeah, you fucking have." She sniffs. "Paul Mulholland was a monster. Seriously. An actual monster. The things he was involved in."

"The women in the basement."

"He was holding them for someone else. Making them work in that kitchen. He was moving stolen goods. Handling dirty money. That's just business. I mean he was an absolute shit of a human being. He broke his last girlfriend's jaw."

"He hit her?"

She laughs. "What the fuck do you think? I mean he hits women, yeah. It's not even one of those moments of rage things. He just does it. That kind of monster."

A psychologist could have a field-day with Natasha, unpicking how she sees the people trafficking thing as 'just business' and the domestic violence as something lower than that, something monstrous. The idea that things are only evil if they could possibly happen to her.

"What happened that night?" I ask.

"Hmmm?"

"The night of the fire. What happened?"

She glances about. It's just us and the car and the road out into the country, housing becoming more sporadic, the landscape opening up into farmland, trees lining the side of the road.

"I'm nearly four months pregnant, I think," she says.

"You've not been for a scan?"

"I could've got rid of it. I've got no interest in starting a family with him. I don't need this in my life right now."

"But you're keeping the baby?"

"You think I'm not capable of giving love to someone?"

"I didn't say that."

"I told Paul about it a few weeks back, not long after Kath died."

"Who's Kath?"

"Shut up. I told him and I thought he'd drive me to the abortion clinic immediately, but he was ... excited. He was fucking thrilled. Can you imagine that? The look on his face was.... Ah, it was nauseating. *I* was pregnant and *he* wanted us to have a baby. It's not his fucking baby."

"I understand." I don't really, not exactly, but she wants me to understand so I'll play along.

"He started putting money aside. Even set up one of them —" she laughs "—you know, a trust fund. He was willing to put money aside for the baby when there's me – me, who's actually owed the money he was looking after for Kath and Brendan – having to beg for every tenner he gave me."

"He owed you six million?"

"He was holding it for a bunch of people. Some real shits. But no one deserves it more than me. Oh, how he made me beg."

"He was controlling," I prompt.

"Yes, but don't think he was clever with it. He was just a greedy evil fucker. And now he wanted us to be a family. Me and him? Makes me fucking shudder."

"Who's swearing?" mumbles Dad next to me.

"Don't worry, Dad. Almost there," I say.

"I'd had enough," says Natasha. "I went over. I was going to take the money we needed, me and the bump here, and leave. Why am I telling you this?"

"Because you want to."

"You're fucking slick, Hannah. You know that. Think you can get your way if you just say the right words."

"I'm just trying to get the right resolution for everyone."

Another laugh.

"I killed him in the kitchen," she says, matter-of-factly. "There were words. He raised his voice. I don't know what fucking audience he thought he was performing to. It was only me."

"You were frightened."

She makes a thoughtful noise. "You can't be frightened all the time. Eventually, you get used to the threats. That's why he always needed to escalate. Shouting isn't enough, so it becomes a slap. That's why he ended up breaking that stupid cow's jaw. No, I wasn't frightened. I'd had enough then. I hit him with a frying pan. Yeah, like in a cartoon. But I hit him hard and he went down. It's not easy to knock someone out. Not really. I was ready to hit him a second time. Maybe switch the pan for a knife. There were plenty of them about. But down he went. Dead or out cold."

"Understandable. He was your abuser and—"

"Don't use that word."

"What?"

"It gives him fucking credit he doesn't deserve. He wasn't my anything. He was the shit on the bottom of my shoe and I'd had enough."

"Okay."

"I went to his office-den-crappy-man-cave thing and got the laptop. He had almost no cash on the premises. I packed it all up and I was going to just head out of there. But then I had to stop. I couldn't leave Paul alive. I couldn't have him coming after me. I sure as fuck couldn't have the people he worked for come looking for me or the money."

"Who did he work for?"

"Bad people. The kind of people your sort never meet. Relentless cunts."

I think of the man with the HDJ registration plate car that I've seen three times now and wonder if those bad people are closer than Natasha realises. Perhaps people who want their share of the six million back.

"I couldn't leave that place and let it look like I'd done ... well, what I'd actually done," says Natasha. "So I set the place on fire." She gives a scoffing laugh. "It's actually hard to set a kitchen on fire when you've suddenly got to do it. The place was filthy. Congealed grease in the duct vents. Should have gone straight up. But I was arsing about with cardboard and plastic tubs and trying to get any of it to catch. I turned on the fryer full of oil up to max. It was pathetic. I think I was panicking at that point. All it needed was time, but I'd gone back to his office to get more paper to fuel it when it caught proper." She laughs. "Yeah. Nearly got caught in my own blaze."

"The women in the cellar," I say.

"What about them?"

"What about them? You knew they were there, right? Did you think of them?"

There's silence from the back seat for a time. "Whose story is this?" she demands.

"Sorry?"

"This isn't about the women in the cellar. I'm not responsible for everyone else's well-being."

"But you knew they were down there?"

"What are you trying to say?" Her voice is suddenly hard, sullen even. "You think you can hold me responsible for what happened? I barely got out with my life. I didn't transport them over here. I didn't decide they should work for no wages in a scummy fast-food kitchen. I didn't do that."

"I didn't say you did," I suggested, aiming for calm.

"Fucking bitch," she mutters. "Making out it's my fault. I barely got out with my life."

She's a clever woman. I've seen that over the past few weeks. She's a bright young thing; but the gulf between her actions and her willingness to accept what she's done is vast. She murdered a man, an evil man perhaps, but she murdered him. She murdered six women she knew were trapped in that cellar. She's given my dad God knows what in order to coerce me to do her bidding.

She thinks Paul Mulholland was a monster.

I'm very much of the opinion that he wasn't the only one in that relationship.

87

Walker sits in the office and stares at the photo Duncan sent him.

It's a candid picture of Ruby Adams; taken, if Walker's not mistaken, in the Lion Pub in New Parks.

Ruby isn't smiling. She's looking across at someone else out of shot.

She's a young woman of average height and build, with loose curls of dark hair around her face. Very average in many ways, but Walker can't help but see the resemblances between Ruby and his daughter Amber. The shape of her nose. The set of her eyes. Sisters. Or half-sisters anyway. Amber has an older sister. Walker's not even doubting the truth of what Duncan told him. He can see it now.

He has three children when he thought he only had two.

Ruby, Amber, Oscar.

Helen is absolutely going to divorce him when she finds out. Their lives have been on separate tracks for a long time now, each in their own pleasant busy world of middle-aged work and hobbies. But to discover her husband – fiancé at the time – had not only cheated on her but had a child in the process... Walker can't see his marriage as anything but over. Though he's still angry for being kept in the dark, he can now understand why Duncan never said anything for all those years.

His phone rings. It's Rob.

"Hey, Rob."

"They're not here."

"At the Douglas-Jones house?"

"They're not here. It's empty."

"Okay. You sure they were there?"

"Mate, I don't know. The front door was open. She's got a dad with dementia who doesn't stray far from home. I've got a bad feeling about this."

Walker pulls a tight face even though there's no one in the office to see it.

"I'd ask the neighbours, but this place is out in the sticks," says Rob.

Rob's the kind of sergeant who will happily take advice from his constables, and despite their relative ranks, he knows Walker's got two extra decades of experience.

"We could make an emergency request for her phone data," says Walker. "You have her number, right? We'd have to get Scabbard or the duty DI to authorise that. Or we cast the net wide on ANPR, see if a camera spots their car anywhere. Except we don't know what car they might be in."

"She drives a Jag." There's a breathy, humourless laugh from Rob. *"I had to speak to her when her dad reported it stolen. Shit. I've probably even got it written down somewhere."* There's rustling on the line. *"Walker. See if you can get hold of a DI to authorise the phone and ANPR. I'll get the reg to you."*

The call ends.

Walker takes several steps towards Scabbard's office even though he knows the detective inspector isn't in. It's Saturday evening. Unless they're on cases with active leads, a lot of CID officers only work Monday to Friday. The Narborough Road fire is an open investigation, but a lot of that has shifted over to Organised Crime under DI Bacon.

Walker finds Scabbard's work mobile number and calls. It rings for a long time.

"Scabbard."

"Sir, it's DC Smith."

"Yep. What is it?"

Scabbard's tone is clipped. There's noise on the line, a general hubbub. Scabbard sounds like he's in a shop. No, a restaurant. Walker can picture him, stepped away from his table, maybe to a corridor or entrance to take this call.

"Sir, I'm calling to ask for an urgent ANPR search and phone location data on a suspect and individuals potentially in danger."

"What suspect?"

"Mulholland case. We believe that his associate, Ruby Adams, possibly linked to the fire, is with Hannah Douglas-Jones, the witness from the fire."

"What?"

"Mulholland case, sir. I—"

"This is the first time I've heard these names, Walker."

This isn't true. The Douglas-Jones woman has been mentioned several times in briefing.

"Ruby Adams is the real name of Natasha Dibello, the survivor of the fire," says Walker.

"How long have you known this?"

"About an hour, sir."

"And what are you even doing looking into this? This is all in

Organised Crimes's hands now. It's fucking Saturday evening, Walker. I am off-duty."

"I know, sir."

"You can't spring shit on me when I'm out on a date. How's that look?"

For the briefest moment, Walker's mind dwells on the word 'date'. Scabbard is married but also, according to office gossip, treats marriage vows as a set of flexible guidelines rather than any ironclad commitment to his wife.

"Sir," says Walker, "I can explain everything but—"

"Yes. Good. You do that," says Scabbard. *"I want a clear report. Bullet points. Not paragraphs. Get that sent over to me and I'll have a look."*

Walker's about to argue, then Scabbard says, *"Shit. Mains are coming. Bitch ordered the most expensive steak,"* and ends the call.

Walker stares at the phone.

Scabbard wants it all written in a report before he'll authorise anything. Bullet points, not paragraphs.

"To hell with that," he says and sets off to find the duty DI.

Downstairs in another suite of offices, he sees a detective sergeant and then, in a side office, DI Neelam Gill, who must have pulled the short straw for this weekend and is the station's duty detective inspector.

Walker raps on her door.

Neelam Gill is young (at least in Walker's eyes) and is both intelligent and principled, a rare combination.

"Ma'am," he says, "can I have an urgent word?"

She deliberately sets aside the mouse she was holding.

"What is it, Walker?"

Outlining the whole case at speed is not easy, not if Walker's going to make any sense. But he does his best. The fire at the Narborough Road house. The one apparent survivor, a student who somehow found her way into Hannah Douglas-Jones's confidence and home. The links between Paul Mulholland, the Degutis gang and, via the O'Malleys, this Ruby Adams character who might have been Mulholland's girlfriend; might even be the mother of his child.

Only then does it occur to Walker that he might not only have a previously unknown child, but also a grandchild on the way.

He leans against a filing cabinet for support as a wave of dizziness crashes over him and he tries to continue with his explanation.

"This Adams/Dibello character is with the Douglas-Joneses now, and possibly means them some harm. She is also potentially our key suspect in the fire that killed Mulholland. Motive unknown."

He realises he needs to stop talking. Gill has already picked up her office phone to make a call.

"You have the car VRM and the phone number?" she asks.

"I do," he says, before checking if that's true.

He looks at his phone. Rob has messaged him both phone number and number plate. He shows her the phone.

"Okay, let's get this done," she says.

88

I drive into Houghton on the Hill. Left at the petrol station.

Dad makes some murmur of recognition, but he's not talking a lot now.

"Dad? You know where we are?"

I don't want him slipping into unconsciousness. I could do with concentrating on Dad, but now I'm picking my way around the winding back streets of the village. It's narrow, and parked cars make it narrower.

"How much fuel is in the tank?" Natasha asks.

I glance at the gauge. That electrical warning light is back on. "About a third of a tank," I say. "You'll get a hundred and fifty miles, easily."

She plans to take the car. On the one hand, I want her to be far away from me, far away from Dad. On the other hand I really do now want to kill her.

"Which house is it?" Natasha asks. "I want you to slow down, but don't stop. You'll drive past it and then come back again."

I do as she says, pointing out Harvey's tall Georgian house on the right.

"On the driveway. Reverse in so it's pointing out."

I park the car and twist around to look at her. I don't know what she plans to do next.

"Out," she says, jerking a thumb towards the house.

"What about Dad?"

"He'll be fine here."

"I'm not sure he will. He might wander off—"

"He's not going to get far in that state."

I'm boiling with anger now. She has no right to be this callous with Dad. He's given her nothing but affection.

"You can't make us do this. It's—"

People talk about things moving too fast to see, but I do not see the punch coming. I'm partway through a sentence and then I'm jerking back, this white hot pain radiating from my nose.

I twist in my seat, hands to my face. My eyes water and I can't stifle a gasping groan.

"You do what I fucking tell you," says Natasha, her voice cold and hateful.

I inspect my hands, expecting there to be blood. There's none.

"Get out," says Natasha. "And don't argue with me again."

I follow her to Harvey's front door. It's painted in glossy dark blue, so shiny it could have been done yesterday. My nose is throbbing violently. I press my fingers to the sides of it as though I can hold in the pain.

Natasha bangs the fancy brass knocker. It makes a thunderous noise.

Harvey appears, his face set to admonish whoever's disturbing the peace; then he sees the two of us, and his expression changes. Something like confusion and distaste are competing for control.

"Hannah. Natasha."

He looks down and sees the knife in Natasha's hand. "What nonsense is this?" he says. "If it's a joke, I don't appreciate it."

"Back inside, you fat fuck," says Natasha.

His mouth hangs a little.

"She's not joking," I say.

He points at the knife like he's somehow in charge. "You can't be out and about with a knife. A blade more than three inches—"

Natasha steps forward and presses the tip of the blade against his belly.

"Ow!" He recoils. The sheer disbelief on his face is unmeasurable. "This is not funny!"

"Inside." Natasha pushes me in ahead of her.

Harvey backs down the hallway. He looks to me.

"This isn't real, is it?"

"I told you we were coming," says Natasha. "We want the money."

He seems to be slowly catching up with the true situation.

"You know I have some workmen in the kitchen?" Harvey says. "Fitting a new counter."

Harvey is not an accomplished liar. Nervousness is making him look like a sweaty, overgrown schoolboy.

"Harvey," says Natasha.

"What?"

"Harvey," she repeats.

He blinks and focuses on her.

"I'm gonna make things absolutely fucking crystal clear," Natasha says. "If there's anyone else in this house, then you have ten seconds to work out how to get rid of them. If you can't do that then we're going to have a problem. Got it?"

She holds the knife upright and jabs it violently in an ultra-realistic mime of gutting a person straight up between the ribs.

Now that he's on the same page as the rest of us, Harvey looks as though he wants to vomit.

"And you're part of this, are you?" he asks me.

"She's drugged Dad," I say, simply.

Natasha raises her eyebrows. "Now. Why don't you take us to where the money is?"

I sense mild unease from Natasha as she glances at the various doorways off the hall. I think she's intimidated by the grandeur of this house. Well, to hell with her and her crippling class consciousness.

Harvey is slow to move. He pulls himself together and moves towards the door that's slightly ajar on the left.

He leads us through into a lounge that's furnished like a cross between a gentleman's club and a hotel lobby. It's all leather armchairs, low lighting and whisky decanters, clustered around a fireplace. The wallpaper is tartan, and there's even a stuffed pheasant under a glass dome. He was clearly going for a look and nailed it.

"Take a seat," he says.

It's a decent effort at asserting some control.

"Shut the fuck," says Natasha, standing. "Where's the money?"

"I don't actually have..." The sentence wilts as he looks at the knife.

Harvey turns to the wall to the right of the fireplace. A gaudy oil painting of some dahlias hangs there. It looks ghastly on top of the tartan wallpaper. Turns out that it's hiding a door.

"An actual hidden safe," Natasha says. "Harvey, you are properly fucking minted, aren't you?"

"It's for my business clients," Harvey says. It's a little too fast, and a little too defensive. Natasha picks up on it.

"Open it up."

Harvey's nostrils flare. "Put the knife down, please. All I'm doing is retrieving Hannah's money for her. There's no need for any theatricals."

Natasha's strides over to him. She's half his size, but he half raises his hands in surrender fashion. The knife flashes and suddenly the tip of it is in the side of his neck and he's screaming.

"It's just a little prick," hisses Natasha.

She steps back. Harvey's hand goes to his neck and he whimpers as it comes away slick with blood.

I want to act. There's no way Natasha can overcome both Harvey and me, armed with only a knife, but she's still the only one who knows what pills Dad has taken.

I see Harvey look at me. His expression pleads for me to help him.

"She's got Dad," I say to him. I shake my head. "Pills. He's taken something bad."

"And time is running out," Natasha says. "Tick tock." She's talking brightly now, as if she's a children's TV presenter. "Open the safe, Harvey. Nice and easy. Get everything out."

"Oh no, I don't think—"

"Everything. Don't make me stab you."

I can't believe that Harvey could be so dumb. He practically spelled out that he's got more in there than just my money. Of course Natasha wants to take it all.

He enters a code on a keypad.

He swings the door open and empties the contents onto a small table.

There's a small cash box, a larger box that looks as if it might be for jewellery, and some stacks of notes.

"Find a bag for that lot," says Natasha. "It's all going with me."

"A bag?" Harvey manages to look as though he doesn't know what one is.

"Kitchen!" Natasha barks. "Just a bag. Bring it all with you."

As she looks around, maybe scanning the room for a suitable bag, I can't be sure but I think I see Harvey furtively take something from the safe and slip it in his pocket.

89

Walker's back at his desk.

He phones Rob while he gets a map up on his screen.

"Rob," says Walker without preamble. "The ANPR data shows Hannah's car going east on the A47. Just passed Thurnby."

Rob's got his phone on speaker. Walker can hear Josie talking.

"*They going to Peterborough*?" she suggests.

"*Not sure*," says Rob, slowly. "*There's a guy who looks after Hannah's money who lives out that way. Houghton on the Hill? She said he lives in some massive house*."

"Do you have a name?" Walker asks.

It takes Rob a few moments to remember the name, or maybe he's consulting his notes. "*Harvey Kenelm*."

Walker's hands clatter over his keyboard as he runs some searches. "He's got a financial consultancy company listed at a Houghton on the Hill address. Looks as if it's a residential property." He gives Rob the postcode.

Rob groans. "*It's a forty minute drive from here or thereabouts.*"

"I'm as close, coming from the city centre," says Walker. "I'll leave now."

He grabs his keys. Neelam Gill appears in the corridor as he's leaving.

"Any results?" she asks.

"Ah, yes, ma'am. We've located the car. It's on the way to the Douglas-Jones' finance guy. Heading there now."

"You have the address?"

Walker nods.

"Do we know if the suspect is armed at all?"

"We don't." Walker tries to make it sound like the lack of any problem, rather than the lack of information, but the DI's smarter than that.

She looks at him and is about to speak, then she pauses and inhales. "Make sure to send me that address before you leave. And I want you to check in with me personally before you engage with anyone. I'll get some uniformed backup to join you."

"Yes, ma'am."

Walker continues to his car, sending the address to DI Gill.

He's not sure what Ruby's end game is here.

Harvey's the money guy. Does Ruby want some of it? Is she heading towards a confrontation?

Hate to think what she might be like when backed into a corner. That's what Duncan Flanagan had said.

Walker hurries to his car.

90

Natasha forces Harvey and me towards the kitchen.

She pauses in the doorway, distracted by its size and opulence. "This kitchen is fucking massive."

It's one of those kitchens where an entire family could entertain themselves while someone's cooking. There's a large table, set into a bay window at the end that faces the garden. There's a huge Aga cooker. It's a sizeable enough room that there's an island in the middle with boards and a knife rack.

Natasha sees me looking at the knives in the block on the wooden counter.

"Don't even think about it," she says.

"You've got the money," I say.

Harvey has got the contents of the safe in his arms. "It's all covered by the insurance," he says, as though that means anything right now.

Natasha's at the Aga now, and she's lifted the boiling

plate. It's the heavy circular lid that exposes the hottest part. I can see glowing hot coals under there.

Maybe I can plant the thought that she's being pursued.

"You've got a head start on anyone who might come after you," I say.

"Nobody's coming after me," she says. "No one."

That 'no one' includes us. Her words chill me, and I know that I need to act.

"Can you at least tell me what pills Dad's taken now?" I ask.

She ignores my question.

"What's in there?" Natasha points to a door off to the side.

"Utility," croaks Harvey.

"Open it. I need a bag. A carrier. Anything." She swings to me. "You get over here, where I can see you."

I do as she says. As her head turns back to Harvey, I manage to snag something from the shelf of implements next to me. I am pretty sure it's a meat tenderiser, a little hammer with a studded head for pounding steaks. I drop my arm to the side, shielding it with my body. Its weight in my grip is a small comfort.

Harvey is in the utility space.

"That bag," says Natasha. "Gimme that."

It's a Waitrose insulated cool bag, but it's big enough for everything in Harvey's safe. "And that bottle. Grab it now." Natasha points. Harvey grabs the cool bag and retrieves the bottle. Natasha snatches it from him. It's a large bottle of pink liquid. Paraffin.

The paraffin. The exposed coals of the Aga. The pieces slot into place.

She has no intention of letting us go. Any of us.

91

Walker thought he might be able to make the journey east over to Houghton on the Hill far faster than Rob and Josie, but Leicester city traffic is crawling. The light-controlled junction where Humberstone Road meets Dysart Way near the Probation Service building is chock-a-block.

He sits in traffic that's bumper to bumper while thoughts cascade in an unstoppable procession through his mind.

Ruby Adams. His daughter.

How could anyone have kept that secret from him?

It's not a hidden little secret, parcelled up in words. This was a baby, a child, a growing girl. More than twenty years and this has all been hidden from him. A life.

She'd grown up and he'd missed it all.

She'd had a mother, but had that been enough?

Walker's memories of Leanne Church were both hazy and crystal clear. Lots of details were missing, yet those key impressions, those vital slivers of memory, remained strong.

Leanne Church was attractive, no doubt about it. She had

a brassy, confident air. She wore clothes that made no attempt to conceal the shape of her body, the round curves. Whatever assets she had, she had them on show and she didn't care who was looking.

Physically and personality-wise she was attractive. To have her attention lavished on you was to be singled out. But the biggest factor of all, the reason that Walker fell into a relationship with her? It was simply that she was there.

They'd spent a night together round at her place after a night at the Lion. Leanne was in her twenties and living with her parents, but the parents were out or away somewhere. Maybe Walker and Leanne attempted sex that night but they were both too drunk. He couldn't properly remember but he was sure nothing at all actually happened. They slept, pressed together on her single bed.

But the next day, as the mid-morning light filtered through the curtains, they'd spooned, dry-mouthed, laughing as they recalled the excesses of the night before. Half-hearted contact became more urgent. They had sex in twisted sheets in the same bedroom she'd been in all her life. Walker had a fiancée – miles away – but in that moment sex seemed inevitable, animalistic. In his stupid, hungover, *young* head it was destiny. Just that once. It had to happen.

And it had happened like that several times. It wasn't romantic – it was something far simpler.

Walker has no idea how he'd have reacted if Leanne had got in touch months later, told him about the baby. He'd have attempted to do the right thing, he's certain. He's not sure what that might have looked like, but his life could have taken a very different course.

But he married Helen. She's his wife. Helen is the mother of Amber and Oscar. That's his current life.

He pictures himself walking into his family home and unleashing this news.

He can't picture it as anything other than an act of extreme destruction.

And that baby? She is now a young woman, grown up amongst criminals, thugs. She's been ignored and abused, so that her anger is honed into a weapon.

He has no idea what she's done recently, nor what she might be capable of.

Walker wants to believe that a child of his would have some inherent goodness, but he knows enough about people to understand that's not how life works. Situations mould people, make them who they are.

And on top of everything, this new daughter of his is pregnant.

A new life.

Walker had imagined becoming a grandparent, of course he had.

This was not the way he'd pictured things, not at all.

His mind shifts the pieces around, trying to see a way that this can all work out well. He's not able to see it.

The lights change and he is up against the bumper of the vehicle in front as they move forward.

92

Natasha's going to set the house on fire with us in it. I just know it.

I need to act.

Natasha puts the paraffin down by the open top of the Aga. She has Harvey bring the bag to the kitchen island and dump the safe's contents into the bag.

She's going to take the items, start getting reckless with the paraffin, then take the Jag with or without my dad in it.

She's going to kill us and escape and right now, unless I do something, she's just going to get away with it.

As she's turned towards Harvey, I step behind her and bring the meat tenderiser down as hard as I can straight on her head.

I am a tall woman, and I put in a lot of strength. I've got a lot of anger to channel. It connects on her head above her ear. There is a solid *thunk* and she staggers. Her hair tangles in the tenderiser as she pulls away. There's blood on the studs of the little hammer, blood in the matted hair

"You..." She grunts, hazily lifting a hand to her head.

Her feet nearly go from under her but she manages to stay upright.

I've not knocked her down. I've not bashed her brains in. She touches the wound. Blood is coming through her hair: oozing, not gushing.

She seems to be struggling to focus.

Harvey is clumsily feeling around in his pocket and produces that thing he'd grabbed from the safe. For a moment I think it's a man's electric razor, then he finds the button on the side and a finger-width of white electricity arcs at the end.

Holy shit. I think it's a taser. Harvey really did have something useful in the safe!

"Get her!" I say.

He steps forward but he's too slow.

His approach forces her to focus. He moves in closer, taser out, but it's a timid action – more like he's offering it than threatening. With her bloodied hand, she bats the taser hand aside, then thrusts with the knife, straight in his shoulder. It sinks an inch.

Harvey yells.

The taser drops to the floor with a plastic clatter.

She whirls on me. The stream of blood from where I hit her covers her ear and is down to her chin.

She grabs the front of my blouse and yanks me forward. I am instantly unbalanced. Natasha pulls me down and brings a knee up into my face.

The pain makes me reel backwards across the kitchen. My hands go instinctively to my face and come away covered with blood.

Natasha has barely broken her stride. She's zipped up the contents of the safe in the Waitrose cool bag and slung its strap over her shoulder.

She takes the top off the paraffin.

And then Harvey's doorbell rings.

93

The three of us freeze in place.

I'm against the sink, clutching my bleeding face. Harvey is slumping, gasping, at the island counter. Blood is spreading through his shirt from the stab wound in his shoulder.

Nastasha, a deranged set to her eyes now, looks at me.

"Maybe it's your dad, Hannah," she muses. She touches the wound in her head again. "Fuck!" She looks at the tenderiser on the floor. "What the fuck is that thing?"

The doorbell rings again.

"We're going to ignore it," says Natasha. "He'll give up and go away."

God, I hope it is Dad. I want him conscious. I want him moving. I have no idea if she gave him enough pills to kill him or not, but I'm frantic with worry.

The doorbell rings again, insistent and urgent.

"It could be a neighbour, worried about Dad if he's got out of the car," I suggest. "They might call the police if they think he's not being cared for."

"I won't be here long enough for that to matter," says Natasha.

And then there's a huge thumping crunch. The door being kicked in.

It must be the police! It's the police with a battering ram! They've come to save us!

I move round the kitchen, holding onto the counter to look down the hallway.

The front door swings on its hinges.

But it's Dad that's coming in. I don't understand.

"Dad!"

Then I realise that he's not alone. The man with the thick blond hair has a hand on his shoulder, propelling him through the hallway and into the kitchen.

"Who the fuck are you?" says Natasha.

I see the blond man has a gun pressed into Dad's spine. A handgun. An actual gun.

The gunman steps fully into the room and pushes Dad aside. I rush to catch him before he falls, but we're as unsteady as one another.

"I don't feel well," says Dad, clutching onto my shoulders with fingers bunched into claws. "Why are we at Harvey's?" He blinks blearily and looks at my face. "You've hurt yourself."

The blond man points his pistol past Harvey and at Natasha.

"Ruby Adams," he says. It's both statement and accusation. Ruby. That's her real name then? "Drop the knife," he says.

Her face is a twisted mask. I can see her fingers grip the handle tighter. Part of me thinks she's just going to go for it, try to tackle the gunman with a kitchen knife.

"What's going on?" says Dad.

I can only guess that this man represents those people who want the same money Natasha stole from Paul Mulholland's house as it burned. I say nothing.

Natasha stares down the barrel of the gun, weighing things up, perhaps trying to make the impossible possible. And then she screws up her mouth, steps back to the Aga and puts the knife down on the counter next to the paraffin bottle.

"You have the Bitcoin," says the gunman.

Harvey is gripping his bleeding shoulder and looking pale. "What Bitcoin?"

Natasha gives the blond man a sardonic smile. "Aw hun," she says. "If only I did."

She is not intimidated by his attitude or his gun.

"You're coming with me," he says. "We need to retrieve that money."

"Don't know what you're fucking on about."

I need them out of here. I need to get Dad out of here and to some medical attention. Harvey is going to need some attention too, but he's at the bottom of my to-do list.

Five of us in the kitchen. Three of us bleeding. One with a stomach full of God knows what. A gun in one hand. A knife on the counter. An open bottle of flammable liquid. A bloodied meat tenderiser on the floor. And there – Harvey's taser. Too many components. An explosive mix.

Think, Hannah. Talk your way out of this one.

"The Bitcoin is on a laptop," I say.

Blond guy looks to me, the gun still trained on Natasha.

"Shut up," says Natasha. That's good. It gives me credence.

"It's in the car outside," I say. "A laptop."

The blond man looks from me to Natasha as though to seek confirmation.

"It's not yours," she says between gritted teeth.

"You need the pass code – the, uh, seed code," I say.

A flicker of a frown on his brow.

"Without it the Bitcoin's totally inaccessible," I add. "Only Ruby and I know the phrase."

"Bullshit!" she hisses.

Fear propels me to dredge up what I can recall. "*Falcon flight, cliff so high. Ocean reef—*"

"Shut up!" Natasha yells.

The end of the gun makes a figure of eight in the air as the man looks between me and Natasha. "This true?"

"It's in the Jag outside," I say. "Take it. Be my guest. Seriously."

He nods at the bag on Natasha's shoulder. "What's that?"

"Cash from this guy's safe," I say.

"You'll bring it too," he tells Natasha.

"Fuck I will."

"My instructions. Dead or alive, you little shit. You owe the bosses big time"

"Owe?" Natasha spits. "I owe you cunts nothing."

"Over here now," he says. As she increasingly loses her temper, he's kept his. But he is holding the gun I guess. "Here, now, or I snap your arm, princess."

She's got no power. The rage that's been burning inside her; the pain of her imagined grievances. They've got nowhere to go.

She's lost.

In one movement, Natasha picks up the bottle of paraffin. She splashes it onto the exposed coals of the Aga and then sprays it in an indiscriminate arc across the room.

Liquid flies. Fire follows.

94

Josie and Rob are heading over at speed, but traffic is a problem. The junctions past the Racecourse were congested. Josie can see that Rob's agitated.

"So, some possible scenarios," Josie says as they speed down Gartree Road. She really wants to keep Rob talking. "Natasha is Ruby. She's pregnant with Paul Mulholland's baby. She survives the fire and assumes this new identity. She's been using Hannah as a way of laying low. Making herself useful, acting as if she belongs. She could have probably spun it out for longer, but she's had her cage rattled now."

Rob nods. "That part makes sense."

"Question is," says Josie. "Whatever she was running away from: was it because she's scared, or because she has something planned?"

Rob's brow creases. "Fear seems like the obvious answer. But this Ruby seems quite calculating."

"Exactly. Like she has a plan."

"Any idea what that might be?" Rob asks.

"No. But I bet it involves money," says Josie. "New baby on the way. Off they go to talk to Hannah's finance guy. Feels like a shakedown."

"Yeah," says Rob. "You can bet your boots that as soon as she gets what she wants, she'll pull that disappearing act again. She's done it once, when she was right under our noses. If she does it again I reckon we'll never find her."

Josie nods. Rob's right. They have to catch up with Ruby before she can make a run for it.

95

Fire moves so fast.

People talk about fire being a living thing. For the second time in a month, I'm seeing up close the snake-like speeds at which it can move.

It leaps in a line across the kitchen in front of me. It burns in the air as it slashes down on the kitchen island then across Harvey and onto the gunman. Shocked, he fires a split second before the chest of his leather jacket catches alight.

The sound is huge in the confined room. A window pane explodes.

Harvey is screaming, his arm is on fire. It's an animal squeal of pain and terror. A scream of sheer horrified disbelief.

The gunman spins as he burns. The gun goes flying and bounces off a wall.

Harvey trips and falls, thrashing.

The blond guy has enough presence of mind to grab his jacket and rip it off.

Dad pushes himself away from me. I make to grab him,

but he's pulling a tea towel off a drawer handle and lunging to smother the fire on Harvey's arm. He moves with the kind of speed and purpose I've not known in him for months, maybe years.

He's shouting Harvey's name over and over again as he tries to put out the flames.

As the blond guy frantically tries to ball up and fling aside his burning jacket, Natasha makes to run past him and out the door. Kitchen cupboards and the curtains on the side window are aflame.

She squeezes past and is at the door when the blond guy, a vivid pink burn mark on his cheek, turns and kicks her legs from under her. She goes down.

Harvey's fire is out but he's still screaming.

The fire is spreading across the kitchen, The smashed window is letting in plenty of air, fuelling the fire as it consumes the curtains.

Natasha struggles to get up, her feet slipping on the floor.

The blond guy, down to a green and white football shirt, calmly looks about and then bends to pick up his pistol.

I can see the indecision in Natasha's eyes. She's caught between trying to flee down the hallway before he shoots her and going for the gun herself. That hesitation is potentially fatal.

She's on her feet but he has the gun.

"Dead or alive," he says.

96

The blond guy is going to shoot Natasha.

This is what I wanted. I want her dead.

The hurt, the harm, the pain.

She's ripped my life open and tried to crawl inside.

What she's done to me is nothing short of torture.

And, if I understand everything, she is a multiple murderer. She not only killed Paul Mulholland but also those people in the cellar. She is monstrous. She is demonic. She is irredeemable.

She deserves to die. And this blond guy, this *gangster*, is the agent of that revenge.

I should let him do it.

But I'm not going to.

Only she knows what drugs are in Dad's system. He might be moving and conscious now but— No, I can't take that chance.

The gangster is pointing the gun at her. I have the tiniest window of opportunity. I need to act, not think. I have no idea how to fight, but I do know how to move swiftly across a room. No end of times I've subtly extricated myself from a conversation and in a second or two been twenty feet away to stop some sort of social disaster.

I lunge across the kitchen. Growing up as the gawky, tall girl means you're aware of your body the whole time. You either make peace with it and learn how to move in a graceful and efficient way, or you turn into someone who visually apologises for taking up space by slouching and sliding. Not my style.

I lunge. I crouch to scoop up Harvey's taser from the floor.

I think I know how to work this thing, there's a button to press once I've placed the contacts against his flesh. Some of them work from a distance and shoot wires across a room. Trust Harvey to have bought the inconvenient type.

Blond guy's not even noticed me. I lift the device to the back of his neck and press the button.

The effect is immediate.

He makes the briefest sound, like a gargled roar and drops to the floor like the proverbial rag-doll. In falling, he knocks against me and I am forced to go to my knees or fall over completely.

The gun tumbles away from his hand.

Blond guy is down and out on the floor. Unconscious. Or he could be dead.

Natasha stares at me in disbelief and then darts for the gun. I half-lean to stop her, but she's nearer and too quick.

She snatches it up and steps back to the door. She has the cool bag of money over her shoulder. There's the laptop in the car. She has everything.

She holds the gun at arm's length and sights along the barrel.

I can feel the rising fire on the side of my face. The

curtains are aflame. The wooden architrave at the top of the window is now alight too. The air is becoming hazy with smoke.

I can feel the sweat trickling down my face. Is it sweat or is it blood?

"I don't understand you," Natasha says. She's wheezing as she says it.

I simply stare at her.

"You have everything anyone could ever want," she says. She glances for a split second at Dad as he cradles Harvey on the floor.

Harvey's eyes are closed and he's gone a strange grey colour. I have never seen a living human take on that colour. No, that's not true. A great-uncle of mine was in hospital with heart failure and I went to visit him as a child. He had that same greyness. He died very soon afterwards.

Yeah, heart attack, I reckon.

But Dad's holding him, like a father with a baby.

Natasha looks back at me. "You have everything. And you don't protect it."

"Please..."

She blinks away the blood that's trickled near her eyes.

"If I had what you had ... I would have done it so much better."

The gun wavers as she moves her finger on the trigger. Then she stuffs her hand in her hoodie pocket, comes out with something white and tosses it at me.

It lands right before me. It's a cardboard medicine box. Zopiclone.

"These?" I say.

"A handful," she says, then she's spun around and gone.

97

The main road through Houghton on the Hill is narrow and Rob takes it at a maximum reasonable speed.

Josie's not been here before. The whitewashed houses. Ivy crawling up brickwork. An old red telephone box. Shit, some of the houses here actually have thatched roofs. This is rich people country.

"Scotland Lane," she says, pointing past a slender war memorial in a little patch of green.

As they turn, movement from one of the nearby houses catches Josie's eye. It's a black car that's just pulled off from a drive and driven away.

"That's the car," says Rob.

"You see the driver?" she says. "Young woman. Think it's Ruby Adams."

"Think?"

The vehicle is round the corner ahead and away before Josie can get a proper look again.

"It's Ruby Adams," she says.

She expects Rob to accelerate after it, but he brakes sharply to a halt.

She turns to ask what the hell he's doing but before she can speak she sees the house, the open front door and the smoke that's coming out.

"Oh, fuck," she says.

Rob's got his seatbelt off. "Get after her. Radio it in. Get back up. No reckless stuff, yeah?"

"Sure," she says, but he's already shut the door.

She could jump out and run round, but it's easier to release her seatbelt, slide over the centre divide and handbrake. By the time she's got the car started, Rob is running down the drive.

She punishes the car with harsh acceleration. She reaches a T-junction. One direction is a dead-end. She takes the other up to a junction with the A47. Which way would Ruby have turned?

Right, she decides. Away from Leicester. This Ruby is trying to make a new start, so she'd heading somewhere different.

Josie puts her foot down.

"Coming for you, bitch," she mutters.

98

Rob radios control before he goes into the house.

"Control, from Tango four-two-four, urgent message. Over."

"Go ahead, four-two-four."

"Control, I'm at the address for Harvey Kenelm in Houghton-on-the-Hill. The property is on fire. Repeat, fire at the scene. Our suspect, Ruby Adams, has made off from the scene in a black Jaguar X351, index unknown. Tango four-two-seven is in pursuit, believed heading north from Houghton on the Hill. Over."

"Received, Four-two-four. Fire service and additional units being informed."

"There may be persons still inside. Request immediate assistance. Over."

He doesn't wait for the reply but enters through the door into a tiled hallway. Several doorways lead away from the hallway. The one at the end, leading into a kitchen is open. Smoke is coming from there, rolling and thick.

He can hear noises ahead, indistinct at first. Then very clearly, Hannah Douglas-Jones's voice.

"Come on, Dad. I'll deal with that."

"Hannah?" Rob calls. "Hannah! It's the police!"

He waves the smoke away and enters the kitchen.

He has no idea what's happened here. The back half of the kitchen is on fire. There are two bodies on the floor. A tall man in a football shirt and an older round chap whose arm is pink and black with burns.

Hannah moves slowly towards Rob. She's got her dad, Donald, on her arm.

"Who else is in the building?" says Rob.

Hannah looks him in the eye. Her nose is bleeding. "Harvey. Not sure if he's had a heart attack. He's not moving."

"And this guy?"

"He was after Natasha. He had a gun. I zapped him."

He wants to ask what she means but there's no time.

"We need to get you all out," says Rob, knowing that's bloody obvious.

"Dad needs help. Natasha gave him some pills. Zopiclone."

"Sure, sure. You get him out."

As Hannah moves down the hall, Rob makes a split decision on who to drag out first. The old guy, Harvey, looks much heavier but he's an innocent bystander and not – Rob assumes – a Degutis thug.

He grabs hold of Harvey's hands and with more concern for speed than personal dignity, drags him out along the hallway.

99

Walker is approaching Houghton on the Hill along the A47.

Free from the city, he's driving at a constant sixty-plus as he overtakes vehicles.

His satnav suggests that he's only a few hundred yards away from the house where Harvey lives.

He radios in. "Control. This is Tango four-two-six. Am approaching Houghton on the Hill. Update requested, over."

"Received, four-two-six. Unit four-two-four at scene. Unit four-two-seven in pursuit of suspect, Ruby Adams, in Jaguar X351 on A47."

"Which direction, control?"

There's a pause. "*Tango four-two-seven last reported heading east along A47 from Houghton on the Hill, over.*"

That's his current direction of travel. The junction for Houghton on the Hill is just there, but Josie's chasing Ruby further down the road.

There's no decision to be made.

"Control, am joining pursuit of suspect," he says. "Alert other units in the area, over."

100

Josie almost fails to spot the Jag until she's upon it.

She expected to see it barrelling down the A47 towards Peterborough and beyond, not in a slip road layby. It's stationary, maybe twenty metres from a mobile trucker's café that's shut up for the weekend.

She brakes swiftly but smoothly and pulls in at the far and turns a tight circle to double back along the slip road towards it.

She notifies control that she's found the vehicle. Patrol vehicles are in the area and will be there soon.

By the red light of a summer's evening, she sees that Ruby Adams is at the wheel and, though she can't hear her, Ruby is swearing violently.

Josie parks, gets out and approaches slowly.

Ruby looks up. That's not a happy face.

She gets out. She's got two bags with her. A battered old gym bag and a supermarket cool bag.

"Shitting piece of junk. It's cut out again." She looks at Josie. "It's my dad's car. It's never been fixed properly."

"Nice try Ruby. Natasha. Whatever you want to call yourself." Josie smiles at her. "I have a lot more questions for you."

Ruby appraises her evenly.

"I've done nothing wrong," she says.

"I've just come from a house fire that might argue otherwise. Now, put those down." She reaches into her pocket for her handcuffs. "Ruby Adams, I am arresting you initially on suspicion of wasting police time. You do not have to—"

Ruby has dropped the bags but retained hold of something she'd possibly had in her hand all along. It's a pistol.

Josie feels a quiver run through her. She's seen guns before but she's not immune to fear.

"Now, come on, Ruby. No need to escalate this. We can chat at the station."

"I'm not going to a fucking police station."

"Is that thing even real?"

Ruby raises it to aim at Josie. Josie curses her big fat mouth. The goal here is not to antagonise the woman.

And now genuine fear has robbed her of the power to think straight.

This is Ruby Adams. Girlfriend or something to Paul Mulholland. This is the woman who very probably set the house on fire on Narborough Road. This is the woman responsible for seven deaths that the police are aware of. Ruby Adams, pregnant with a dead man's child. This woman is a dangerous unknown quantity.

A car goes by on the main road beyond the strip of grass. Who is going to spot two women talking in a lay-by? Who is going slow enough to see the gun one is pointing at the other?

Not for the first time in her career, Josie considers the possibility that she might die.

She is surprised that in this moment she has nothing resembling regrets. She is definitely afraid. She is certainly angry. But there are no regrets. And Josie knows that it's not because her life is in order and she is at peace with things, but because her life is such a disappointment to herself that there are no pieces to cling to, no places where regret could find a home.

Her hands are out in front of her, open-palmed, begging for calm.

"Ruby. We need to calm down. We can talk."

"Fuck talking. I need your car."

"I mean it's Rob's—" Her eyes can only focus on the gun. "I mean, sure. Yes. The car is yours. But you don't want to make things worse, do you?"

Ruby scoffs. "There's no worse than this." She grabs the bags and shakes them. "This is all I've got."

"And your baby."

"Shut the fuck up. Walk." She steps forward, gesturing brutally for Josie to lead the way back to her car.

There's no escape for Ruby now. Police cars will be closing in. Unless this woman wants to run through the trees at the side of the road and take her chances in the fields of Leicestershire.

Only Josie's safety and survival is uncertain here.

"The keys are in the ignition," says Josie.

There's the crunch of loose stone under tyres.

A car is rolling into the far end of the lay-by, coming up behind Josie. It's not a patrol car. It's Walker.

101

As he drags out the big blond guy, Rob realises that the man is wearing the green and white striped kit of FK Žalgiris football club. It's enough to almost make him laugh. A Degutis man advertising his Lithuanian credentials with his home team football shirt. If only all crooks would be so obliging.

The man is stirring and moaning as he's pulled out onto the driveway.

There are people at the end of the driveway. Villagers. Locals. Some are chatting. A couple are filming the burning house on their mobile phones.

Hannah is on the driveway with her dad and Harvey.

Donald Douglas-Jones sits on a raised bank of lawn, arms on knees, head slumped as though he's dozing or about to throw up.

Harvey Kenelm lies on his back. Hannah crouches over him, doing CPR chest compressions.

Rob wants to go help but he's got this guy. He's waking

slowly, and if he's the threat Rob suspects he might be, he doesn't want this man awake and free.

"Listen, mate," he says. "I'm going to cuff you now because I can't safely monitor you. You're currently under arrest for..." he reaches for something "...let's call it breaking and entering. I'm going to read you your rights, but I'll read them to you again when you're compos mentis, got it?"

The man groans. Rob has no idea if that's in response or not. Doesn't matter. Procedure is all.

When he's got the man secured, Rob goes over to Hannah. He radios in the medical situation. Ambulance is ten minutes away. A first responder might be quicker.

"Want me to take a spell at that?" Rob asks Hannah. "Takes it out of you, doesn't it?"

As he takes a turn at the chest compressions on Harvey, Hannah turns to the gawkers at the end of the drive.

"Oi! You lot! Is there a defibrillator in the village?"

There's muttering. One person points. Another says, "In the phone box."

"Then stop fucking filming us and go get it!"

Most of the people don't move. A couple of women hurry off.

Hannah goes to her dad. She grips his hand and he seems to come to life for a moment.

"Natasha's run off," she says to Rob.

Harvey isn't breathing, but Rob just needs to keep going with CPR.

"I know," he says.

"She's not even who she says she was."

"Yeah. We figured that out," he says. "Eventually."

"She took a load of money out of Harvey's safe. She ... she played me, Rob. She completely played me."

"You showed kindness to a stranger," he says.

"More fool me."

He shakes his head vehemently. "No. Kindness is never wrong."

She makes a noise. He looks over. There's a faint smile on her face. Hannah looks like she's been through the wringer and the smile is a bit crazed, but it's a smile.

There are sirens in the distance.

"You're a strange cop, DS Joseph," she says.

"I'll take that as a compliment," he says and keeps on with the chest compressions.

102

Walker appraises the situation as he stops his car to the side of the Jag.

A worse situation he could not imagine.

Josie and Ruby stand in the lay-by. Ruby has a gun trained on Josie.

Ruby glances back at him but keeps the gun aimed at Josie.

It's her. His daughter.

She's there.

She's dishevelled, blood on her face and her expression feral. But it's his daughter.

"Control from Tango four-two-seven. Urgent assistance. Over."

"*Go ahead, four-two-seven.*"

"Control, I'm in a lay-by off the A47 between Skeffington and Tugby. I have Ruby Adams on scene armed with a handgun – repeat armed with a handgun – threatening DC Josie Kaminski. Immediate threat to life. Require urgent firearms and back-up. Over."

He gets out. That's not procedure. He shouldn't additionally put himself in danger. But this moment demands action.

"Back off, mister," says Ruby. "This has got nothing to do with you."

"Yeah, we've got this all under control," says Josie. "Ruby here is taking my car."

Walker takes a moment to get the words out.

"No. You need to stop."

"Fuck off." Ruby waggles the pistol at Josie. Josie walks back.

"You carry that gun, armed officers are going to shoot you, Ruby," he says. "They're on their way right now."

She cocks her head, pretending to listen for sirens.

"They're coming and..." Walker swallows hard. The gun might be pointed at Josie but fear has turned his guts to jelly. His knee creaks as he takes a step forward, as though his body wants to remind him of his own mortality. "I don't want you to get hurt, Ruby."

"Like the fuck you care," she says.

A gasp of breath escapes his lips, a stillborn laugh.

"Actually, I do care, Ruby. I care *a lot*."

"You don't even know me, mate."

"I do. I know you. I ... I knew your mum."

She gives him the swiftest glance, trying to keep her eye on both of them.

"No, you fucking didn't."

"Leanne Church," Walker says. "I knew her back in the old days. She was bright and bold and didn't take crap off anyone."

"You don't know my mum!"

"I did. Very well indeed. I cared for her a lot."

"Who are you?"

"Everyone calls me Walker," he says.

Josie's by the car she came in. She puts a hand on the door.

"How old are you, Ruby?" says Walker.

"What the fuck is that question?" says Ruby.

Even Josie is giving him a quizzical look.

"How old?" he repeats.

She shakes her head. "Twenty-two."

"Right," he says. "I knew your mum twenty-two and a bit years ago."

Ruby's feet stutter and are still on the broken tarmac. "What the...?"

"Yeah, Ruby..." he begins to say.

She turns, eyes wide and watery with disbelief. The gun, for a moment, is pointing at no one.

Josie leaps forward and tackles Ruby from behind. She grabs the wrist of the hand holding the gun.

Walker ducks to the side, away from the direction of the gun and hurries to circle Ruby.

Ruby growls like an animal as she tries to fight against Josie. Ruby has fury, but Walker sometimes thinks that Josie operates constantly on a level of barely controlled rage. And she's got police combat training too.

Ruby tries to force her way from Josie's grip like she's a circus strongman breaking chains. But Josie has her.

They whirl. Josie smashes Ruby's hand onto the bonnet of her car. The gun is knocked away. Ruby screams. Josie gives her a little room. Ruby pulls and Josie uses that momentum. She lets Ruby move away and, still holding her arm, twists. It's a savage twist, possibly enough to dislocate a shoulder, and then with the woman's arm pinned, slams her with great force against the side of the car.

Ruby goes down on her knees, her growls turned to gasps of pain.

Walker notes the location of the gun in the grass verge and comes over to help Josie.

"Nah," Josie pants. "I've got this."

She snaps a cuff onto Ruby then pulls round the other hand to cuff it too. Ruby is swearing. And sobbing.

Walker wants to leap in – to help, to soothe, to cradle his daughter.

Josie looks up at Walker. "What the hell was that?"

"Huh?"

"That weird shit, mate. What the hell?"

He has no answer.

Josie, regaining her breath, reads Walker's daughter her rights.

"Ruby Adams, I am arresting you..."

103

A fire engine has appeared at Harvey's house to tackle the fire in the kitchen.

Three ambulances and an 'enhanced paramedic' turn up not long after. Emergency vehicles fill the narrow road. Gawking neighbours have been moved away, out of sight.

I am strongly tempted to complain when the first ambulance crew go straight to Harvey when my dad is right there in need of assistance.

They're working on Harvey with the defibrillator on the lawn when the second ambulance comes along. I almost physically grab them and drag them over to Dad who has slipped in groggy insensibility again.

I show them the Zopiclone and they inspect dad.

"How many did he take?" says the enhanced paramedic.

"A handful," I say, which I know isn't a number.

"Okay," he says. "Good news is that these aren't going to kill him. Sedate him, sure. We're going to need to observe him, but all he's going to need is time. Isn't that right, Donald?"

He pats Dad's hand but Dad is away with the fairies again. I think he's actually snoring.

Harvey is placed in the back of an ambulance and it drives off. I have no idea if they got his heart going again. I want to not care but I guess human emotions don't work like that.

The paramedics take their time with Dad, placing him on the stretcher and then into the ambulance. The enhanced paramedic goes to check over the blond guy who's come round from his tasering. They've put him in a police vehicle somewhere. I didn't see where.

I realise DS Rob Joseph is beside me.

"So, at some point we'll need to do the whole statement thing," he says.

I look at him. I find his sincere gaze strangely compelling.

I cough lightly. "I need to go with Dad to hospital."

"Of course. Want to fill me in briefly?"

The confrontation at home seems like a world away now, but I attempt to give some details.

"It was as if she'd taken off the mask and decided to show me who she really was." I sigh as I recall the whole thing. "Do you know what she did? She saw the inside of my house, took note of all the things I like. Photos of me with an old haircut, books that I read, the things that are important to me, and she built her entire personality around them. She invented Natasha Dibello and it was a person designed to appeal to me and my stupid ego."

"Not stupid," says Rob. "That's pure manipulation."

I want to tell him that I should be immune to that stuff,

that I know all about it. That it's my job, but the truth is nobody's really immune.

"Did she mention the fire, or what made her do whatever it was she was doing?" Rob asks.

I nod. "Oh yes. She was on a roll by then. I think she has a real chip on her shoulder when it comes to class."

He peers at me intently. "Go on."

I wonder what that look means. It feels as though DS Rob Joseph has his own thoughts on the matter of class. It would be interesting to know what they are.

"She was angry at me. Angry because of who I am. The privilege of being me. I had opportunities that she never did. All of that. But she was angry before she even met me. She was angry at being pregnant by Paul Mulholland."

"She didn't want a baby?"

I screw up my face, trying to remember how she expressed it. "It was maybe a bit of that, but it was more to do with the way he thought he owned her, or had a say in what she did next."

"Oh." He rocks back slightly. "Is that what she was running away from?"

I nod. "She wasn't just running away from the situation. She caused the situation. She started the fire."

Rob exhales slowly. "She told you that?"

I nod.

"Bloody hell," he whispers, blinking.

For a moment, Rob Joseph looks as lost and human as any of us. It's quite an attractive look on him.

"We must talk again," I say.

The ambulance is ready to go. I climb in beside Dad. I turn to say something else to Rob but the doors are closed.

104

Saturday nights at Mansfield House police station are busy enough, but today is something else entirely.

More than a dozen CID officers who thought they were having a quiet night off, now suddenly find themselves back at work. DI Scabbard, in the one glimpse Josie had of him as he headed into a meeting with DI Bacon, DI Gill and the detective super, looked mightily pissed off. Walker mentioned he'd been out for the evening, a dinner engagement with a woman who was not his wife.

There are two people in custody.

Ruby Adams will possibly be charged with seven counts of murder in relation to the Narborough Road fire, maybe a couple of attempted murders, plus arson, robbery and more besides.

In another cell, "Mindy" Minaugas Petrauskas, known associate of the Degutis gang, is looking at a potential life sentence purely on the charge of possession of a firearm with intent to cause fear of violence. Other charges will be added.

Under the supervision of DI Neelam Gill, each of the

Duncans has provided a detailed statement of their actions that evening.

In the Dead End Duncan's little corner of the CID office, Rob has broken out the expensive instant coffee sachets. He keeps promising to buy the team a coffee machine, but that day hasn't quite materialised.

Coffee is consumed, statements are written. Eventually DI Gill declares she is satisfied with their accounts and leaves them alone. It's nearing midnight.

"Man," says Rob, slumping back in his chair. "Are we actually done?"

Josie positions herself on the desk-edge next to Rob and looks at Walker.

"Are we done, Walker? Anything else to share?"

Walker gives her a look like he doesn't know what she means. Maybe it's an act. Maybe it's not.

Walker takes a huge, heaving breath. "Yeah."

"Yeah?"

"I need to tell you both something," he says.

"Oh?" says Rob. "What is it?"

It takes Walker a while to summon the words. "Ruby Adams is my daughter."

Josie had guessed as much from his words in the lay-by but it's still a shock.

"What?" says Rob.

Walker shrugs. "I only just found out. Today was the first time I met her."

There is a long silence.

Rob tilts his head. "You're gonna have to talk us through that, mate. What's the story?"

"It's a long story, but if you're willing to listen..."

105

Walker is in Scabbard's office.

He has just delivered a piece of news that is likely to end his career. He knows this.

He's even come in this morning in his better suit, his shoes shined. If he's going to get the bollocking of his life and then be fired, he might as well look smart while he's doing it.

He had to tell someone the truth. If he'd carried on working the Ruby Adams case without disclosing that he is Ruby's father, it could jeopardise whatever convictions they get, so he's had to come clean.

Ruby is still in custody downstairs. Someone higher up has granted an extension to thirty six hours for questioning. The Crown Prosecution Service have approved every charge they plan to lay at her feet. Final charges will be put to her within the next two hours. There will be no bail for Ruby Adams.

Having delivered his confession to Scabbard – full and with no omissions – Walker waits for judgement from his superior.

Scabbard, uncharacteristically, thinks before speaking. The look on Scabbard's face has been building to a crescendo. Walker's not sure whether it will end in a heart attack, a stroke, or an actual explosion. Scabbard's face is extremely red.

"This thing..." he says slowly.

"Yes?" Walker says.

"That you just told me."

Walker nods. Braces himself for whatever the consequences are. Dismissal, investigation, intense press interest when it all comes out.

"I never want to hear you utter those words again."

"Sorry, what?"

Walker was not expecting this.

Scabbard lays his hands on the desk, fingers splayed. "We can go ahead and do all this, if you insist, Walker. We can invite the circus that will accompany this revelation. Or we can just assume that this conversation never happened."

"Pardon, sir?"

"I think we can go about our business as police officers without introducing our own personal dramas."

Walker is taken aback.

Is Scabbard seriously suggesting that Walker actually *wants* the attention that this would bring?

"But, sir – I know the suspect. I'm her dad."

Scabbard recoils, a hand raised.

"Please. Shut up, Walker."

"But the things I did. The *thing* I did."

"Shut up, Walker. No one wants to think about you putting your junk in someone else. It was a long time ago and, besides, the bitch is dead."

Walker shuts up.

"You don't invite trouble," says Scabbard. "This is your little fuck up and it's yours to carry. Forever." He jabs a finger at Walker. "And don't go mouthing off to DI Gill or some old golfing buddy you've got higher up. I'll deny all knowledge and you'll be out on your arse. How long have you got to retirement?"

"A bit under three years, sir."

"Then think on that."

None of this was what Walker expected when he came in this morning, but if Scabbard wants to put a lid on it, then that sort of works. Walker would like to stick around until his pension's due.

Walker stands. "There's just one thing, sir," he says.

Scabbard looks at him. "Go on."

"I'd like the chance to talk with her. I don't think she knows that I'm, you know, her dad."

Scabbard emits a small breathy hiss. "Course you would. I can arrange a nice candlelit dinner, so the two of you can exchange your life stories. How would that be?"

Walker lets the sarcasm wash over him. "Sir. Just the briefest window, that's all I ask."

"Fine. Fifteen minutes." Scabbard flicks a hand to dismiss Walker.

"Thank you."

106

Dad spent Saturday night and much of Sunday in Leicester Royal Infirmary before he was allowed home, seemingly no worse for wear.

One of my tasks on Sunday was phoning Marissa to try and make amends, if such a thing is possible.

And then on Monday I'm back at Leicester Royal. Ward twenty on the first floor.

That's where Karolina is.

She's conscious and she's able to have visitors.

I settle into the big blue chair next to the hospital bed.

Karolina has had surgery to stabilise her spine, so she's finally allowed to sit propped up. She's got healing wounds on her face, a nicely developing scab down her cheek. Her accident doesn't seem to have dented her demeanour.

"What did you bring me?" she asks without hesitation.

I produce a bunch of grapes from my bag. I do it with a flourish, offering it like a bunch of flowers.

"Fucking grapes." She scowls, but takes one anyway, with her good arm, and pops it in her mouth.

"Grapes are like little tiny nuggets of health," I tell her. "Eat them all and you'll be out of here in no time."

She arches an eyebrow. "Grapes will do physio for me, huh? Best course of treatment for me, Doctor Hannah, would be a luscious Danish pastry."

"Well, it's a good job I went to medical school then, isn't it?" I say as I pull a box out of my bag and place it on her little wheeled table, next to the grapes."

Her eyes light up at that. "Let me see."

"Eat some more grapes first," I tell her.

"You're enjoying this. Just you wait 'til I get out of here," she grumbles.

"I honestly can't wait," I tell her sincerely. "So much has happened. And yes, I know that I should have listened to you."

"Tell me then," she says, putting another grape in her mouth. "I am the most captive audience you will ever have. Tell me how the whole thing happened."

She closes her eyes and continues to feed grapes into her mouth while I try to put things in order in my mind.

"Well, first of all, we must forget the name Natasha. She was never called that. Her name is Ruby, and she was in a relationship with the man who owned the burned down house, Paul Mulholland. Sounds a little bit coercive, and maybe a little bit like a convenient arrangement. Whatever it was, Ruby got pregnant and it all changed. Paul wanted to play happy families, and all Ruby could see was a trap. She convinced herself that she needed a way out, with a pot of money."

"And burning down a building was the way to achieve that," murmurs Karolina, with a disbelieving shake of her head.

"She either didn't know about, or more likely didn't much care about the collateral damage in the form of those women in the cellar." I'm shaking my own head now. "Then along comes Hannah, swooping in. I find her on the street after the fire, I give her a drink and a T-shirt. That could have been the end of it, but no. I seek her out later because I can sniff a business opportunity."

Karolina opens her eyes at this point. "What I don't understand is why she went home with you? She had a place. She could have gone back there."

"It sounds as though she wanted a complete new start. A blank slate. One thing that I'm certain about with Na – with Ruby, is that she's very quick to learn. Very adaptable."

"Like a sociopath."

"Is she?"

"She pushed me into traffic. I get to decide the labels."

I grunt in acknowledgement. "So when I let her stay with me, she saw a new set of possibilities. She didn't need to go on the run. She could set up a brand new life, supported by me. I gave it to her on a plate."

"She could have just done that. Been your assistant."

"Yep. That might have happened. But I pushed her buttons, didn't I? Took her back to the fire. Made her talk to the police."

"So she made a new plan."

"Honestly? I think she made several new plans. I think she was going to coast along as my useful assistant. Then she was ready to stage a coup – set herself up as a business rival, and steal my clients. Finally, she saw no other choice than to rob me. And rob Harvey."

"How is Harvey?"

I gesture upwards at the hospital around us.

"Apparently, he's here somewhere. He's alive."

I don't know what more I have to say about it than that.

"What about the money?" says Karolina, chewing. "The money she stole from Mulholland?"

I think for a moment. It honestly hasn't crossed my mind.

"It's on the laptop in Bitcoin. She couldn't remember the, um, seed phrase – is that what it's called?"

"Just twelve to sixteen words to unlock it."

"I heard her singing some words at one point. I thought it was nursery rhyme."

"You remember all of them?" says Karolina, giving me a wolfish smile.

I smile. "And make myself a multi-millionaire? I guess the police have the laptop in evidence now. And the money... I guess it just stays in the cloud."

She nods and shuffles up slightly. "Now. See how many grapes I have eaten. Let me see in the box."

I give her a nod and slide the box of pastries closer to her.

107

Walker sits across from Ruby.

They are in an interview suite, but he's moved his chair so that the table isn't between the two of them.

"Ruby. I'm Patrick Smith. Most people call me Walker."

She's tired after nearly two days in police custody but not so tired she can't muster a scowl.

"Yeah. I remember you."

How are you doing?" he asks.

"How am I doing? About as well as you'd imagine. Accused of murder and locked up in this shithole."

Walker tries out a sympathetic nod. He's aware that any attempt at empathy will look shallow and insincere. There's a blood connection between them, but their background and life experience couldn't be more different.

"Are you comfortable, though?"

"What, you're like the housekeeper here, are you?"

Walker smiles. He examines her mannerisms as she speaks. Recognises flashes of Leanne.

"I need to talk to you about your background, Ruby."

"Not this shit again."

"I did know your mother."

She's quiet now. Why? She heard him say this in the lay-by. But has she had time to process it, to put the pieces together?

There's fear in her eyes. Whether it's fear of what's about to come out of Walker's mouth, he can't be certain, but he needs to say it anyway.

"I'm your father, Ruby."

"Fuck off." She shoves the chair backwards, scooting across the floor to create physical distance between them.

"I didn't know about you until a couple of days ago, Ruby. I'm so sorry that I haven't been there for you."

"So what? Now is when you choose to show up?"

"Timing is ... not great."

"Fuck lot of good this news is gonna do me. Unless you're going to help me escape. Are you gonna do that?"

"No," says Walker. "But whatever I can do to help, I want to do it."

"Yeah? Well, the way you can help right now is by leaving me the fuck alone. I managed without you this far, didn't I?"

Walker knows that she's right. He gets up from the chair and steps back to the door.

He turns. "In case it's of any interest, you have a half-brother and a half-sister. Oscar and Amber."

She is silent for an extended beat.

"You're telling me that you have a nice little nest somewhere in the suburbs? Where you dote on your *real* family?" She's furious now. "You want to give me a glimpse of the life I could have fucking had?"

"I didn't meant that."

"Oh, you bastards are all the same. In your nice safe houses and your nice little gardens and you make out that you've got your own problems when you don't know what it's fucking like for the rest us. You watch us squirming in the fucking dirt and you think you can lift us out of it and dust us down and we'll be fucking grateful? To be in your world for just a moment!"

"Ruby, I just wanted to—"

"Oh, fuck off, copper. Just fuck off."

108

Wednesday night, Josie and Walker are at a secure cargo terminal at East Midlands airport.

They walk across the tarmac together.

"Looking smart," Walker says to Josie.

She nods. She thought carefully about her outfit for this job – even considered wearing her police uniform, but opted in the end for a charcoal trouser suit. It feels slightly ironic given that nobody's here to see it, but she wants to pay her own quiet respects.

They are accompanying the bodies of the six Chinese women in the official handover to the airline that will transport them back to China. The two of them were selected for this job because it's taking place at three o'clock in the morning. The intense media interest drives the unsocial timing. The unsocial timing means that it's a job for the Duncans.

The number of local, national and international agencies involved in this transfer is high. The paperwork has been considerable.

Thankfully, all that Josie and Walker need to do is witness the handover, maintain the chain of custody and keep their eyes peeled for any unwanted intrusions.

Mei Lin-Jones, a middle-aged woman from the repatriation agency, stands close by.

As far as Josie can tell, she is the one who has triple-checked the paperwork and tirelessly smoothed the way for this to happen.

Mei exudes calm authority. She will make the long journey herself, ensuring that everything goes without a hitch until each one of these women is returned to their families.

The individual coffins have been brought here in an unmarked refrigerated van, and now they are being transferred into a freight container that will go into the belly of the aircraft.

The moment of transfer is orchestrated with dignity. Mei pauses the transfer so that all of the people involved can bow their heads and reflect for a moment. This includes ground support staff wearing hi-vis, the Chinese consular official, the Border Force representative, and Josie and Walker.

Mei is satisfied and she indicates that the loading may be completed.

The last that Josie sees of the bodies is the loader platform lifting the container up towards the hold of the aircraft.

It is done. With almost no words and several sheets of paperwork. But it is done.

Josie and Walker make their way out of the area.

"I'm just going to say it," she says.

"What?"

"That's a crappy way to die."

"It is," he says. "Playing on your mind?"

She shakes her head. Not because he's wrong but because that's not what she meant to say in the first place.

"To come over here. Trafficked, whatever. And then working in a nothing, nowhere kitchen for our takeaway restaurants while back at home in China, there's a family. And they're just waiting."

"They're all someone's daughter, someone's sister," says Walker.

"That. Flung out into the world to die."

"Trying to make a better life for themselves."

She shakes her head again. The world is a mess. "I hope their families can ... I dunno, find some peace when they're back home."

Walker cracks a sad smile. "Families are never at peace. That's part of the deal."

Josie wonders if he's talking about himself and his family.

"You told your wife? About the—"

"Yeah, yeah," he says. "I told her about Ruby."

"Did it go well."

He laughs out loud now. "It did not."

"Do you need a place to stay?"

"No, Josie. Thanks."

"Oh, I wasn't offering. I've got no room anyway."

"Right."

He raises his key fob to unlock his car door.

"You know," she says. "There's this truck stop café down the M1 on the way back near Shepshed. Serves a cracking breakfast, even this time of night."

He looks at her. "We're not truckers."

She smiles, nose wrinkling. "I know the guy. He's fine."

Walker goes round to the driver's side, visibly mulling it over.

"Full English," she says. "Fried bread. Black pudding. All that disgusting shit. And you can tell me about how awful your life is now."

Walker considers this.

"All right," he says.

"You're buying, obviously," she says.

"Obviously."

109

Rob pulls up outside Hannah Douglas-Jones's house the following morning.

As he waits at the front door he can smell something. It's a plant that's growing up a trellis. The flowers are small for the amount of scent that they give off.

He's in the act of checking when Hannah opens the door. He straightens awkwardly while she gives him a questioning look.

"Sorry, I was just wondering about the smell."

"So you knocked the door to ask?"

She's toying with him. She steps back and invites him inside.

"I was wondering how you are," he says. "You and your dad."

"Well you can see for yourself while I make some tea," says Hannah, showing him outside to a courtyard area.

Rob nods, then goes over to take a seat at the cast iron table.

Hannah's dad is sitting there with a newspaper.

"Donald?" he says. "How are you doing?"

He looks up at Rob. "Who's this? Come to read the meter?"

"DS Joseph helped us when all that nastiness happened at Harvey's," says Hannah.

Donald Douglas-Jones looks round. "Is Harvey here?"

"No. He's elsewhere," says Hannah. From her tone of voice and what's she's told Rob, that's probably the only answer Hannah will ever give her dad on the subject of Harvey Kenelm. He's still in the ICU, and whether or not he comes out is a coin-toss.

"You came when we had that trouble with the car," says Donald, remembering, although quite possibly remembering the business when Rob gave them a lift to the gala a fortnight ago.

"That's me," says Rob.

"Is it all fixed now?"

That's a bigger sounding question than Donald realises. The personal, emotional and social fallout from recent events is probably far from being resolved.

Rob looks to Hannah. "Will your business recover from the things that happened?"

Hannah makes a see-saw motion with her hand. "It's on the way. Tyrese Jali is back in the fold. He's a simple creature when it comes right down to it."

"You got some football gossip to share."

"No gossip here." She wags a finger. "This other client I pretty much lost as soon as I landed him – Todd – he's at least talking to me again. I think I can win him over. Fingers crossed."

"Good news."

"Now listen, Dad. Marissa said that she'd make you some

of that eggy bread that you like. Want to go into the kitchen and make sure she does it right?"

Donald levers himself up out of the chair. "Damn good idea that. Leave you young people to it."

Rob's smile breaks out. "Not been called a young person for a while."

"Oh yes," says Hannah. "It's a key advantage of hanging out with older people."

Rob's taking pleasure from being here in the sunshine with Hannah. She is well-suited to a sunny day, he thinks. She tilts her head back to get the sun on her face, stretching out her neck in a way that makes his pulse pick up.

"You here on official business then, detective?" she says.

He shakes his head. "Ruby is being remanded in prison pending trial. It's all paperwork now for us."

Hannah is way smarter than he is.

"So, this is a final official visit or perhaps a first unofficial visit?"

She's making it easy for him, and he is grateful.

"Maybe an unofficial visit," he says.

"For unofficial reasons." She says it in a deliberate manner holding his gaze.

Rob rolls his eyes. Time to stop pussyfooting about. "It's against police regulations for me to ask out someone who is a witness in a live case."

"Oh?" She sounds genuinely interested. "And when does it stop being a 'live' case?"

"After Ruby has been convicted or acquitted."

She narrows her eyes. "That could be a long time."

"It could."

She nods slowly. "So, if you did ask me out, it'd be a long time before we could go on a date. Officially."

He lets out a sigh. "Sadly."

She wrinkles her nose. "I mean, it's distinctly possibly that we go on that first date and we don't hit it off at all."

"I suppose."

"So, rather than commit ourselves to a long wait we perhaps ought to go out for a test date just to see if we hate each other or not."

"We could," he says. "Unofficially."

"Unofficially," she agrees.

Rob smiles. He can't believe she's said yes. A woman who's so obviously out of his league.

"And it's jasmine," she adds.

"Sorry?"

"The plant by the front door that smells nice. Jasmine."

"I love it," he says.

ALSO BY BECK LEWIS

SAFE SPACE

When your memories are missing, how do you know you're not the one to blame?

A year after a carbon monoxide accident left five people dead, Cassie O'Donnell wakes from a coma to find her life erased. She's homeless, unemployed, and her mind is filled with shadowy memories she can't trust.

Desperate for answers, Cassie joins a support group run by the survivors - a safe space where they can grieve and heal together. But then one member of the group dies of an apparent drugs overdose...

An ex-girlfriend begs DS Rob Joseph to investigate this latest death and he secretly joins the support group. But he soon discovers that the survivors are all carrying secrets.

Both Cassie and Rob begin to suspect that someone inside the group knows what really happened in that house on the night of the accident - and is willing to kill to keep the truth buried.

One tragedy. Five survivors. No one is safe.

Safe Space

* 9 7 8 1 0 6 8 2 4 1 8 6 4 *

BV - #0333 - 050526 - C0 - 198/129/23 - PB - 9781068241864 - Matt Lamination